David Wishart studied Classics at Edinburgh University. He then taught Latin and Greek in school for four years and after this retrained as a teacher of EFL. He lived and worked abroad for eleven years, working in Kuwait, Greece and Saudia Arabia, and now lives with his family in Scotland.

Praise for David Wishart:

'Ancient Rome's shrewdest and most sardonic detective . . . the best balance of mystery and history yet.' *Kirkus Reviews*

'An entertaining read . . . an enjoyable romp.' *Historical Novels Review*

'Drawn with great dash, and the one-liners are as good as ever. Genius.' *Good Book Guide*

'Wishart takes true historical events and blends them into a concoction so pacey that you hardly notice all those facts and interesting details of Roman life being slipped in there . . . Salve! To this latest from the top toga-wearing 'tec of Roman times!' *Highland News Group*

'It is evident that Wishart is a fine scholar and perfectly at home in the period.' *Sunday Times*

'A real gripping mystery yarn with a strong vein of laconic humour.' *Coventry Evening Telegraph*

DAVID WISHART

PARTHIAN SHOT

nel

NEW ENGLISH LIBRARY
Hodder & Stoughton

A CIP catalogue record for this title is available from the
British Library

ISBN 0 340 82737 8

Typeset in Plantin Light by
Phoenix Typesetting, Auldgirth, Dumfriesshire

Printed and bound by
Clays Ltd, St Ives plc

Hodder Headline's policy is to use papers that are natural, renewable
and recyclable products and made from wood grown in sustainable
forests. The logging and manufacturing processes are expected to
conform to the environmental regulations of the country of origin

Hodder and Stoughton
A division of Hodder Headline
338 Euston Road
London NW1 3BH

DRAMATIS PERSONAE

**(The names of historical characters are given in
bold upper case)**

CORVINUS'S HOUSEHOLD

Bathyllus: the major-domo
Lysias: the coachman
Meton: the chef
Perilla, Rufia: Corvinus's wife

ROMANS

GAIUS CAESAR ('Prince Gaius'): Tiberius's heir-
apparent; the future emperor (Caligula)
ISIDORUS of Charax: Rome's official Parthia-watcher
Lippillus, Decimus: commander of the Public Pond Watch
TIBERIUS ('The Wart'): the emperor
VITELLIUS, LUCIUS: head of the senatorial commission
treating with the Parthian embassy.
(He was the father of the later Vitellius, last of the three very
short-lived emperors who succeeded Nero in AD 69)

THE EMBASSY

Callion: Greek, from Seleucia
Osroes: a Magian
Peucestas: a eunuch
Zariadres: the embassy leader; a nobleman from Ctesiphon

NON-ROMAN POLITICALS

ARTABANUS: currently Great King of Parthia

MITHRADATES: exiled brother of the Iberian king Pharasmenes, and marked out for the Armenian kingship

PHRAATES: an elderly Parthian prince; Rome's candidate to replace Artabanus

TIRIDATES: Phraates's nephew; also a Parthian prince

OTHER NON-ROMANS

Anna: a prostitute working at the Three Graces

Damon: Phraates's son by his mistress Polyclea

Helen: owner of the Three Graces

Isak: an Ostian gang-leader

Jarhades: one of the family of jugglers and tumblers. His wife is Erato and their son and daughter are Batis and Calliste

Nicanor: son of the Syrian merchant Anacus. His sister was Sebasta

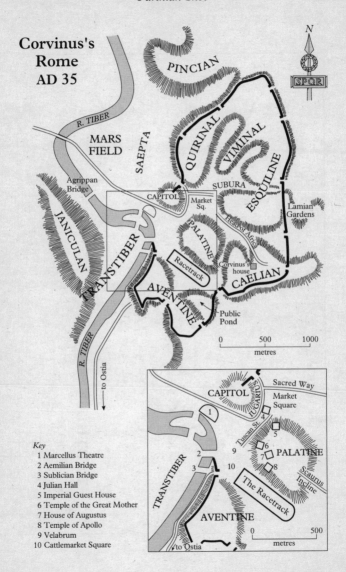

Corvinus's Rome
AD 35

N
SPQR

R. TIBER

PINCIAN

MARS FIELD

SAEPTA

QUIRINAL

VIMINAL

ESQUILINE

Agrippan Bridge

CAPITOL

SUBURA

Market Sq.

Lamian Gardens

JANICULAN

TRANSTIBER

PALATINE

Head of Africa

Racetrack

Corvinus's house

CAELIAN

AVENTINE

Public Pond

R. TIBER

to Ostia

0   500   1000
metres

CAPITOL

Sacred Way

Market Square

TRANSTIBER

Tuscan St.

PALATINE

The Racetrack

Scaurus Incline

AVENTINE

to Ostia

0   500
metres

Key
1 Marcellus Theatre
2 Aemilian Bridge
3 Sublician Bridge
4 Julian Hall
5 Imperial Guest House
6 Temple of the Great Mother
7 House of Augustus
8 Temple of Apollo
9 Velabrum
10 Cattlemarket Square

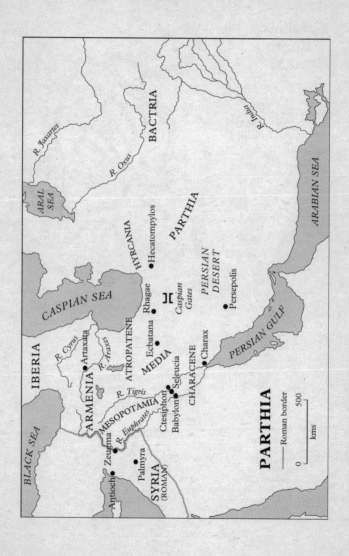

R. Jaxartes

R. Oxus

R. Indus

BACTRIA

ARAL
SEA

HYRCANIA

PARTHIA

ARABIAN SEA

Hecatompylos

ATROPATENE

CASPIAN SEA

Rhagae

Caspian
Gates

PERSIAN
DESERT

Persepolis

PERSIAN GULF

R. Cyrus

Artaxata

R. Araxes

Echatana

MEDIA

IBERIA

ARMENIA

CHARACENE

Charax

R. Tigris

Seleucia

BLACK SEA

Ctesiphon

MESOPOTAMIA

Babylon

R. Euphrates

Zeugma

PARTHIA

Antioch

Palmyra

——— Roman border

SYRIA
(ROMAN)

0   500

kms

For the French contingent at Glargin: May and
Andy Halkett and Pierre and Lily Halter.

May the wines in your cellars always be
good ones.

I

Accounts days only come two or three times a year in the Corvinus household; they rank with blots on the religious calendar like the anniversaries of Cannae and the Allia, and they involve a lot of creative swearing. Me and numbers just don't get on, and never have. Pythagoras, unless I'm mixing up my philosophers, believed the universe was made up of the little buggers, which says a lot about Pythagoras. Anyone silly enough to spread dangerous ideas like that around deserves to come back as a clam.

I'd just totted up the column on the latest tablet for the third time and got my third different answer when there was a knock on the study door and Bathyllus put his head round. Cautiously, which is par for the course on accounts days: our super efficient major-domo knows perfectly well that interrupting the master when he's wrestling with household income and expenditure can lose you teeth. Especially since when I'm balancing the books I have to keep off the fermented grape juice. Wine and arithmetic don't mix.

'Ah . . . I'm sorry to disturb you, sir . . .'

'Then don't, pal.' I reversed the pen and drew the blunt end savagely through the wax at the foot of the column. 'Jupiter sodding bloody God Almighty!'

'. . . but you have a visitor.'

Hell; that was all I needed. Visitors when I'm slaving over a red-hot abacus I can do without, and Bathyllus knows it.

'Pass them on to Perilla.'

'The mistress has gone out, sir. To the Pollio Library. And the gentleman wants to speak to you personally.'

Bugger. Double bugger. I sat back in my chair. 'This "gentleman" have a name, by any chance?'

That got me a sniff; not much of one, mind, because like I say even our sarky, full-of-himself major-domo doesn't take unnecessary risks on accounts days. 'Yes, sir. Lucius Vitellius.'

My eyebrows hit the ceiling. We don't get many visitors, or I don't, rather, because Perilla's got her own network of intellectual geeks and literary weirdos who pop in and out to exchange anapaests, but even among the ones we do get ex-consuls don't figure all that prominently. And Lucius Vitellius didn't figure at all. The likelihood that one of Rome's top senatorial heavies – in both senses of the word – had just dropped in in passing to swap the latest barber-shop jokes over a mouthful of wine and a few nuts was on a par with flying pigs above the Capitol.

'He tell you what he wanted?' I said.

'No, sir. Only that it was important and if you were at home it was essential that he see you.'

Essential, right? Shit; I didn't like the sound of this, not above half. When movers and shakers like Vitellius use the word essential it means trouble. 'Okay,' I said, laying the pen down. 'Wheel him in. And bring the wine tray. If I'm going to be interrupted I might as well get something out of it.'

'Yes, sir.' Bathyllus prepared to exit.

'Uh, Bathyllus?'

He turned. 'Yes, sir?'

'Before you go, pal.' I passed him the accounts tablet. 'Just cast your eyes over this, will you? What do you make the total?'

He took it and glanced at the figures. His lips moved. 'Eight thousand three hundred and forty-six,' he said finally.

'You're sure?'

He gave me a look like I was a mentally disadvantaged prawn. 'Quite sure.'

Oh, hell. That made total number four. Maybe I did need a break after all. 'Fine,' I said. 'Off you go.'

He left.

Vitellius came in like a homing hippo. 'Large' didn't do the guy justice; he barely scraped between the edges of the study door either side without taking the frame with him, and I reckoned nine-tenths of what lay under the sharp broad-striper mantle was pure solid blubber. Most fat men are just fat; Vitellius was a positive triumph of adiposity.

'Corvinus,' he said. 'Good of you to see me. Not inter-rupting you at all, am I?'

Yeah, well, maybe he had missed the abacus, the pile of wax tablets on the desk, the chewed pen and the clumps of torn-out hair littering the floor, but I wouldn't be placing any bets. Litter-carrier's nightmare or not, not even one of the Senate's leading lights could be that unobservant. 'No problem,' I said. 'You, uh, want to sit down?'

The study only has one couch, but there is a chair for visi-tors. Quite a substantial one, luckily, and armless or it would've been a non-starter. He pulled it up and sat. The legs creaked and I heard a faint groaning as the leather straps underneath took the consular strain.

'You're doing the accounts?' Vitellius nodded towards the mess on the desk. So he had noticed after all.

'Yeah,' I said. 'Or I was, anyway.'

'Try to avoid it myself. Get my secretary to do it. Sharp young Greek lad with a proper head for figures. You have to watch the bugger, though. Some of these accountants are too damn constructive for their own good.'

'Right. Right.' Bathyllus knocked and came in with the

wine tray, deferential as hell. 'Fine, little guy,' I said. 'Just pour for us and then go and buff up the cutlery, okay?' That got me another sniff; if there was a prize for Rome's top snob Bathyllus would win it at a slow canter; on his scale consulars rate pretty high, and left to himself he tends to make the most of them. I waited until the door closed behind him with a frustrated click. 'So. What can I do for you?'

Vitellius took a swallow of the wine. The huge jowls wobbled as he smacked his lips. 'Not bad stuff, this. Who do you deal with?'

Bugger; I hate this pussyfooting around. I could cheerfully do without Vitellius, too, even if the alternative was cerebral torture. 'A guy in the Argiletum. It's all right. Now I'm sorry to be pushy, but—'

'Got a little job for you. At least, not me personally.' He paused. 'In fact, Corvinus, this isn't my idea at all and we may as well get that straight from the start, all right? No offence meant, but there we are.'

Jupiter! Yeah, well, on the few occasions our paths had crossed we hadn't exactly hit it off, but there was a sourness to his tone that didn't suggest the relationship was set to improve. Still, he was the one sitting in the visitor's chair drinking my wine, not the other way about. I leaned back against the couch-end. 'Yeah?' I said. 'What kind of job would that be, now?'

That got me a long, slow, jowly stare: evidently in Vitellius's book answering questions was something other people did, preferably when he was doing the asking. He took another gulp of wine and set the cup down, like he was drawing some kind of line. 'I'm just the messenger-boy,' he grunted. 'Isidorus'll explain things to you personally.'

Yeah? Well, that was a delight to know, anyway. 'Who's Isidorus?'

'The man who wants you to do the little job.'

'Really? All of that?' I said brightly. Shit; break over. Two minutes into the conversation or not, I'd had enough of this lark. Throwing the bugger out on his very substantial beam-end would take a lot of muscle, sure, but I could always call in some of the bought help to give me a hand. And finding out whether he bounced or just came down with a nice hefty thud would set me up very nicely for the rest of a very boring morning. 'Now listen, pal. You may not be aware of this, and it's not your fault if you aren't, but you chose a really terrible day for giving me the run-around. Bearing that in mind, and considering the possible resultant consequences of an unconsidered reply, suppose we try that last one again. You ready? Good. Now. Who the fuck is Isidorus? And why should he think I need any sort of a job?'

The jowls purpled and quivered. I could see the guy was within a hair's-breadth of coming back at me in spades – not that I'd've minded – but he just reached for his cup and took another gulp before he answered. Interesting; ex-consuls aren't exactly easy-going at the best of times, and that little bit of lèse-majesté ought to have got me blistered. Vitellius was holding himself in so tight I wondered he didn't rupture. The question was, why?

'Isidorus of Charax,' he said shortly.

I nodded. 'Right. Right. That is *really* informative, pal. So far we've got the length of a name and a place of birth. Now maybe you'd like to go a little bit further and tell me what the guy actually does.'

The purpling went up a notch. 'Jupiter bloody best and greatest, Corvinus! If this were up to me . . . !'

'You'd spit in my eye. Yeah. I'd sort of worked that one out for myself, and to tell you the truth I'm wondering why you don't. Seriously wondering, because Isidorus has to be Greek, Greeks in Rome don't rate consular messenger-boys, and if they ever did the bugger in question sure as hell wouldn't roll over and take it like you seem to be doing. So I'll ask you again: who's Isidorus?'

Pause; *long* pause, while we glared at each other. Then, suddenly, Vitellius grinned; not a pleasant grin, either, even allowing for the three or four blackened teeth that showed when he smiled.

'Oh, dear,' he said. 'I am *really* going to enjoy this.'

He reached into his mantle-fold, pulled out a sealed letter and handed it over. Then he reached for his wine cup, took a hefty swig and sat back, his eyes on my face.

I broke the seal, and my eye went straight to the authorising signature . . .

Tiberius Julius Caesar Augustus.

Aka the Wart.

Oh, shit.

I read the thing through from the start. Not that there was much of it; just the bald request that I be good enough to put myself at the disposal of Isidorus of Charax and the Roman Senate, on a matter that would be explained to me.

I raised my eyes to Vitellius's face. He was smiling so hard there could've been a hinge in his neck.

'The litter's waiting,' he said.

I took a long slug of my untouched wine before I stood up. Something told me I was going to need it.

The Wart, eh?

Fuck.

2

Litters I hate, but it was throwing it down outside, and, besides I was still too much in shock to object. The four chair guys and the half-dozen outwalkers that Vitellius rated were sheltering beneath the branches of the big beech tree that grew the other side of our garden wall and overhung the pavement. I thought I heard one of them swear as we came down the steps – understandable, seeing what the poor bugger was faced with hefting on the return journey – but they were over and ready to go almost as soon as we'd climbed in. Vitellius, I noted, didn't bother to give any instructions.

'Where are we going?' I asked. 'Or is that a secret too?'

'Palatine.' Vitellius was beetroot-faced and breathless with the effort of climbing over the sill. He grunted and heaved himself upright against the cushion facing me. The litter rocked and, outside, someone swore again. 'House of Augustus.'

Yeah, right; well, that made sense, anyway. Taken together with the letter, a lot of sense. It meant that whoever this Isidorus was – I'd've guessed, from his name, he was a freedman, but maybe I was wrong, because even the most trusted imperial freedman didn't have that much clout – he was on the imperial side of things. Fifty years back when Rome's first First Citizen had been handed his major slice of the administrative cake by the Senate he and Livia had worked, as it were, from home, and built on accordingly; with the result that a lot of the purely imperial business was done on the Palatine, while Capitol Hill tended to be senatorial or shared. Most of it was pretty high-powered, too; certainly too important to trust to just any broad-striper whose family connections might've got him the city judgeship or consulship but who still couldn't be relied on to find his backside three tries out of five with both hands and a map. A Greek was pushing things, mind, freeborn or not; which made Vitellius's tight-lipped play-it-by-the-book attitude doubly weird.

He wasn't very forthcoming on the journey, either. Not that I pushed, mind. I was still in shock.

I'm not all that familiar with the Palatine. There're still some private houses up there, sure – I used to own one of them myself – but most of these are on the outer slopes. Since Augustus's day the central area has gradually been becoming state-owned, and there're more libraries, picture galleries and temples than you can shake a stick at. Plus, of course, the various properties that technically belong to the imperial family but are mostly used by the imperial administration, like Augustus House itself.

The rain was slackening off as we parked the litter and mounted the steps, but by the looks of the sky there was plenty more to come, which didn't bode well for the Augustalia in three days' time. We were met in the cool, tastefully decorated atrium by a cool, tastefully decorated secretary. A couple of mean six-foot-tall by three-foot-wide Praetorians glowered at us under their helmets from either side of a staircase that was all coloured marble and polished cedar.

'Morning, Quintus.' Vitellius nodded to the secretary. 'This is Marcus Valerius Corvinus. We've an appointment with Isidorus.'

'Ah, yes. Indeed.' The guy gave me a long, cool stare. Yeah, well; at least this time round I was looking respectable. I hadn't changed my tunic but I had on one of the new mantles Perilla buys me every Winter Festival and I hardly ever get round to wearing. 'You're to go straight up, sir. Alciphron!'

An exquisitely barbered slave unfolded himself from a stool by the wall. I raised an eyebrow at Vitellius – I'd expected he'd know his way well enough to do without an escort – but he didn't seem particularly surprised. Maybe this Alciphron had a pocketful of doggie biscuits to get us past the Praetorians.

We set off up the stairs. Forget the pocketful: if our gopher had been handing out doggie biscuits he'd've needed a sack. It could've been a hangover from Augustus's own day – although from what I'd heard of the old buffer he'd been far too smart to give the impression of a closely guarded autocrat – but there were sentries stationed every few yards. Seriously armed sentries, too. Impressive. Finally, we reached a pair of oak-panelled doors. The gopher tapped gently, waited, then opened the doors and stood aside to let us pass.

I had to stop myself from whistling. I've been in plenty of government offices in my time, sure, but this one had them all beat hollow. My bet was that in its day it'd been Augustus's private library. Certainly it was grand enough: bronzes by the cartload and more book cubbies let into the walls than you'd see in Rome anywhere outside the Pollio. Fully stacked, as well. At the end of the room was a big desk with a huge window behind it, the shutters drawn back either side to show a canopied balcony and the city beyond. Nice; and that grade of view wasn't wasted on clerks.

The guy sitting at the desk didn't fit with the surroundings at all. Isidorus – it had to be Isidorus – was a little, nondescript, balding man with ears that stuck out like lugs on a wine jar, a snub nose and a scrawny neck bare and wrinkled as a plucked chicken's. In that room he looked as out of place as a freedman's nag in a racing stable.

'Ah, Lucius,' he said. 'You've brought him. Well done.' The bland face turned in my direction. 'Come in, Valerius Corvinus. Have a drink. I've managed to get you some Caecuban. It's one of your favourites, so I understand.'

'Uh . . . yeah,' I said. 'Yes, it is. How did you . . . ?'

'Very good. The jug's on that table to your right. Help yourself. And one for Lucius, if you don't mind. I won't, myself.'

Feeling slightly unreal, I went over to the side table, poured two cupfuls from the snazzy silver jug and took them over to the desk. Vitellius was already overflowing one of the guest chairs. I handed him his wine, and he grunted.

'Now. Sit down, my dear fellow. Make yourself at home.'

I took the second chair. Now I was closer I noticed the guy's tunic. It was the lounging type, and practically worn through in places; the sort of old, comfortable thing you hang on to despite your wife's and major-domo's best efforts to get rid of it. That impressed me like hell, even more than the fancy surroundings. Dress sense on the Palatine or the Capitol's important. Government officials wear formal mantles, the sharper the better, because they like to score over the underlings and visitors on the other side of the desk. It's only the *really* senior types – and I'm talking imperial family here – who can wear what they damn well like because impressing visitors isn't something they need to worry about. Isidorus wasn't a blood-imperial, sure, of course not, but the principle was the same. I'd bet that if he stood up and walked around he'd have on the down-at-heel party slippers to match.

The other thing I noticed was his eyes. They were pale

grey, and very, very smart. You didn't see that too often either.

Yeah, right. Forget freedman; whatever position Isidorus held in the imperial hierarchy, the guy *rated*. That was clear as daylight.

I sipped the Caecuban . . .

The stuff went past my palate and down my throat like liquid silk: real spice-route silk, too, not the Coan variety. Any Caecuban's good, sure, if it's the genuine article, which a lot of it isn't, but this wasn't just any Caecuban; this was the real stuff, from the Caesars' private cellars. I'd tasted it once or twice before, and believe me there is nothing comes near it, not even the best Falernian. 'Managed', hell; I'd bet springing a jug of that nectar took clout in the five-star, gold-edged super-executive class. That was a clincher, if I'd needed one, which I didn't. I reckoned if we weren't quite at the top of the movers-and-shakers tree here we were as close to it as made no difference.

The ice settled on my spine. First the Wart's letter, now this. What the hell was going on?

Isidorus waited for me to put the cup down. Then he said, 'Lucius will've given you very little information, Valerius Corvinus. On my instructions, so don't blame the poor man. That's right, isn't it, Lucius?'

Grunt.

I gave my erstwhile litter companion a sharp sideways glance. Shit; he hadn't said a word since we'd come in, and he was sitting nice as pie sipping his wine like a dowager. My neck prickled. I just *knew* the guy had been warned in advance to keep his lip zipped and let Isidorus do the talking. The interesting thing was that he'd done it without a whimper. And consulars, like I say, don't take a back seat for nobody . . .

'Now.' Isidorus sat back. I couldn't see his feet, but I'd bet they were swinging clear of the floor. 'No doubt you're wondering what this is all about.'

'Uh . . . yeah,' I said. 'Yeah, you could say that.'

'Fair enough. You've heard, I expect, of Prince Phraates?'

'Who?'

Vitellius might've been playing dumb man-in-the-middle, but he grunted again like someone had shoved a pin into his ample rump.

Isidorus ignored him. 'No, then,' he said. 'Well, it doesn't matter. Phraates is the youngest son of a former king of Parthia, although the term *young* is no longer appropriate.' He paused, then said cautiously, 'You, er, have heard of Parthia, haven't you, Corvinus?'

Beside me, Vitellius choked on his wine.

Well, I appreciated the guy's delicacy, and there wasn't so much as a smidgeon of sarcasm in the tone, but even with my grasp of geography I couldn't't've missed a bloody great empire stretching all the way from the Syrian border to India.

'Sure,' I said. 'Of course.'

Isidorus smiled. 'Good. I'm relieved. Phraates, then, is a Parthian prince. He was sent here by his father, partly as a hostage and partly for his own safety, sixty-odd years ago in the Divine Augustus's day.'

Sixty years! Gods! 'And he's still alive?'

'Oh, my goodness, yes, very hale and hearty. He lives with his Greek mistress and son in a villa over on the Janiculan; a very nice property, very nice indeed, or so I understand. His survival, though, is very much to the point. Two days ago, on his way home from a dinner party in the early hours of the morning, he was attacked by a gang of knifemen.'

I sat back in my chair. We were into things here that I understood.

'He was *what*?' I said.

'The attack happened not far from the Esquiline Gate,

near Maecenas Gardens. Fortunately it was beaten off and the attackers never reached the prince's litter, but three of his bodyguard were killed outright and one died later.' The smart grey eyes hadn't left mine, not for an instant, and there wasn't even the hint of a smile now. 'There. Your comments, please.'

'It doesn't make sense,' I said.

'Really? Now why would you say that?'

I was being tested, and I knew it. I wasn't looking at Vitellius, but I could feel him watching me. 'Jupiter, where do you start? You might as well've said that the guy'd been raped by a passing walrus. Knifemen don't operate in gangs. They're solo artists, or they work in threes or fours at most. Second, they go for pedestrians, usually lone drunks. They steer clear of heavily guarded litters and carriages because taking on opposition like that just isn't worth the risk. And last, in that part of the city even at that time of night there's plenty of well-heeled traffic about with protection of its own that would wade in and sort the buggers out. Will that do you?'

The smile came back, but the eyes behind it were still cold and level. 'Oh, yes, Valerius Corvinus. Thank you, very concise. That will do very well indeed. And yes, I agree that it makes no sense; I agree absolutely. The problem is that it did actually happen. Now. We'll move on. There's something I haven't told you which may have a bearing on matters. And I must emphasise that the information is totally confidential.' He glanced at Vitellius. 'Five days ago, three days before the attack on Phraates's litter, a Parthian delegation arrived in Rome. If negotiations with them are successful then Prince Phraates will be sent east with Roman military backing to be made Great King of Parthia.'

My guts went cold.

'Oh,' I said. 'Oh, fuck.'

Beside me Vitellius gave a sharp, pained grunt and closed his eyes. Yeah, well; as diplomatic expressions go it probably did leave something to be desired.

'Quite.' Isidorus cleared his throat. 'That aside, you see now, of course, the significance of the attack. And its implications. If Phraates had been killed – which was certainly the intention – then our whole plan for replacing Artabanus would have become unworkable at a stroke.'

'Uh . . . Artabanus?'

'Do forgive me, Corvinus. Artabanus is the present Great King.'

'Of Parthia,' Vitellius muttered. His eyes were closed again, so he missed Isidorus's glare.

Well, if you don't ask you never know. 'Right. Right,' I said.

'Artabanus isn't popular at present with a fair percentage of the Parthian nobility. Hence the delegation.'

I took another sip of the Caecuban. 'Uh. . . . this may be a silly question, but why should the Parthians send to us for a king?'

'Because they've no choice. When Artabanus came to power he had all his potential rivals executed. Which left Phraates who was beyond his reach. Or has been up to now.' He was watching me closely. 'I'm sorry, Corvinus. I have tried to simplify things, but the situation really is quite complex. That will do us for the present, but if you have any questions of your own I'd be glad to answer them, or try to.'

Fair enough. 'Just the one,' I said.

'Ask away, then.'

'It's simple. I'm no diplomat, I'm not even political, and it's obvious what I know about Parthia you could write on the back of a bust sandal strap. Whatever you want doing in this business, the Roman bureaucracy's full of sharp cookies a lot more qualified than I am. So why choose me?'

Isidorus rubbed his temples. 'Ah,' he said. 'Yes. A fair point. My instructions came directly from the emperor.' He turned to Vitellius. 'You did show Valerius Corvinus the letter, didn't you, Lucius?'

I shifted in my chair. 'Yeah, he did, but still—'

'Tiberius gave me no explanation – as, naturally, was his right – but I would imagine his choice of you in particular was based largely on, ah, certain events that took place a few years back.' He cleared his throat again. Vitellius's attention, I noticed, was suddenly on his wine cup. 'Events which we won't go into here. I understand, though, that in the course of them you met the emperor personally.'

'Ah . . . yeah.' Sure I did. My balls still shrank at the memory.

'Then you obviously made a lasting impression on him.'

I swallowed. Shit; now *there* was an uncomfortable thought. Just the mere notion that I figured anywhere at all in that cold, calculating, abacus-minded bastard's world view made my skin crawl. 'Okay. Fine. Forget me as such. Why anyone outside government circles?'

'Because sixty years in Rome or not Phraates is still a bloody Parthian.'

I blinked; not at the mild swear-word, although I hadn't expected it from Isidorus, but because of the tone. For the first time in the guy's bland delivery I detected what sounded very like a note of exasperation. 'Very illuminating,' I said.

Isidorus gave a tight smile. 'Corvinus, I'm sorry. You're quite right; in itself that answer was *not* particularly helpful. Still, it's the one you want. As a guest of the Roman state, Phraates is under our protection and eligible for our help – our *official* help – as and when necessary. As following the attack on his litter it now is. You'd agree?'

'Uh . . . sure,' I said. 'Obviously.'

'Obviously. Yes. I would have thought so too. The

problem is that Prince Phraates is having none of it. Neither the protection nor the help.'

'Why the hell not?'

'Because he's a Parthian. Parthians may ask for Roman help – the delegation is a case in point – but they don't do so lightly. Also, there's a certain amount of professional pride involved. Phraates has always had a private bodyguard: technically illegal on Roman soil, of course, but under the circumstances we're not going to be picky. He also has his own espionage system; again unofficial, naturally, but which, to be fair – and I'm speaking professionally – is not one to be sneered at. He considers both these factors to be quite sufficient for countering any threat and has told us in no uncertain terms that he will look after his own safety. Which, from Rome's – from *my* – point of view is extremely worrying. You're with me?'

'Yeah. Yeah, sure.'

'On the other hand, Prince Phraates for all his faults is very much the pragmatical diplomat. As am I. The two of us may have our own opinions and priorities, but in this instance like it or not we have to agree on a common policy and course of action. His sticking point was and is that he wants no official nursemaiding – the word is his – because that, as he sees things, would compromise his new status as prospective Great King. He is, however, willing to accept an independent investigator with no vested interest in either camp. The compromise – as suggested by the emperor – is you.'

I kept my tone and my expression neutral. 'Is that so, now?'

'That, I'm afraid, is so. Your task, of course, would be to find out who is trying to kill Prince Phraates before he succeeds.'

Yeah, well; I'd assumed that might be it. Still, it was as well to have it out in plain Latin. Nonetheless . . .

'You don't ask for much, do you, pal?' I said.

That got me a level stare. 'Trust me, I know exactly how much I'm asking. Although I'd remind you the idea did not originate with me.'

'And, uh, things would depend on me agreeing, naturally?'

The grey eyes were still fixed on mine. 'In theory, yes. In practice . . . well, I'm afraid that in the light of circumstances you would be a very brave man to refuse.'

'Yeah. Yeah, right.' Well, at least the guy was being up front about it. And he was spot on. Saying no to the Wart was about as smart a move as taking a stroll through a snake-pit.

'Believe me, Corvinus, I'm no happier about the situation than you are. I dislike having to use amateurs at the best of times, and on this occasion it worries me very much.' He must've seen something in my expression, because he held up a hand. 'No. Don't misunderstand me. I don't mean to be disparaging, I'm simply stating a fact. As you'll discover for yourself, dealing with Parthians – Parthian aristocrats, especially – isn't easy. They're touchy, vain, two-faced as Janus, and it takes a lifetime's study to understand the way their minds work. If you ever get that far.'

'No different to Roman senators, then, right?' I glanced at Vitellius. He coloured to the eyeballs but didn't bite.

'Oh, a great deal more complicated than that. I never said your task would be easy. What I am saying is that it's important for Rome. And, I believe, for Parthia.'

'Not to mention for this Phraates.'

His lips twitched in a smile. 'Quite.'

'One last question?'

'Go ahead.'

'It's the obvious one, sure, but it has to be asked and answered. This King Artabanus; he have any spies – agents – operating in Rome?'

Isidorus leaned back. Obvious question or not, he took his time answering. 'No,' he said finally. 'He does not. Not that

I am aware of, certainly. And before you ask, I would, Valerius Corvinus, be *very* aware of something like that, believe me.'

Well, you didn't get much more definite, and from Isidorus I'd take it as final. No one had told me what the guy's exact job was, but I'd bet a sturgeon to a pickled walnut he knew what he was talking about there. 'Fine,' I said. 'So. When do I get to talk to Phraates?'

'Ah.' Isidorus turned briefly to Vitellius. 'This is where Lucius comes in.' Yeah; I'd been wondering – barring the messenger-boy angle – why our broad-rumped consular had been invited to this little confab. 'Lucius is heading the imperial sub-committee negotiating with the Parthian envoys. That side of things doesn't affect you, of course, but fortunately it does provide you with an excellent natural opportunity to meet the prince and certain . . . others.' There was something in his tone, and in the hesitation before that last word, that made me frown, but the eyes discouraged questions. 'Lucius?'

Vitellius shifted his massive weight in his chair and leaned forward. The wooden joints of the chair creaked. 'We've put the Parthians in one of the imperial guest-houses, Corvinus,' he said. 'West slope, facing the Capitol. They're giving a dinner there tonight for Phraates and a couple of the other local eastern bigwigs. I'm invited, and I've cleared it with Phraates for you to come too. As my aide.' He scowled. 'Which last fact you'll remember, please, and act on accordingly, because as far as the delegation's concerned that's all you are at present. That clear?'

'Uh . . . yeah.' Jupiter on a trolley! 'It's clear.'

'Fine. Don't forget it, then.' The scowl didn't lift. Obviously, my fat pal the consular wasn't any more tickled to have me aboard the good ship Diplomacy than his boss was. Only Isidorus covered it better.

Isidorus stood up. I'd been right about his lack of height; the top of his head was about level with my chin. 'Excellent,' he said. 'I wish you luck, Valerius Corvinus.' He held out his hand and we shook. 'Luck, and success. Incidentally, I'll have a word with Quintus on the front desk. If you do need to see me at any stage without Lucius here in attendance you should have no trouble.'

Meeting over, evidently. I drank the last of the Caecuban at a gulp – that I wasn't going to waste – and got to my feet.

'I'll pick you up at sunset,' Vitellius growled. 'Wear your best mantle.'

Well, that was the easy part over. Now I had to explain things to Perilla.

3

Perilla was in when I got back, copying out the notes she'd taken at the Pollio Library. I carried Bathyllus's welcome-home jug and cup over to my couch, planting the usual smacker on her raised lips in passing.

'Marcus, where on earth were you?' She put the pen down. 'Bathyllus just said you'd gone out. I thought you were doing the household accounts today.'

'Ah . . . yeah. Yeah, I was.' Gods! This wasn't going to be easy. 'I got sort of sidetracked. You . . . ah . . . have a good time?'

'Oh, yes. Very interesting.' She consulted her notes. 'Did you realise that the goby can stop a ship under full sail dead in the water, just by fastening itself by its jaws to the hull?'

'Uh-uh. What the hell's a goby?'

'A small carnivorous marine fish, two inches long.'

'Shit. Where did you find that?'

'In Trebius Niger. Seemingly one of them immobilised Antony's flagship at the Battle of Actium. He also says that swordfish exist that sink ships by puncturing them. And don't swear.'

'Trebius Niger's a credulous prat.'

She frowned down at the wax tablet and closed it. 'Yes, perhaps you're right, dear. I wasn't totally convinced by the goby, I must admit. I mean, why would it bother? Some of him's quite good, though. Niger, that is. Oh, and apropos of fish, Meton asked me to tell you that he's got a basket of lampreys. We're having them for dinner tonight.'

My blood ran cold. Hell; I hadn't even *thought* of Meton. Our prima-donna food-fixated chef needed three days' notice in writing for an ordinary skipped meal. A few hours and a special fish evening combined put the potential repercussions into the mythical bracket, up alongside the punishment of Sisyphus. 'Er . . . I won't be in for dinner tonight,' I said.

Her eyes met mine; the lady had got the implications as well as I had. 'Oh, *Marcus*!' she said.

'Don't worry; I'll speak to Meton.'

She was still staring at me in horror. 'Marcus, he will go *berserk*! Do you know how often he has a whole basket of lampreys? I mean, these things cost a fortune. When you can even get them.'

'Yeah, well . . .'

'Where are you going?'

'The, uh, Palatine. With Lucius Vitellius and a few, ah, Parthians. It's a sort of . . . diplomatic dinner.'

The temperature in the room suddenly dropped below freezing. Perilla set the tablets down carefully on the floor.

'Tell me,' she said, very quietly.

So I told her.

'At least there isn't a body this time,' I said when I'd finished and the spiders had come out of cover. 'The guy survived.'

'Corvinus, this is politics!' You could've used the line of the lady's lips to slice marble. 'You know how dangerous politics are. I'd have thought you would've learned your lesson after Sejanus. Why on *earth* didn't you tell them to find someone else?'

'That wasn't an option. In any case, this time's different. It's official, and I'm on the right side of the line.'

'You think that matters?'

'Perilla, the letter was signed by the Wart himself. I can't buck that.'

She turned away. 'Marcus, why does it always have to be *you*?'

'Maybe I'm just lucky.' I saw her shoulders stiffen. 'Joke.'

'Was it really?' She still wasn't looking at me. 'Has it ever occurred to you, Marcus Valerius Messalla Corvinus, that anyone who is capable of murdering or assassinating or otherwise disposing of another human being or attempting to do so might just have no compunction about adding to their score whoever is stupid enough to shove his nose into their business?'

'Ah . . . yeah. Yeah, it has. Usually in the middle of the night after too much cheese last thing.'

'Will you please, for one minute, be serious!'

Pause; long pause. I got up, went over and put my arms round her. She was shaking. Uh-oh; this was a bad one.

'I think,' she said softly, her forehead against my chest, 'that one of these days I am going to be upstairs working on a poem, or sitting reading, or doing something equally innocent and inane, when Bathyllus will come in and tell me you've been found in an alleyway with your throat cut or your head pulped, and that will be that. It's happened – or almost happened – once before, when it was a hole in the ribs. The next time it will be real, and it will be permanent. Now tell me I'm wrong.'

Jupiter in tights! When Perilla's in this mood – and it doesn't happen often – then all you can do is sit it out.

'You want me to put in for some government office, lady?' I said quietly. 'Spend our evenings discussing grain quotas and the latest contract proposals for manufacturing sediment traps in the public water supply?'

'No, of course not. You'd hate that sort of life, I know that. But it still doesn't mean you have to—'

'Okay, then. How about business? I'm a narrow-striper; there's nothing to stop me setting up a shipping company. You choose the product: Syrian glassware, for instance. You know the breakage and loss statistics on the Antioch/Puteoli run for Syrian glass and how that'd affect the mark-up? I could give you really fascinating nuggets of information like that over the fruit and nuts after dinner. Or there's farming. Good solid purple-striper tradition, farming. I could set something up with Alexis the botanical whizz-kid, breed a new kind of super-radish—'

She hit me. Not hard, just a gentle punch, but she meant it all the same. 'Marcus, stop it. All right, point taken. You've got to do it, I know that. Get yourself involved. Still, knowing doesn't make things any easier.'

I kissed her. 'Yeah,' I said. 'Yeah, well . . .'

Crisis over. I knew the signs. The thing is, if I ever did turn respectable – or what my father would've called respectable, anyway, which meant boring-conventional – it would hit Perilla bad. Whether she admitted it to me, or to herself, or not I was as sure of that as I was of anything. And that would be that.

Not that she didn't have a point, mind.

'So.' She pulled away and wiped her nose. 'What are your plans? Besides talking to this Prince Phraates at the wretched dinner?'

I shrugged. 'I hadn't really thought. Maybe pay Lippillus a visit.' Decimus Lippillus was the local Watch head at Public Pond and an old friend. He was also smart as paint, and the Esquiline mightn't be his own patch but he'd have contacts. 'See if I can trace the knifemen responsible, work back from there to whoever set the attack up.'

'Knifemen,' Perilla said. I skidded to a mental halt. Bugger. Now *that* had been a mistake. 'Uh . . . yeah. Not that I'm thinking of tracing the actual knifemen themselves, of course, no, no, perish the thought, but—'

'Corvinus, you are so transparent that it is not true!' She laughed; not altogether a happy laugh, but a laugh nevertheless. The laugh died and she was suddenly serious again. 'Well, no doubt I'm being silly and I'll get over it. Don't forget, though, will you, that silly is not the same as stupid. Not the same at all.'

'No.' I kissed her again. 'No, I won't forget.'

'Good.' She kissed me back. 'Now perhaps you'd better have that word with Meton. Before he decides on what sauce to serve with the lampreys.'

Oh, hell. Still, there was no point in putting it off. Bite on the shield-strap, get it over. 'Yeah, right,' I said.

I turned round and yelled for Bathyllus.

The little bald-head soft-shoed in within ten seconds flat. He hadn't been eavesdropping, I knew that: Bathyllus, like all the best major-domos, has the uncanny ability of materialising where he's wanted, when he's wanted, from whatever part of the property he's been in before. Me, I've given up wondering how he does it. It's a mystery, like how vultures conceive or how senators manage to tie their sandal straps.

'Yes, sir.'

'Fetch Meton in, would you, pal?' There was *no* way – no way – that I was going to beard that surly bugger in his own kitchen. Even if he'd let me over the threshold.

I'd tried to sound offhand, and Bathyllus's expression didn't change, but I noticed his Adam's apple went up and then down briefly, the way someone's might if you said to them: 'I have grave news concerning your grandmother and a patch of spilled oil at the top of the stairs.'

'Yes, sir,' he said, and exited in the direction of the kitchen.

I went back to my own couch, lay down and took a large, nerve-steadying swig from my wine cup. Shit! This wasn't how it was supposed to go between the master and the bought help. Technically, as the warped, evil-minded, misanthropic bugger's owner, I had literal power of life or death over him. I could sell him to a male brothel, have him flogged, sent to the mines or the quarries, thrown to his own bloody lampreys as a special dinner course himself, recycled for cat meat. I could—

'Yeah, what is it? Only I got a stock simmering that has to be skimmed every five minutes.'

I refocused. Not that Meton was a pretty sight to focus on. 'Uh . . . right. No problem, pal. None at all. I just wanted to talk to you about dinner tonight.'

The proto-human that was probably one of the best chefs in the city glowered, which for Meton passes as a beam. 'The mistress told you about the lampreys, then?' He glanced at Perilla, who'd picked up her tablets again and was studying them like Trebius Niger was the greatest thing since Aristotle. Traitor.

'Yeah. Incidentally, where *did* you get them from?'

'Special cut-price deal, bankrupt goods. A friend's master died sudden and the old bugger had a cash-flow problem. He let me in on the ground floor.'

Oh, shit; a horrible thought struck me: lampreys were notoriously unfussy feeders. 'This, er, master, Meton. He didn't happen to die by drowning and/or being digested, did he?'

'Nah. Hit by a lump of tenement down the Subura.'

'Fine. Fine. Just checking.'

'They're prime fish. Practically full-grown. Real beauties.' Meton's eyes under their solid eyebrow matting gleamed. 'I reckon slow-stewed in Pramnian with bay, peppercorns and a touch of lovage, then reduce the stock as a gravy. Or I might do some of them—'

'Meton—'

'. . . sliced and pickled in juniper-berry vinegar, then set in a fennel jelly with capers. I picked up a few crayfish in the market this morning. Crayfish'd go nice on the side split and grilled *au naturel* with—'

'Meton—'

'. . . a basting of cold-pressed extra-virgin oil, some rosemary and a touch of good fish sauce. Valentian, not Tarraconian, that bloody stuff's overrated. Then there's—'

'Meton, pal, I'll be eating out tonight.'

He stopped like he'd run into a brick wall. He didn't say anything, he just . . . *looked*. The effect plus the hair was unnerving.

'Uh, it's an unexpected dinner party. I didn't know anything about it until this morning.'

Silence. Dead silence. The colour had drained from Meton's face. What I could see of it, anyway. Then it began to spread back up, starting from the neck and working its way north to the eyebrows. The huge hands began to twitch like matted spiders . . .

'Tomorrow's okay, though,' I said quickly. 'Tomorrow would be fine. Lampreys'll keep for a day easy, right?'

The fingers were beginning to curl. The guy still hadn't spoken, but everything visible and non-hirsute above the tunic top was an interesting puce.

'You could . . . ah . . . Perilla won't be coming.' I was babbling now, to fill the awful vacuum of silence. 'She'd be happy with just the crayfish. Or maybe you could do just half the lampreys, the ones in wine, and we could have the cold ones in jelly tomorrow. How does that sound, pal? Nice, eh? That okay with you, Perilla?'

Her nose was still buried in the tablets so all I could see was the top of her head.

'Yes, dear,' she murmured. 'That would be lovely.'

Oh, great, so much for conjugal support. Hell, I was

beginning to sweat in earnest. 'It's, uh, a really important dinner, Meton. *Really* important. You see, there're these Parthians, and . . .'

The brows came down like feral caterpillars. 'Parthians?' he said. 'You're eating with fucking *Parthians*?'

'Uh . . . yeah, as it happens. A . . . uh . . . delegation of Parthian aristos.' Bugger; so much for confidentiality. Still, Meton was safe; you could tell Meton that the Wart had sneaked back into Rome disguised as a pork butcher and he'd've asked what kind of sausages he'd brought with him. 'They're having a special dinner.'

'A Parthian dinner? With Parthian food? *Real* Parthian food?'

'Could be. Could be.' I was watching him closely. The fingers had uncurled and he was almost smiling, or doing what for Meton amounted to smiling, which wasn't scowling too hard. Maybe we were going to come through this yet. 'I . . . ah . . . didn't think to ask at the time.'

He looked at me with total incredulity, then shook his head. Yeah, well; people have different priorities. If you can categorise Meton as people.

'You think there might be guinea-fowl?' He'd taken on a sort of inward look. 'Parthians have this stuffing for guinea-fowl with dates and pine nuts, see. I've heard of it, sure, but I've never come across a recipe.'

'Is that so, now?' I hadn't seen the bugger so animated since he'd got his hands on a giraffe left over from the Games. We had recognisable grammar and syntactical cohesion, for a start. I began to breathe again. 'Great. Look, Meton, let's do a deal, okay? We leave the lampreys for tomorrow and I have a word with the Parthian chef, see if he can help. How about that, eh, pal?'

The simian brows knotted. 'They've got this other thing, a dessert. It's a compote of apples and pears with ginger, poppy seeds and mountain honey done in a pastry shell.'

'Just leave it with me, pal,' I said quickly. 'Have we a deal or not?'

'Dessert included?'

'No problem.'

He stuck out a massive hairy paw, and we shook.

'Great,' I said. 'You'd best go and, uh, stock the skim.'

'Skim the stock, Marcus,' Perilla murmured, eyes still fixed on Trebius Niger.

'Crawl back under your stone, lady. Okay, Meton, that'll be all.'

He left, walking like the marble floor was blue empyrean, and I breathed a sigh of relief: first crisis of the case over. Second, counting Perilla.

I just hoped the Parthians hadn't gone native and we were eating Roman.

4

Vitellius arrived prompt at sunset, as promised, in a very up-market litter with more than the usual complement of escort, complete with enough torches to make for a decent-sized comet: evidently we were representing Rome here, and out to impress. Me, I'd rather have indulged my hatred of litters and hiked it; although the clouds were building up from the north, promising a seriously wet night, it wasn't actually raining, and the Palatine wasn't all that far. However, as per instructions I was wearing my best party mantle and carrying my snazziest pair of party slippers under my arm, and if the heavens did actually open before I got there my contribution as half-drowned rat to Rome's diplomatic brownie points would've been zilch.

Not, it transpired, from the sour look Vitellius gave the mantle as I climbed in opposite him, that I was likely to figure among the high scorers anyway.

'That the best you can do?' he growled.

'Yeah, that's about it,' I said equably. I cast an eye over his effort, which had dinky little designs picked out in seed-pearls. 'You look as if you've mugged an oyster-bed, pal.'

His mouth opened, then shut in a tight, hard line. The bearers took the strain, which was nine-tenths Vitellius, and we were off.

For the first part of the journey, Vitellius sat and sulked, which in a large, jowly man is not a beautiful sight. I gave it ten minutes, then I said, 'Ah, maybe you'd better fill me in about who we're going to meet here.'

He looked across at me like I'd made the most bloody inane suggestion in the universe. Finally, when I'd decided he wasn't going to bother answering, he did.

'Fair enough. Pin your ears back. Phraates you know about. There're four delegation members. The leader's a noble from Ctesiphon – that's the Parthian capital, Corvinus, if you didn't know, inasmuch as these buggers have a capital – by the name of Zariadres. Oily chap, a courtier to his finger-nails, don't trust him an inch even for a Parthian. Then there's Osroes. He's a different kettle of fish entirely, not a courtier, one of those bloody Magians from the back country near the Caspian that've been pushing their way on to the Royal Council recently. He—'

'What're Magians?'

Vitellius glared at me. 'Jove's balls, you're hopeless! If I was as bloody ignorant as you are I'd slit my wrists.'

'Yeah, well.'

'They're a religious sect, or maybe an elitist social group. Either or both, whatever you like to call the buggers they're trouble. We don't have an equivalent at Rome, unless you think of a cross between an ultra pukkah, old patrician family and the high priesthood of Jupiter, and even that doesn't go far enough. Sunny, open, tolerant personalities they aren't, and Osroes is a fair representative sample. They're narrow-minded as hell, they've got all sorts of bees in their bonnets, and they hate everything that comes from the wrong side of the Syrian-Parthian border. Plus a lot of what goes on inside Parthia, to boot. Currently, they're trying to become a power at court whether Artabanus likes it or not, which by all accounts to give him his due he doesn't. Osroes knows that and he takes considerable exception. Which explains Osroes.'

'Okay. So who else have we got?'

'Peucestas. He's a eunuch.'

My face must've shown my feelings, because Vitellius grinned in the half-light of our flanking torchbearers. 'Get this through your skull now: there's no stigma attached to having no balls in Parthia. Quite the reverse. Eunuchs have a special place, and it's a highly respected one at that. You'd best get used to the idea.'

'Uh . . . fine. Fine.'

'Peucestas is okay. At least he looks normal, and he isn't effeminate. Like the other three he comes from a top aristocratic background. Family is – or was – big in Eastern Media. They chose the wrong side in a wrangle over the kingship twenty-odd years back when we were pushing another claimant. Artabanus broke them and Peucestas was one of the prime victims. He hates the Great King's guts, which is one reason why he's here.'

'Who's the fourth guy?'

'That's Callion.'

I blinked. 'He's a Greek?'

'One hundred per cent pure-blooded, both sides. And don't you forget it, boy, especially if you're talking to him and the subject comes up in conversation because you won't be popular if you do. Callion is not – I repeat *not* – a Parthian, not in his own view. There've been Greeks in Parthia since Alexander's time, when it was still Persia and the Parthians were just a bunch of hooligans living in tents out in the sticks. Callion's descended from a Macedonian cavalry commander who fought at Issus. His family's the richest and most influential in Seleucia.' He paused. 'Seleucia. That's a very big Greek city just across the Tigris from Ctesiphon, incidentally. In case you were wondering, which no doubt you were.'

I ignored the sarcasm: yeah, I had been wondering, as a matter of fact. The only Seleucia I knew was the port for

Antioch. 'Parthia has Greek cities?' I said. 'I mean *real* Greek cities?'

'Juno's bloody tits!' Vitellius shifted irritably on his elbow, making the litter shake. I felt the bearers stagger. 'Corvinus, don't you *dare* come out with a half-assed remark like that in Callion's hearing, okay? Ignorance is one thing but bloody stupidity's another. Look. Parthia's like us in one way: we've both got a lot of different peoples inside our borders and it saves hassle to allow them a certain amount of latitude in self-government. Right?'

'Uh . . . right,' I said.

'Only there's a difference between us and the Parthians where our provincials are concerned. We can draw a sharp line. If the buggers step across it they get hammered. We know it, they know it, there's no argument and no beefing. So they generally stay quiet and do as they're told. You're with me?' This time I didn't answer. 'Parthia can't do that because the Great King doesn't have the military clout. Seleucia may not be independent but she's big enough to warrant respect and careful handling. The Seleucians've always been awkward bastards where the Parthians are concerned, and being so close to Ctesiphon doesn't help matters because the king can't ignore them. On the other hand, it means they can't ignore the king either. Especially these days.'

He was still looking and sounding tetchy as hell, but I could appreciate that the guy was doing a conscientious job. This was all stuff I needed to know, and despite the grumbles he was giving it to me straight. Also, in a perverse way, I was interested.

'Uh . . . "these days"?' I said.

'More or less. I'm trying to simplify things for the sake of your weak brain, Corvinus. There's an anti-Greek push on at present, and the Seleucians are edgy because they reckon

– quite rightly so – that they've been sold out. And unless there's a change of regime things can only get worse. Hence Callion. You understand?' He grinned suddenly, revealing a mouthful of bad teeth. 'Oh, Parthian politics are endless fun. Keeping track of them beats banging your head against a brick wall any day.'

'Uh . . . yeah. Yeah, right.' I sat back against the cushions. I'd seriously underestimated Vitellius. Ten-ton broad-striper or not, the guy was no fool, and no slouch. He'd done his homework, he obviously knew what he was talking about, and for an off-the-cuff thumbnail sketch what I'd just had wasn't bad at all. I wasn't surprised that the Wart had chosen him as his prime dickerer. Tiberius was no fool either. 'Isidorus mentioned some others.'

'Right.' Vitellius glanced through the curtains, and my eyes followed his: we were past the top of Scaurus Incline now and onto the crest of the Palatine proper. 'Two in particular. Tiridates and Mithradates. Tiridates is Phraates's nephew.'

'He's a Parthian prince?'

'Damn right. He knows it, too. Cocky young bastard. Like Phraates he's been here since he was a kid, which isn't that long. And as you'll no doubt find out he doesn't like his uncle at all.'

'Uh-huh.' Interesting. 'So who's Mithradates? Another Parthian?'

'No. He's the younger brother of the Iberian king.'

Shit, I wished I could get my head round this foreign geography. I'd enough trouble with our variety. 'Okay, tell me,' I said. 'Where the hell's Iberia?'

'In the Caucasus, to the north of Armenia. The kingdom's got Greek connections, or so they claim.'

'What's he doing in Rome?'

'Keeping out of his brother's way. They hate each other's guts.'

'Is that so, now?' I wasn't unduly surprised: hating relatives' guts seemed to be endemic in the eastern world. 'So why the invite, if he's not a Parthian?'

'You heard of Armenia?'

Shit! 'Of course I've heard of bloody—'

'Fine. Then you'll know that whoever holds Armenia holds the key to Parthia. That's why it's changed hands more often in the last hundred years than a whore at a glee club party. Currently, the kingship's vacant. Artabanus has sent his son to take it over, but we can't have that. The emperor's on the point of backing Mithradates as king, with his brother's active support because that way he's rid of the sod. And a future king of Armenia is worth a Parthian dinner ticket, right?' Vitellius scowled. 'Look, Corvinus, this isn't for general consumption, so keep your bloody lip buttoned. Understand?'

I didn't bother to answer. Gods above! Talk about complexities! And I was definitely moving in high political circles here. It's not often you're invited to dinner with not one but two potential kings. Plus the aristocratic extras.

Vitellius was looking out of the window. 'Incidentally,' he said, 'just remember that you're in the diplomatic corps. Temporarily, but you follow the ground rules all the same. Play the smartass and I'll have your balls. Agreed?'

'Sure,' I said. 'I'll do my best.'

'You'll bloody well do better than that, boy, if you know what's good for you. And you can start now, because we've arrived.'

5

I got my first taste of what I was in for as soon as the door-slave opened up and we crossed the threshold. Normally, the vestibule of a house is pretty bare, with maybe some lamps on a portable stand so the evening guest can take in the host's pricey floor mosaic and possibly a mural or two without squinting and avoid the embarrassment of groping his way through to the atrium. I'd never actually walked on a carpet before: you get them in Rome, sure, but mats aside they're strictly wall decoration, and not that common, either. This one was big, covering practically the whole floor, and your feet just sank into it: a sort of woollen mosaic with a hunting scene worked into the pattern. In the wall niche to one side was a perfume-burner which filled the lobby with what I'd reckon was the equivalent of several gold pieces' worth of very expensive smells.

'Nice,' I said to Vitellius. He didn't bother to answer, just gave me a nasty look. Yeah, well: maybe diplomats on the job aren't supposed to notice these things.

The door-slave took our cloaks and outside sandals. I'd expected him to be locally grown bought help, part of the furniture and fittings that came with the house, but he was some sort of easterner. Obviously the delegation had brought their own staff.

'Drinks are being served in the atrium, sirs,' he murmured in Greek. 'If you'd care to go on through.'

We did; and if the lobby had been an eye-opener, the atrium was a real gobsmacker. Government guest-houses are generally bare places, not least because statues and the more portable items of furniture tend to disappear pretty quickly into some of the rougher guests' diplomatic bags and don't get replaced. Neither Isidorus nor Vitellius had told me how the delegation had travelled to Rome, but judging by the amount and appearance of the furniture and fittings my guess would be they'd hired an Egyptian grain barge. 'Travel fast, travel light' obviously wasn't a Parthian maxim; nor, for that matter, was 'You can't take it with you'. From the looks of things, these Parthian buggers had done just that, and they hadn't skimped themselves, either. There were more carpets, on the walls too, this time; more perfume-burners; and the number of lamps burning would've powered Alexandria's lighthouse.

'Stop gaping, you fool!' Vitellius muttered as we crossed the threshold. 'Remember, you're a fucking Roman diplomat!'

'Ah . . . right. Right.'

The atrium was full, and just glancing round I could see that I'd been wrong about Vitellius's mantle. If anything, he was underdressed. Most of the other men in the room – there weren't any women – had on long, brightly coloured embroidered tunics over silk trousers. Their beards – most of them were bearded – were curled and glistened with what was probably perfumed oil. What with that, the burners and the heat from the oil lamps I reckoned if I could get through the evening without keeling over I'd be one step ahead of the game.

'Ah, Lucius Vitellius! Welcome, my dear! Welcome!'

One of the beardies had detached himself from a nearby group and was homing in on us like a gilded barge. Before I knew quite what was happening he'd grabbed Vitellius by the shoulders and planted a smacker on each of his pendulous jowls, then a third full on the mouth. I winced, but Vitellius didn't seem fazed at all. Yeah, well: they do things different beyond the Orontes. Mind you, if he'd tried it in the Subura he'd've got himself decked.

'Good evening, Zariadres,' Vitellius said. Right; so this was the delegation leader, the smoothie from Ctesiphon. 'You're well, I trust. May I introduce Marcus Valerius Messalla Corvinus?'

Zariadres turned to me with a smile. I stuck out my hand quickly: diplomacy has its limits. We shook. His hand was soft, but not flabby: there was a strong grip there, and the eyes were sharp as knives. Right, then; scrub first impressions.

I hadn't fazed him, either. Smoothie or not, I reckoned Zariadres could keep up with the best of them.

'Oh, yes,' he said. 'Your aide, Vitellius. Prince Phraates did mention that you'd be bringing him.' We were speaking Greek, of course, but I'd expected that, and after a few years in Athens it was no problem. Zariadres's was standard Ionian: more liquid than the Athenian version, but completely fluent. 'A pleasure to meet you, Valerius Corvinus.'

'Uh . . . likewise.'

Without turning, Zariadres snapped his fingers. A slave – another easterner – materialised with a wine tray. Jupiter! They must even've brought the ordinary house slaves with them!

'Help yourselves to a drink and join us. We have a few minutes before dinner.'

I took a glass – they were Syrian, a matching set, and they must've cost a bomb – and sniffed the contents while Vitellius glared at me. In that company I was half expecting date wine or some aberration with honey in it, but the stuff was Caecuban. Not quite up to Isidorus's imperial standard, but pretty good all the same. I sipped appreciatively.

The other guys in the group Zariadres had left – there were two of them – had turned to us politely. The first was an old man in his late sixties, bearded, wearing a fetching embroidered tunic with a broad belt that dripped rubies and emeralds and made even Zariadres's get-up look dowdy. His hair and beard were oiled and curled, and he wore a headband with a single huge pearl at the front. That last was the giveaway. This just had to be Phraates. Only royals were allowed the diadem – even I knew that – and as prospective Great King the guy was obviously making a statement.

'Vitellius. How are you, my dear fellow?' he said in Latin. Then he looked at me and his eyes narrowed briefly. 'And Valerius Corvinus. A pleasure to meet you.' He changed to Greek. 'This is Callion.'

It seemed that Phraates wasn't the only one making a sartorial statement here. The second guy looked as out of place as a duck next to a peacock; or maybe 'swan' would be better, because although he was wearing a plain Greek mantle it was the best, whitest Milesian wool with only its edges embroidered. Right; the Seleucian of the party, the definitely-not-Parthian descended from Alexander's cavalry commander. He was tall – six foot, easy – good-looking in a sort of hard, chiselled way, late twenties, slim as a whip and clean-shaven, with his dark hair cut short as a wrestler's and unoiled; serious, unsmiling. He nodded to Vitellius and held out a hand to me. Phraates, I'd noticed, hadn't offered to press flesh: kings, even if they were only prospective ones, are above that sort of thing.

'A pleasure to meet you, Corvinus,' he said. I shook: a hard hand, this one, and there were muscles under that soft mantle. Wrestler was right, or maybe athlete, because his nose was intact. In any case, I'd bet he kept himself fit and that he was probably fanatical about it. 'You're Vitellius's aide, so I believe. Strange; I haven't seen you at any of our official meetings. Now why would that be, could you tell me?'

'Valerius Corvinus isn't directly concerned with the negotiations,' Vitellius said smoothly. 'He's a newcomer to the service.'

'But most welcome all the same.' Phraates shot Callion a glance that carried a definite message with it. The Greek smiled.

'Of course,' he said. 'That would explain it. You've been out east, Corvinus?'

'Sure. I lived in Athens for a few years. And I spent a while in Antioch.'

'A beautiful city. Then you know Daphni, of course? Just outside, in the hills?'

'Yeah. Daphni's okay.'

'You'd like Seleucia, then. Seleucia-on-the-Tigris, I mean. My own city. It's equally old, and just as beautiful as Antioch, if not more so.' He glanced at Phraates. 'We Greeks are very proud of Seleucia.'

'I haven't been there myself, naturally,' Phraates said. 'Nor indeed to Antioch. However, I quite understand your feelings, Callion. You have every right to be proud. Parthia owes an enormous debt to Greece and the Greeks – a fact that my cousin Artabanus doesn't seem fully to appreciate. You'd say the same, Zariadres?'

'Oh, yes, lord.' Zariadres bowed his head. 'Definitely. Where would we be without the Greeks?'

A man with his back to us talking to another group turned round. 'Perhaps in the happy state of discovering that we were Parthians, with a perfectly good culture of our own,' he said. His Greek, like Zariadres's, was perfect, but his accent was thicker. 'Or was the question rhetorical?'

I felt both Zariadres and Callion stiffen, although the man was smiling. Phraates didn't blink, but something about him shifted. I had the impression of a steel blade drawn from a sheath.

'Osroes,' he said quietly, 'I am sorry, but you're being unreasonable. Greek culture and Parthian differ, certainly, but they're complementary and always have been. We learn from each other, and the learning benefits both sides, don't you think?'

'Oh, yes, lord. When it goes equally both ways. Certainly.' The new guy – he'd be Vitellius's Magian – dipped his head as Zariadres had done, but although I might've been mistaken the bow was just a shade less deferential. 'Achieving a balance, though, if you'll forgive me, is sometimes difficult. That's my view, at least. Up to now . . . well, living in Rome for so long, sire, you may not altogether appreciate the fact, but hitherto the balance has been more than a little askew. Personally, I think the Greeks have had it their own way for rather too long. No slight intended to my colleague, naturally.' He bowed to Callion.

I'd been watching the to-and-fro carefully. Phraates's expression didn't change, not a whisker, but Callion coloured up and Zariadres looked like he'd swallowed a bad oyster. These two, the court politician and the Magian, were pure cat and dog, I could see that: Osroes didn't even glance at Zariadres. And Callion was looking fit to be tied. Not that that was particularly surprising, mind.

'Surely that's a matter for the Great King to decide.' Phraates was smiling too, but the tone slammed down hard-edged as an axe blade. 'Also, a dinner party is no place for politics. Or this one is not. You'd agree, I hope.' Osroes's eyelids flickered. He half bowed in acknowledgment but said nothing. 'Now. We'll leave the subject, if you don't mind. Let me introduce you. Lucius Vitellius you know, of course, but you won't have met Valerius Corvinus here. Corvinus, this is my very good friend Osroes.'

Yeah, sure, and I was Cleopatra's grandmother. If this guy was very good friend to anyone, least of all Phraates, then I'd eat my sandals. I could see he'd be a real bastard; not old – he was barely into his thirties – but he'd a mouth like a rat-trap, a nose so aquiline any self-respecting eagle would've curled up and died for it and eyes like flint chips. And he was sure of himself as hell. That came across in spades. Osroes might take a put-down from a future Great King of Parthia, but that's what it would need. I'd bet that anyone else trying it on would have to watch their back.

'Pleased to meet you,' I said.

I got a nod that was barely polite, and Vitellius didn't do much better. Whatever else he approved of, Osroes evidently didn't have much time for Romans, and he didn't much care who knew it.

'I must compliment you on how you've fixed this place up, Zariadres.' Vitellius turned to the embassy's leader.

Zariadres shrugged: an elegant lift and fall of the shoulders. 'This is nothing,' he said. 'When you dine with the Great King' – he bowed again to Phraates – 'in his palace at Ctesiphon you'll see real splendour. You Romans despise luxury, or you embrace it and let it dominate you, which is equally a mistake. Appreciating softness without becoming its slave is something that you can learn from us.'

'True. That, Zariadres, is very true indeed.' Phraates smoothed his beard and I caught the sudden, strong whiff of perfume. My nose must've wrinkled because he smiled at me. 'Don't fall into the trap, Corvinus, of thinking that we Parthians are soft just because we wear silk and jewellery and like fine scents around us. We can do without them if we have to. And the Parthian warrior is the finest of his type on earth. You wouldn't disagree, Lucius?'

'Certainly not, Prince,' Vitellius grunted. 'Your mounted archers are superb. Joined with our legions they'd make an army that would be invincible.'

Phraates laughed. 'As we'll see, no doubt, before too long. To my cousin Artabanus's discomfort.' A gong sounded quietly. 'Ah. That'll be dinner. You'll now have an opportunity, Corvinus, if you haven't experienced it before, of sampling Parthian luxury in another form. I hope you enjoy eating. Perhaps we can discuss your opinion later. I'd be very interested to hear it.'

Osroes shot me a dark look; Callion, too, although his was more considering. Yeah, right; well, I hadn't made any bosom friends there. I stepped back politely and Phraates moved towards the dining-room.

I thought for a moment I'd walked into some sort of up-market club. The couches were laid out in the usual horseshoe arrangement, sure, but there were more of them, they were shorter than normal and separated off by clear space, and instead of a big central table each pair of guests had their own smaller version. The whole layout faced a sort of stage at the far end of the room beside the serving door. Odd, but perhaps this was standard Parthian practice; I didn't know. In any case, Phraates had already reclined in the centre, with Zariadres on his right. A slave led Vitellius and me to the couch immediately left of centre; Callion had his back to us beyond, at the left-hand tip of the horseshoe, while Osroes was at the opposite tip on the extreme right, next to the serving door. As I reclined and another slave poured scented water over my hands I looked round the room at the faces I hadn't seen yet.

Vitellius held out his own hands over the slave's basin so our heads were close together. He nodded towards the couch to our right, past Phraates's and Zariadres's. 'Okay,

Corvinus,' he murmured. 'Just so you know where we are here. The nearest man to us is Tiridates, Phraates's nephew. His couch-mate's the Iberian.'

I glanced across. Tiridates was a comparative youngster, mid-twenties, in full Parthian fig, with a short curled beard. He had his back turned to his uncle – understandable, sure, given the seating arrangements, but there was something about the way he was lying that suggested his positioning was deliberate. Phraates hadn't so much as looked in his direction, either, even before the dinner, or not that I'd noticed. I doubted there was much love lost there, which didn't come as all that much of a surprise given what Vitellius had told me about the relationship between the two. He was holding his own hands out to be washed, ignoring the slave and talking volubly to Vitellius's Iberian, the future king of Armenia . . .

I gave the guy the once-over, and straight off I felt the ice bunch in my guts. Mithradates was a bad 'un, a *real* bad 'un. I could tell that from just one look. He reminded me straight off of Aelius Sejanus, and you didn't get much worse than that long-gone bastard; not so much physically as by the set of his body and the expression on his face. Mid-thirties, black-bearded but with the beard uncurled and unoiled, hair tied back in a pigtail, bare arms thick and muscled and hairy as a gorilla's, and a sneer that said to the world: 'I can take you any time I like. Want to see me do it?'

'Nice,' I said. 'Mithradates, I mean.'

Vitellius grunted. 'Right,' he said quietly. 'He's a proper bastard, born and bred. Tough as hell and twice as nasty. Got the young prince dangling from his little finger. Tiridates may put on the high-and-mighty Parthian prince act but he's soft as butter underneath. The two of them run around together.'

My eyes shifted to the couch nearest ours. 'Who's the lad next to Callion?'

Vitellius lowered his voice even further. 'That's Damon. Phraates's son by his Greek mistress. You remember? Him I wasn't expecting. Why he's rated an invitation tonight I'm not sure.'

I did a quick recap. Yeah; Isidorus had mentioned Phraates had an unofficial family on the Janiculan. I looked more closely. Damon was a watered-down version of Tiridates. Half-Greek or not, he'd chosen to come in Parthian dress, but even at first glance I could see he wasn't comfortable in it; or maybe it was the typical Roman wide-boy's short trimmed beard with no moustache that didn't quite fit in with the rest. That was a mistake, for a start. The guy was no youngster, not even close; I'd put him late thirties at best, twenty years too old for that style, although his sulky face practically yelled 'spoilt teenager' over the wine cup he was already swigging from. I noticed by the way that one of the fingers of the hand he held the cup with was missing.

'Uh . . . who made the seating arrangements?' I asked Vitellius.

'No idea. Why the hell should you want to know something like that?'

'Just curious.'

He shot me a look from under his brows, but I didn't elaborate: now wasn't the time, and it probably wasn't all that important, anyway. I carried on with my inspection of the room. There was only one name I hadn't fitted to a face, and only one face to fit it to: the second man at Osroes's table, on the extreme right tip of the horseshoe. 'That's the eunuch?' I said, pointing discreetly.

Vitellius looked, screwing up his piggy eyes: he must be short-sighted. 'Peucestas. Yes, that's him.'

Jupiter! I hadn't had much experience of eunuchs, but that guy didn't measure up to the little I had at all. Forget your smooth-cheeked effete priests of Cybele: Peucestas had a full

beard and even reclining I could see he held himself like a
soldier. He wasn't fat, either: solid, sure, but I'd reckon it was
beef and muscle, not fat.

'He, uh, looks normal.'

'I told you, Corvinus. There's nothing effeminate about
Peucestas. He's all right.'

'But the beard. It's fake?'

'Not that I know of, although I wouldn't risk tugging it to
find out myself.' Vitellius chuckled. 'He would've already
had it when he was castrated twenty-odd years back for
choosing the wrong bloody side.'

I stared at him. 'That's when it was done?'

'Of course. When did you think? That's Parthians for you.'

Oh, shit! I didn't answer, feeling the ice in my own balls.
The guy must've been in his twenties at the time; thirty,
maybe. Sweet holy gods! No wonder he hated Artabanus!

The slaves brought round the starters, one set for each
table. Most of them I recognised, even if they were at the
luxury end of the market like pea-hens' eggs and larks'
tongues in aspic. One or two, though, were strange, like the
bowls of what looked like curdled milk with green bits.

'Ah . . . what's that stuff?' I asked Vitellius.

'Yoghurt with salt and mint. You eat it with the flat bread.'
Vitellius was digging into the quails: you didn't get his size
on salad. 'It's the traditional Parthian beginning to the meal;
a sort of—'

'Curdled milk.' So, I'd been right. Yeah, well; that particular delicacy I'd pass on. Definitely one for Mother's chef
Phormio. 'And how about these?' I pointed to a collection of
amber-coloured lumps artistically arranged on a small silver
platter.

'Deep-fried locusts in honey.'

'Is that so, now? Ah . . . someone told me once that locust
was also the name of a fruit.'

'Not in this case.'

'Got you.' Feeling slightly queasy, I reached for the jellied larks' tongues. At least they were decently Roman. I hadn't forgotten my promise to Meton, sure, but crispy-fried insect was one Parthian recipe that we could safely give a miss to.

I was helping myself to the tongues when I realised that everyone was looking behind me at Phraates's table. Or looking but trying not to be caught looking, rather, if you know what I mean. I dropped my napkin off the side of my couch and leaned down to pick it up, allowing me the chance to eyeball the prince myself.

A guy – obviously a slave – was leaning over his shoulder, tasting each of the dishes while Phraates sat smiling, waiting until he'd finished. Meanwhile Zariadres was looking on, not saying anything but with an expression like he'd had a very long poker inserted in his rectum.

I straightened, clutching the retrieved napkin, brain buzzing. Not only had Phraates very carefully refrained from telling the delegation what my particular job was, but he'd brought a food-taster with him.

Interesting, right?

6

'It's the standard royal custom, Corvinus.' We were speaking Latin, of course, but Vitellius had still lowered his voice to a whisper. 'The Great King never eats anything that hasn't been tasted first. Very sensibly, given these buggers' hands-on approach to the succession.'

'Yeah? Then how come as the so-called Parthian expert you're the only one who isn't batting an eyelid while all the real Parthians have their eyes out on stalks?' I shelled a pea-hen's egg and dipped it in fish sauce. 'Me, I can see their point. If I invited a guy to dinner and saw him check the porridge for rat poison I'd feel pretty pissed off too. Phraates is no fool, he knows he's putting backs up, so why—'

'Look, just shut up, will you?' Vitellius hissed. 'Gods, man, this is a bloody diplomatic dinner! Ignore it! Later, if you must, when we're alone, but not now!'

I shrugged. He was right, of course: it wasn't any of our business. Still, it was odd, and I hadn't been mistaken about the reaction. Nor could Phraates himself be unaware of it. So what the hell was he playing at?

The rest of the meal was uneventful but good. Me, I'm a wine man, mostly, but I know good food when I taste it, and this was the real thing. One of the dishes just had to be Meton's guinea-fowl, and I came to a private arrangement with our waiter re sneaking me the recipe; plus another that caught my fancy, of paper-thin slices of lamb marinated in herbs and wrapped around a minced wild boar stuffing.

We'd got to the fruit and nuts stage and were filling up the corners when the girls slipped in. Three of them. If it'd been a Roman dinner party – at least a certain kind of Roman dinner party – I wouldn't've been all that surprised because girls with the dessert are pretty much standard, but at diplomatic dinners you don't expect that sort of thing. I didn't, anyway, and although Vitellius never said a word he choked on a mouthful of wine, so maybe he didn't either. Wherever they'd sprung from they were stunners, two eastern-looking ones and a tall negress. I could've predicted which couches they'd head for: one – the negress – to Damon, Phraates's ageing problem teenager, one of the easterners to Tiridates and the other to—

But the third girl – a real honey with long unplaited jet-black hair and perfect bone structure – didn't go to Mithradates's couch after all. She crossed the room and joined Callion.

I dug Vitellius in the ribs. 'Ah . . . would this be standard diplomatic practice?' I murmured.

'No.' He dabbed fiercely with a napkin at where he'd spilled wine down his front. 'No, it bloody wouldn't! Still, they aren't doing any harm, and female company – not wives, of course, they don't count – isn't unusual at Parthian dinner parties. They're none of our business. Ignore them.'

'Fine. You're the one throwing your wine around, pal, not me.'

'Shut up.'

There was a whoop from the direction of the serving door. I turned just as the slim, long-legged girl in the G-string and bra who was responsible came out of the backward roll that'd taken her on to the stage, bounced to her feet and reached for the baton which the man following her was already throwing . . .

She muffed the catch. The baton skittered across the floor

and came to rest against the wall behind her. The girl covered well, walking backwards and hooking it up with a twist of her bare foot to send it spinning among the other three the pair were tossing between them now, but she'd spoiled their entrance and I could see she knew it.

'Ah,' Vitellius said. 'The entertainment. Zariadres did say they'd booked a troupe of tumblers.'

I settled back to enjoy the show. Sure, call me simple, but tumblers and jugglers I've always liked; as far as I'm concerned in terms of entertainment value they leave soulful-eyed crooners and these bloody ballet dancers who pretend they're finding their way round an imaginary wall nowhere, while stand-up comics are beyond the pale. That initial slip aside, these ones were pretty good, among the best I'd seen for a long time. The guy – like the woman, he looked an easterner – gradually fed in more batons until there were a full seven of them. At that point he snatched the first out of the air and replaced it with a sword which may've been fake but looked sharp as hell. Then he did the same with the second baton. Finally, there were only the swords.

That was when the second girl came in. She was a dead ringer for the first, but a younger version, maybe early teens: it was only now, when I saw them together, that I realised the original girl – woman, rather – had to be far older than she looked. Obviously, mother and daughter. She stood facing us halfway between the other two, just behind the spinning swords, and as each passed her she reached out, caught it by the hilt and tossed it behind her. Finally, when the last sword was grounded, the three turned together and bowed.

I'd thought that was the end and I was getting ready to clap and whistle when another guy came through the serving entrance. He was no tumbler, this one, even I could see that: big and broad as a door, pectorals like you see hammered out on fancy parade armour and a set of biceps that looked more like polished rock than muscle. The first two of the troupe, probably mum and dad – although I couldn't see much physical resemblance between the elder man and the Last of the Titans here – stepped aside, leaving the stage to the youngsters.

If the juggling had been good, what came next was amazing. Like I say, the second guy was no tumbler and didn't even make a token effort in that direction – he just played the part of the anchor-man while she did all the fancy work – but they made a good team. They finished their act with a sort of human hammer-throw. The guy held the girl by the waist while she wrapped her legs round his torso; at which point he began to turn, slowly at first, then faster, all the time playing her out like a rope until his hands were almost gripping her ankles. Finally he gathered her in again inch by inch and began to slow, until they came to a stop and she climbed down to take a shaky bow.

I applauded with the rest; as an exhibition of sheer strength, grip and balance it'd been impressive as hell. The two kids were beaming and red as beetroots. Quite rightly so.

'That wasn't bad.' Vitellius was slitting a peach.

I glanced at him. 'Not bad? It was brilliant!'

'That's what I said.'

The other two had made their bows as well and the troupe was backing towards the serving door when Mithradates stood up.

'Wait a moment,' he said. 'Stay where you are.'

They froze. I noticed that the woman had bitten her lip while the younger guy was glowering like thunder, saucepan-lid hands clenched. Uh-oh.

Mithradates pointed to the girl. 'You,' he said. 'Come over here.'

The girl darted a quick, scared glance at the others. The older man's expression had set hard as concrete. He put out his hand and grasped her wrist. His wife was staring right at Mithradates; and if ever I saw hate on a face I saw it on hers.

Mithradates's eyes were still on the girl. 'Over here,' he repeated. 'Now.'

The girl shook her head numbly. The big guy's hands flexed and he leaned towards us; I could see he was within a hair's-breadth of running forwards and catching the Iberian by the throat, which in this company was not a good idea.

I stood up myself. 'Hang on a minute, pal.'

Beside me, Vitellius murmured, 'Sit down, you bloody fool!'

I ignored him.

Mithradates turned slowly to face me. I'd seen eyes like that before, when Sejanus had stared me down after my father's funeral. Same expression too, of absolute, total disbelief, like a worm had reared up and bitten him.

'I beg your pardon?' he said.

I kept my tone low-key and reasonable; no point in pushing for trouble. 'The show's over,' I said. 'The girl's done her part. Now let her go home.'

Mithradates's brows came down like hatchets. He raised his hand, finger levelled at me. 'You,' he said. 'You just—'

'Mithradates,' Phraates interrupted in a mild voice that cut like a razor. 'Valerius Corvinus is quite right. It was a good show, but it's over.' He reached into his belt, pulled out a purse and flung it for the elder man to catch. 'Now. You will sit down, please.' Then, when the guy didn't move, he snapped, 'Sit down! Now! You shame us!'

The silence was absolute. Slowly, never taking his eyes off mine, Mithradates lowered himself on to his couch. I could hear pent-up breaths go out all around the room.

The four entertainers bowed and sidled out through the serving door. I lay down too and reached for my wine cup.

'Corvinus, you gormless bastard,' Vitellius muttered,

'when we're alone I will personally rip your guts out. That is a promise.'

Now it was finished I wasn't feeling too proud of myself, either, and the whole room was staring at me. 'Yeah, well,' I said.

Phraates leaned over towards me. 'You must forgive Mithradates,' he said quietly, in Latin. 'He gets rather overexcited.'

I glanced across. Overexcited wasn't exactly the term I'd've used. I was getting the death stare. Shit; I'd made an enemy here, and no mistake. 'Right. Right,' I said.

Vitellius didn't say another word to me the whole evening. He saved it all up until we were in the litter and out of earshot of the Parthian domestics who'd escorted us out.

'You bloody fool! I warned you! Mithradates is the next sodding king of Armenia! What the hell did you think you were doing there?'

I held up both hands, palm out. 'Okay. Okay! Point taken! I only—'

'What would it matter if the bastard had had the girl anyway? She's just an entertainer! She's probably been had already a dozen times since the Winter Festival!'

'Yeah. Yeah, I know. I'm just not a diplomat, pal. I told you, I—'

'Too bloody right you're not!' He punched the cushions behind him and threw himself backwards so hard I felt the litter-bearers stagger. 'That's the understatement of the fucking century! Wait until I see Isidorus! He'll have you out so fast your head'll spin, Phraates or no Phraates! Holy bloody sodding Jupiter, what a mess!'

I was feeling just a little tetchy myself by this time. 'Pal, this wasn't my idea in the first place, remember? If Isidorus wants to pull the plug then it's fine by me.'

'Seconded, by God! Carried nem. bloody con.!' Vitellius was calming down now; at least, he'd stopped throwing himself around the litter and was just sitting breathing hard and glaring at me. 'Corvinus, do you know what you've *done*?' he said finally. 'I mean, as far as Rome and me personally are concerned?'

'Uh . . . no. Not altogether.'

'No. You fucking well wouldn't.' He took a deep breath. 'Well. For your information I am now in a situation where the future king of Armenia, with whom I may later have to deal both officially and socially, has seen me seeing *him* publicly humiliated in a petty wrangle over a whore.'

'She wasn't a whore, she was a—'

'Shut up. The person responsible for his humiliation being my aide, who presumably, the gods help us, was under my control and instruction. How do you think Mithradates is going to feel the next time we meet? And remember that the next time may involve sensitive political dickering vital to Rome's fucking interests.'

'Ah . . . right.' I swallowed. 'Look, I'm sorry, pal. Really sorry.'

Vitellius turned round and punched the cushions again, savagely. 'Not a tenth as sorry as I am. Or as much as you soon will be, if I have my way.'

'At least Phraates backed me up.'

His head came round and he stared at me. 'Corvinus, you really haven't got a clue what day it is where diplomacy's concerned, have you? What the hell else could he do? Let the two of you slug it out on top of the candied pears? Phraates couldn't've cared less about the girl, and quite right too. As it is, by forcing him publicly to take Rome's side – which is what you did – against one of his most important future allies you've dropped him in the shit as well. Definitely with Mithradates, and probably with the Parthians to boot. Don't think they didn't understand what was happening, because they did. They'll remember it, too.'

'Even so, if Mithradates had wanted a girl he could've got one with the others.'

'Holy immortal Jove!' Vitellius raised his eyes to the ceiling of the litter. 'Don't be an even bigger fool than you are! Of course he sodding could! He and his mates are in and out of the cathouse those girls came from like bloody weavers' shuttles! But he didn't. *Why* he didn't, I don't know, although my guess would be he wanted to embarrass Phraates and lower his stock with the embassy. For reasons of his own, probably involving Tiridates. And you, you gormless idiot, gave him what he wanted so easily he must've thought it was his fucking birthday!'

Things clicked horribly into place. Vitellius was right, absolutely right: the conniving bastard had manipulated me straight down the line. 'Yeah,' I said. 'Yeah, fair enough. Well, all I can do is apologise.'

Vitellius gave a bark of laughter. 'Marvellous! Oh, that really helps a lot! Isidorus will be so bloody delighted that you've done that! Now shut up. I don't want even to listen to you any more.'

While he fumed quietly in his corner I glanced out of the window. We were coming down the Palatine stretch of Scaurus Incline. 'Uh . . . why Callion, incidentally?' I said.

'What?'

'He was the only one of the embassy to have a girlfriend. Why him?'

'Jupiter, Corvinus! They're not bloody celibate! And Callion's a real lady's man. The first thing he asked for when he got here was the address of a decent brothel. Now button that mouth of yours. I've had enough for one evening.'

We subsided into silence again, and I lay back against the cushions to think. The seating arrangements; those had been interesting. Mithradates with Tiridates, that fitted, especially after Vitellius's hints. Osroes as far away from Zariadres as he could get; that fitted too, from what I'd seen of the chemistry between the two men. Was there any significance in the fact that he'd chosen to sit with the eunuch Peucestas? That I didn't know, because I hadn't met the guy. And Callion, the outsider of the group, out on a limb with Damon, Phraates's son; also a bit of an outsider . . .

Then there was the question of why Phraates had made a point of bringing a taster with him to a friendly dinner. I hadn't had the chance he had half promised me to talk things over in private, when I might have asked him direct, but under the circumstances – and after Vitellius's little analysis of the position – that was understandable.

Something else nagged. It was a minor twinge, and probably not worth a rotten anchovy, but still, it nagged.

That troupe of entertainers had been top-class professionals to their finger-ends; like I say, the best I'd seen for a long time. Prime acts like that didn't make elementary mistakes.

So why had the woman muffed that first catch?

Ah, hell, the whole thing was probably academic now anyway, because after Vitellius had finished outlining his opinion of my ancestry Isidorus wouldn't touch me with three pairs of gloves and a long pole.

Which suited me just fine. If that was a sample of diplomatic life then I'd had enough of it to last me until I was ninety.

7

Perilla had been in bed and asleep when I got back, and she was still flat out when I woke up the next morning. That lady's capacity for sleep never ceases to amaze me: Perilla's no night owl, but she's definitely not an early morning person either. Which, this morning anyway, suited me perfectly. After blowing my diplomatic street-cred at the dinner party I might well be out on my ear with Isidorus, but until I knew that for certain I had a conscientious duty to push on with the case. The next stage was to pay a call on Decimus Lippillus down at the Public Pond Watch-house re the knife gang that'd hit Phraates's litter. Knifemen being currently a sensitive issue with Perilla – plus the fact that I wasn't too anxious to tell her about my brush with Mithradates – meant that slipping out of the house while she was still an unconscious and uncritical lump under the covers was pretty sound policy.

I grabbed a crust of bread to eat on the way and set off down Head of Africa. It was still early – just after dawn – and the eastern sky was full of red clouds: we'd had a real belter of a rainstorm the night before, and although that'd passed the gutters were still running like streams and everything was soaked. Early morning was the best time to catch Lippillus, although I'd still probably cut it fine: unless something special had come up overnight, he usually spent the first hour or so after his dawn start dealing with the paperwork and general admin stuff. The knifemen aside, I was looking forward to the chat: Lippillus, as well as being far and away the smartest and shortest Watch commander in Rome, is good company, and after Vitellius and his Parthian mates I needed a palate-cleanser.

Just after dawn's a good time to be walking in Rome. It's cool, the streets aren't crowded, and the only traffic tends to be pedestrian, which means in the narrower alleyways – and the city has plenty of these – there's less of a chance you'll get stuck behind a fancy litter squeezing its way between the shops that spill out into the thoroughfare. I came down off the Caelian whistling, crossed Appian Road and headed along the slopes of the Aventine towards the Watch-house itself.

The squaddie on the desk grinned at me over his working breakfast. 'Hard luck, Corvinus. You've just missed him. Break-in at a tenement near Aqueduct Junction.'

Bugger. 'He liable to be there long?' I said.

'No idea. If you're going over ask for the Cloelian Building. It's the first floor front.'

'Thanks, pal.' Well, it could've been worse: Aqueduct Junction wasn't all that far, the point where the Appian Water crossed Appian Road. I left the guy to his egg roll and went off on my travels again.

I found the tenement finally. It was a new one in an up-market block, the ground-floor shops looked pretty prosperous, and the balconies had flower pots and trailing greenery instead of the usual strings of washing, which meant the tenants were rich enough to have their smalls done for them elsewhere. First floor front was a good address, too, and it explained why Lippillus would be involved personally. Sure, actual purple-stripers didn't go a bundle on tenement accommodation, even the top-of-the-range variety like this example, but it was a growing market for up-and-coming plain-mantle businessmen who needed to be close to Market Square and the city centre. There was even a porter on the door, rigged out in a smart blue tunic: again a sign that we weren't in boiled-cabbage country here. I checked I'd come to the right place and went on up.

The door was open. Lippillus was talking to a thin, sharp-faced woman in a pricey mantle and bangles. Although she wasn't all that tall, she towered over him by at least a head and a half. He glanced round and his face split in a grin.

'Hey, Corvinus! What brings you here?'

I held up a hand: this could wait, and the guy had work to do. He said something to the woman and came out.

'Problems?' I said.

'The usual.' He nodded towards the open door. 'Family were out for the evening. The bugger crowbarred the lock and helped himself to everything that wasn't nailed down.'

'What about the porter?'

'He's clean, as far as I can tell. These guys have to be. Our lad used his crowbar to force the back door of the building where they make deliveries and got in that way. All the same, it took planning, and this wasn't the only flat that got taken. Could still well be an inside job.'

'You want me to come back later?'

'No. It'll keep, and the other flat was empty. Tenant was a single man away on business. Now. What can I do for you?'

'Uh . . . there somewhere private we can go?'

'Not here. There's a cookshop a few doors down that looked quiet enough, if that'll do you.'

'Sure.'

'Just give me a few minutes to mop things up and I'll join you there. Okay?'

'Fine.' I glanced over his shoulder at the thin woman with the bangles. She was glaring at us. Yeah, right: I knew the type. The thief had probably cleaned out her very considerable jewel-box, and she'd be holding the Watch personally responsible for getting the contents back. I didn't envy Lippillus. 'See you, pal.'

I went downstairs, past the porter and outside. I hadn't noticed the cookshop, so it was probably further on in the next block. On the way I thought about just what I could reasonably tell Lippillus. This was going to be tricky. On the one hand, any info re the Parthian delegation – even the fact that it existed – was classified, so that was out. On the other hand, I had to have a reason for asking him about the attack on Phraates. I'd no intention of lying to the guy, none at all, not even for Isidorus – he was too good a friend for that, and besides he was far too smart to be taken in for a moment – but all the same I couldn't give him anything near the whole boiling. I'd just have to play things by ear.

I found the cookshop and went in. It was pretty basic, definitely greasy-spoon standard; you get a lot of these places in tenement areas catering for the early morning tunic trade: workmen who need a good hot meal inside them before they start, because that's usually it until sunset. The rush was over – most of the clientele would be at work by now – and I had the place to myself. I checked what was on offer, ordered grilled sausages for two with bread and a side dish of fried onions and took the plates over to a table in the corner. I'd scarcely sat down when Lippillus came in. He wasn't looking too happy.

'The lady give you a hard time?' I asked, pushing the plate of sausages over.

'You could say that.' He took the bench on the opposite side. 'Her brother's on the staff of the City Prefect. That's where she and her husband were last night. One of the things they talked about over dinner was burglaries and how useless the Watch was. I got the whole conversation repeated, blow by blow. These people make me sick.'

'How's Marcina?' Marcina was Lippillus's common-law wife. 'She had the baby yet?'

'She lost it.'

'Oh, shit.' Both of them had really wanted that kid, unexpected as the pregnancy had been. 'I'm sorry, pal.'

He shrugged. 'These things happen. So. What brings you down to the Pond?'

I scooped up some of the onions on a crust. 'I was hoping you might be able to help me find out more about a knife attack three days ago near the Esquiline Gate. The Maecenas Gardens side.'

'That's Third Region. Gaius Hostilius's patch.'

'Yeah. I know. All the same, I thought I'd come to you first.'

He grunted and cut a slice of sausage. 'You have any details?'

'Sure. It happened in the early hours of the morning. Gang of knifemen jumped a home-going litter party and four of the slaves were killed.'

I'd given it to him deadpan and poker-faced, but I'd been expecting the reaction I got. He set down the sausage knife and stared at me. '*What?*'

'Yeah. Right. And don't tell me that sort of thing doesn't happen because this time it did.'

'Who was the guy in the litter?'

'A Prince Phraates. He's—'

'I know who Phraates is. Jupiter's holy balls! Was he hurt?'

'Uh-uh. The gang was beaten off. But, like I say, three of his bodyguard were killed outright and one died later.'

'Sweet gods! How do you fit into this, Corvinus?' I didn't answer at once, and he scowled. 'Okay, no sweat. It's political, isn't it?'

'Probably. I don't know for certain, but it seems that way. There're political sides to it, sure, or there might be. I'd rather not tell you about them.'

'Fair enough. That's fine with me.' He was still scowling. 'You watch yourself, though. Politics is the dirty end of the stick. I'd've thought you'd have more sense than get mixed up with that business again.'

'No choice of mine, pal. So. Can you help?'

'Maybe. That depends on what you want, doesn't it?'

'A lead on the guys who did it. Names, if possible. People to talk to, find out who was behind the attack.'

He whistled softly. 'Sure that's enough, Corvinus? You don't make things easy, do you?'

I said nothing.

'Okay. Let's think this through. Like I said, the Third Region is Hostilius's patch. He's no ball of fire, that's putting it mildly, but I can have a quiet word with him, see what he says, get the inside angle. Mind you, I'll bet you now a month's pay to a poke in the eye he won't be able to help much.'

'Yeah? Why's that?'

'You said it was a gang. How many would that be?'

'I don't know actual numbers, but I'd reckon ten or a dozen.'

'Right. There aren't any gangs that size operate on the Esquiline or anywhere near it. Sure, whoever set the thing up may've done his hiring piecemeal, but that'd be tricky to arrange. My guess would be they weren't a local bunch, that chummie brought them in on contract. That'd make them harder to trace, too.'

'Brought them in from where?'

'Most of the city's big gangs belong to the dockland area south of Cattlemarket Square, or across the Sublician in Transtiber. There're a couple on the Aventine, too, but that's not such a strong possibility; Aventine villains tend to be solo artists. Same goes for the Subura.' Lippillus impaled a piece of sausage with his knife, popped it in and chewed. 'So the docklanders and the Transtiberans're your best bet. They don't normally operate in big groups, sure, unless they're fighting each other, but they've certainly got the organisation. You get a lot of protection racket activity over that way, so finding a set of professional heavies wouldn't be too difficult.'

'If you had the contacts.'

'That wouldn't be a problem. Not if chummie was persistent and had money. Serious money. All he'd have to do was put the word around in a few wineshops, make it clear he was willing to pay, and the lads'd find him soon enough. It'd be pricey, mind. The gangs don't like operating off their own patch, for obvious reasons: you don't know whose toes you're treading on, and mixing it away from your home ground is always risky. In fact, that could be our best way in.'

'Yeah? How do you mean?'

'Maybe Hostilius can help after all. Crooks may be crooked, but they've got strong views on where belongs to who, and they get pretty pissed off if foreigners muscle in on their territory. I'd bet there're quite a few Esquiline heavies who'd like to see your knifemen pals pegged out for the crows. And if they do know anything there's a good chance they won't be too reluctant to pass it on.' He cut another piece of sausage. 'Leave it with me. I'll put out feelers and let you know if I come up with anything. Now. How're things otherwise?'

We chatted for a bit and finished off the sausages; they weren't bad, not bad at all; they might even have been pork like the cookshop owner claimed, although maybe that's pushing things. Then I let Lippillus get back to his break-in and headed for home.

Well, that was conscience salved: I'd opened up the most likely avenue of investigation, and there wasn't a lot I could do now but wait to see what came of it. Unless, of course, after talking to Vitellius – and maybe Phraates – Isidorus decided to scrub the whole thing, in which case like I'd said to Lippillus I wouldn't exactly be crying. Nor would Perilla.

She was in the dining-room when I got back, finishing off what even for her was so late a breakfast it was practically lunch. I leaned over and gave her the usual homecoming kiss.

'Hello, dear,' she said. 'How was your dinner last night?'

I settled down on the opposite couch. 'Okay.' I wasn't going to give her even the expurgated version before I had to. And if Vitellius had any clout whatsoever with Isidorus even that mightn't be necessary now.

'No problems?' She sounded suspicious. Jupiter, the lady was psychic!

'Uh . . . no. No problems. And the food was great.' Which reminded me: the recipes. I hadn't had time to see Meton before going out that morning, and the terms of our deal meant that a personal transfer was in order. I turned to the hovering Bathyllus. 'Bathyllus, ask Meton to step in for a second, would you? Unless he's otherwise occupied, of course.' Best to be safe. Make it sound too like a summons and if the bastard was doing something important, i.e. anything from breathing forward there'd be Consequences. 'Oh, and bring me those sheets of paper I left on the study couch last night.'

'Yes, sir.' The little bald-head exited.

'So what happened?' Perilla said. 'Marcus, you aren't usually so reticent. You're sure there was no trouble?'

Hell. Nose like a bloodhound. I took a sip from the wine cup Bathyllus had handed me when I came in; just a sip, because with nothing else going on I might as well have another shot at tackling those bloody accounts this afternoon. 'Sure I'm sure. It was just a dinner, nothing special. There was a good tumbling act, though. Really impressive. They had this guy who—'

'So where were you this morning?'

'Down at Public Pond, talking to Lippillus.'

'About the knife gang?'

'Uh . . . yeah. I told you.' Shit; I was beginning to feel uncomfortable. 'Perilla, just what is biting you?'

She didn't answer at first, just ducked her head and fiddled with a crumb of bread on the table. Then she said in a small voice, 'I don't know. I just have a feeling that something's wrong. Or something's about to be wrong. Badly wrong.'

I tried a grin. 'Maybe it's because this time round there's no body. If—'

'*Don't!*' Her eyes came up. 'Marcus, don't joke about it, please. No, I can't explain why this business gives me the shivers, but it does. For some reason I keep thinking of Aelius Sejanus.'

I had to work to keep my expression neutral, but I felt the tingle up my spine all the same. Oh, gods; psychic was right! She didn't even *know* about Mithradates! 'Sejanus is dead.'

'Yes, but—'

'You wanted to see me?'

I turned round.

'Ah, yeah. Yeah, Meton. I've got the recipes for you, pal. Bathyllus is bringing them.'

The eyes beneath the matting gleamed. 'Hey! That's great!'

'So we can, uh, have the lampreys tonight, can we? You decided how to do them? Pramnian and lovage, wasn't it?'

Pause; long pause. Then he said, 'The lampreys got nicked.'

I thought I'd misheard him. 'What?'

'The lampreys,' he repeated slowly, 'got nicked. There are no lampreys. Somebody nicked the lampreys.'

'They *what*?' I was goggling.

'Yeah. Walked into my bloody kitchen cool as you please

through the back door while I was out at the market and liberated the whole fucking basketful.'

'How the hell—'

'So you're having meatballs tonight. Minced pork's all I've
got in. Now if you'll excuse me I've got the sundries to see
to.'

He left. Perilla and I stared at each other.

'That,' I said, 'was one of the weirdest conversations I've
ever had with Meton. Which is saying something.'

'Hmm.' She was looking thoughtful and twisting a lock of
hair. Well, if nothing else that little slice of domestic drama
had pulled her out of her mood, for which I was grateful.
'Yes, it was strange, wasn't it? He hasn't even waited for his
recipes.'

'A whole basket of fucking lampreys! No wonder he was—'
I stopped.

'Was what, dear? And don't swear. Just because Meton
does it doesn't mean you have to.'

'Upset. Only he wasn't, was he? Not so's you'd notice.'

'No.' She tugged at the lock. 'That's what I meant by
strange. I would have thought that losing a basket of lampreys
would have sent him running for the cooking wine. Not that
I'm not grateful that it hasn't, mind, but . . .' She went quiet
for a moment. 'Marcus, how often does something like this
happen anyway? Especially on the Caelian? Someone just
walking into a private kitchen on the off-chance of it being
empty and stealing a basket of very valuable fish?'

'You see a blue moon out there, lady?'

'Exactly.'

Just at that point Bathyllus shimmied in with the recipes
and, for some reason, a clean mantle over his arm. 'Here you
are, sir,' he said. 'And—'

'You know anything about this phantom lamprey-napper,
Bathyllus?' I said.

I'd caught him on the hop, which was the intention. A look that was indefinable passed over the little bald-head's face before it changed to his usual bland major-domo expression.

'No, sir,' he said.

'You sure? Spit on your granny and hope to die?'

'Yes, sir.'

Yeah, well; thousands may have believed him, but I didn't; the bastard was a pure, hundred-on-hundred prevaricator if I ever saw one. Which was odd, because Bathyllus and Meton were cat and dog, at each other's throats for half the time and not on speaking terms for the other. Covering for our anarchic chef was something Bathyllus just did not do. Hell; what was going on here?

'Look, pal,' I said. 'If you—'

'There's a litter outside, sir, with the consular Lucius Vitellius in it. He wants you to join him immediately. I've brought you a clean mantle, in accordance with the consular's instructions.'

I stared at him and swallowed. Oh, shit; Augustus House, here we come. Well, the Great Lamprey Mystery could wait for an hour or two while I got my balls very deservedly chewed off by Isidorus. Still, I wasn't looking forward to this.

'What's it about, Marcus?' Perilla said.

I shrugged while Bathyllus loaded me into the mantle. At least if I was pulled off the case Perilla would be happy. I wouldn't be too upset myself, either: the diplomatic world and I could do without each other, and head-to-heads with bastards like Mithradates I didn't need.

'Search me, lady,' I said. I got up and planted a kiss between nose and chin. 'I'll see you later.'

Sure enough, the litter with its quota of official outwalkers was standing outside. I pulled back the curtain and squeezed into what little space Rome's best and greatest had left me.

'Hiya, Vitellius,' I said. 'Okay, let's get this over with. If Isidorus wants to kick me off the team then—'

'Fuck that, Corvinus,' Vitellius growled. 'We aren't going to see Isidorus, we're going straight round to the delegation house. Some bugger's murdered Zariadres.'

8

'*Zariadres?*' I said.

'That's right.'

Oh, hell; we'd got our body after all, only it wasn't the one I expected. 'What happened?'

There was a lurch as the litter-bearers took the strain and we were off. At a cracking pace, too: Vitellius had obviously given the lads their instructions beforehand, and they were practically sprinting.

'His throat was cut in his sleep. And before you ask, Corvinus, that's about all I bloody well know myself at present, all right?' Vitellius sounded distinctly unchuffed. 'I wouldn't even know that if we hadn't had a meeting scheduled for this morning to which the bugger naturally failed to turn up and after a great deal of humming and hawing the others vouchsafed that he was dead. It took some little time subsequently to screw the extra information out of them that he hadn't exactly keeled over from an apoplexy.' He snorted. 'Fucking Parthians! Wouldn't give you the time of day if they were standing next to a bloody sundial!'

'They know we're coming?'

'Sure. This is Rome, not Parthia. Isidorus insisted on it in the emperor's name, you're the expert here and Phraates has given his gracious but reluctant agreement to co-operate. Not that we'll be too welcome, I can tell you that now. Especially since one of the other three has to be the killer.'

'*What?*'

'We're not fools, boy. The delegation's not official, so there's no Praetorian standing outside the front door, but they're important foreign nationals all the same. Isidorus had men in plain clothes watching the house front, back and sides last night, and no one went out or in. Zariadres was killed by one of his colleagues.'

I was still digesting that particular gobbet of information when we arrived. The slave who opened the door and ushered us into the lobby was a different one from the last time, big and thickset with straight black hair, yellowish skin and slanted eyes.

'Lucius Vitellius and Marcus Valerius Corvinus,' Vitellius said to him. 'Your masters are expecting us.'

The guy stared at us like he was two tiles short of a roof.

'Don't waste your breath. He's Hyrcanian; he doesn't speak Greek.' That was Osroes, striding in from the atrium, aquiline nose well to the fore and looking annoyed as hell. He snapped something guttural at the slave, who cringed back bowing into his cubby. 'Come in, if you must.'

Yeah, well, not exactly a smiling welcome with open arms, but then Osroes hadn't struck me as the cheerful, back-slapping type last time we'd met, either, and now he had even less cause to blow the squeaker. I could see this visit turning out to be a real bundle of laughs.

'Just a moment, pal,' I said. I ignored the resulting glares – Osroes's and Vitellius' – and examined the inside of the door. In addition to the normal lock there was a hefty pair of bolts, top and bottom. Fair enough. A lock can be picked from the outside, given favourable circumstances – and I was keeping an open mind on that one – but there ain't no arguing with two three-foot lengths of iron. If, naturally, they'd been in place at the time. 'Where's the other slave?' I said. 'The one who was on the door last night?'

Osroes shot me a look the full length of his nose. 'He's dead. On my instructions.'

Oh, shit. I could see that even Vitellius was taken aback. 'Uh . . . you like to tell me why?' I said carefully.

I thought he wasn't going to answer, and for an uneasy moment or so I wouldn't't've given long odds against him spitting in my eye.

Finally, he said, 'I found him asleep and the door ajar.'

'Uh-huh,' I said neutrally. 'And when would this be, now?'

That got me a look that would've been appropriate for a mentally disadvantaged prawn. 'This morning, of course. When we discovered that Zariadres was dead. Do you think under ordinary circumstances I'd have had a valuable slave killed just because he'd left a door open?'

Maybe it was supposed to be a rhetorical question, but me, in this bastard's case, I wouldn't give odds. I glanced at Vitellius, eyebrow raised. He didn't say anything – obviously this was my show and as far as he was concerned I could damn well sink or swim – but he made a slight negative movement of his head. So. Vitellius hadn't known about the open front door either. I wondered what else he didn't know. I turned back to Osroes.

'Ah . . . you don't think that killing the man before anyone had a chance to talk to him was a little premature?' I said.

Osroes smiled briefly. 'Oh, I talked to him first, Corvinus. Very urgently. And I assure you if he'd known anything about anything he would have told me. Especially towards the end.'

My skin crawled. 'That so, now?' I said. I was having a struggle to keep the dislike out of my voice. Again, sure, given the circumstances the master of a Roman slave would have an equal right to question the guy under torture, but even allowing for that the matter-of-fact tone made me feel sick to my stomach. 'So what *did* he tell you?'

'Only what I knew already. That he'd been asleep on duty.'

'Soundly enough for someone to take the key from his belt, unlock a door and slip back two heavy bolts three feet away without waking him?'

'Yes. As soundly as that.'

'Was he deaf?'

'No. Of course not.'

Our eyes met, and for a split second the barriers were down. We both knew what he was saying, and what the implications were. It was possible – given, like I say, favourable circumstances – that someone might've picked the lock or unlocked the door from the outside using a duplicate key, sure, but drugging the door-slave and slipping the bolts were another matter. Nothing had really changed: we were still looking at an inside job, even if we did now have the added question of why the door had been opened at all. And that was something, *pace* Vitellius, that Osroes wouldn't admit to; certainly not to me, or to any Roman. After that split second, his expression settled into a careful blankness.

'So why have the poor bugger killed if it wasn't his fault?' I said.

I thought for a moment he was going to damn me for my impudence. However, he only said, 'Because he failed in his duty. That was reason enough. Now if you're quite finished . . .'

'Who leads the delegation, by the way, now that Zariadres is dead?'

He'd been on the point of turning, assuming the conversation was over, and I thought the question might catch him off-guard. In the event, he didn't so much as blink, but he took his time answering, and when he did his tone was cold as a Riphaean winter. 'In practical terms,' he said, 'as the next in seniority I do. Does that answer your question?'

'Yeah. Yeah, thanks.'

'You're welcome. Prince Phraates was very insistent that you should be satisfied. You must ask what you like. This way, please.'

He led us into the atrium. *Satisfied.* Interesting choice of word. I wasn't too sure about the way he'd said the prince's name, either. Maybe it was my imagination, but I had the distinct impression that he didn't think all that much of Phraates. Not that that meant a lot, mind: I doubted if this sour-natured bastard thought much of anyone besides himself.

The other two delegates were lying on couches. Callion was wearing a short-sleeved Greek lounging tunic that showed off his muscles, and he was giving me a stare that was definitely unfriendly. Peucestas – the only one of the three I hadn't met – had on what was probably the Parthian equivalent of Callion's tunic, a soft woollen affair sleeved to the wrist over baggy cotton trousers. The close-up view confirmed what I'd seen at the party: he must've been a very powerful man in his day, and he still looked more solid muscle than fat. A soldier; maybe a wrestler or some sort of athlete, although whatever games he'd be good at would be ones where heaviness and strength counted more than speed and agility. His dark, almost black eyes rested on me expressionlessly.

'Make yourselves comfortable, gentlemen.' Osroes waved us to two more couches and pulled up a cushioned chair for himself. Slaves came forward silently and set cups of wine and plates of fruit on the tables beside us. 'Now.'

I glanced at Vitellius, but he was already digging into the fruit, oblivious. Quite deliberately so, too; the more I saw of Lucius Vitellius the more I appreciated that he was a much sharper cookie than I'd originally taken him for. Yeah, well; this was my job, after all, and from the way they were ignoring him and concentrating on me all of them clearly knew it, whether I had any official standing or not.

'Maybe you can just start by telling me what happened,' I said. 'Who found the body?'

'I did,' Peucestas said. It was the first time I'd heard him speak. His voice was soft and controlled, a light tenor, not the squeaky treble I'd expected. 'The door was open. Zariadres was lying in bed with his throat cut. When I saw that he was dead I roused the others.'

Callion glanced sharply at him, and a message passed that I couldn't read. Interesting. 'What time was this?' I said.

'About an hour after dawn. The time I usually wake.'

Right. Well, all that was pretty straightforward. 'Ah . . . by the way. Where's the body now?' I said.

Osroes's lips pursed. 'We arranged for it to be preserved in honey. For eventual shipment back to Parthia.'

'He's not being cremated? That'd be easier, surely?'

I knew I'd made a mistake as soon as the words were out of my mouth, although what it was I didn't know. Osroes positively hissed, Peucestas looked scandalised, and Callion – for the first time – grinned widely. Vitellius was glaring at me from behind a bunch of grapes.

Bugger, I thought. Here we go again. 'Uh,' I said quickly, 'that is—'

Vitellius trod on my foot, hard, and I shut up like a clam. Then he said smoothly, 'Forgive my colleague, gentlemen. His knowledge of Parthian custom is very limited. If you'll excuse me a moment, please?' He turned and whispered in rapid Latin, 'Listen, you prat! To a Zoroastrian – and two out of the three of them are just that – fire's the most sacred bloody thing there is! Burying a corpse is bad enough, but suggesting that they should burn it is like suggesting they should share the bugger out for breakfast! Now shape up, you stupid bastard!'

'So, uh, what do they do with the corpses?'

'They lay them out for the vultures and collect what's left

after the fucking birds have finished. What else would they do?'

I felt faintly sick. Oh, shit; the east-west divide had never seemed so broad. I took a slug of the wine the servants had left and we hadn't touched, then turned back to Osroes. 'Uh . . . right,' I said. 'Let's start again. I'm sorry if I caused any offence. I really didn't know.'

Peucestas nodded stiffly, but Osroes was still giving me a look like I'd pissed on his lunch. Callion glanced at him, and his grin widened. Yeah, right; he was a Greek, and so normal. Well, at least I'd broken the ice there.

'Of course you didn't know, Corvinus,' he said. 'Unless you were being intentionally crass, that is. Nevertheless, if I were as ignorant about Parthian customs as you seem to be I'd be seriously wondering what I was doing in the diplomatic service.' Grin or not, there was that questioning look in his eye I'd noticed when we'd first met. I had the feeling that Callion couldn't quite place me, and it was worrying him.

'Hear bloody hear!' Vitellius murmured, in Latin.

'I, uh, assume no one heard or saw anything?' I said quickly. 'Where the actual murder was concerned, that is?'

'Zariadres's room was down a corridor of its own to the left at the top of the stairs,' Osroes said. 'Our rooms are all to the right, well to the other side.'

'What about the slaves?'

'They sleep in the kitchen, or in the attics.'

'And there was no one else in the house?'

Osroes was still looking at me like he had a month-old fish under his nose, and it was Callion who answered.

'No one,' he said.

'Perhaps you'd like to see over the house yourself now, Valerius Corvinus,' Osroes said. 'I'd be very happy to show you.'

That I didn't believe for one minute, but at least he'd made the offer and saved me the embarrassment of asking. I got up. 'Vitellius? You coming?'

'I'll stay here,' he grunted. 'I've got things to discuss.' Then he added, in fast Latin, 'You just remember, boy: we're here on sufferance. So no more screw-ups, right?'

'Right,' I said. Yeah, well, I'd sort of taken that on board already, especially where Osroes was concerned. Sufferance was a good word. I nodded briefly. Callion was still grinning. I wondered if he'd understood. He was smart enough, certainly.

Osroes rose to his feet. 'This way, then.'

We went through the passage at the back of the atrium into the small hallway beyond. One of the doors leading off it, I knew because I'd been through it myself, was the dining-room. There was a staircase straight ahead and a corridor on the right next to the dining-room itself.

'This part of the house we don't use,' Osroes said briefly. 'A smaller reception room, a study, some general rooms. You can see them if you like.'

I opened the doors one by one and looked inside. The rooms had that too-neat, empty, stale feel to them that all unused rooms have. 'Where does the corridor lead?' I said.

'To the kitchen and the side door.'

Uh-huh. I went down it. There was a line of store cupboards, mostly empty, along the right-hand wall, and then on the left – past where the dining-room would be – the entrance to the kitchen. I glanced inside. A guy was shovelling out the ash from the top of the cooker, chatting in a language I didn't know to another man who was peeling onions. They looked up, saw me and Osroes beside me and were suddenly very quiet and very busy. Osroes ignored them.

The side door was beyond. It had two massive bolts, which were firmly shot and locked into their guards. Yeah, well; no mileage there. Still, for the sake of completeness I pulled them and looked outside. The door opened on to the garden; not the pretty-pretty part, that was on the south side of the house where it'd get the most sun. This bit was purely functional: herbs and salad stuff and dug-over ground. There was a high, blank wall beyond.

'This part of the property is none of our concern either.' Osroes was looking over my shoulder with his month-old-fish-under-the-nose expression on. 'I'm afraid our cook has a very poor opinion – fully justified, I'd say – of the quality of your Roman vegetables and salad leaves. If you've quite finished we'll go upstairs.'

Supercilious bastard. I closed the door and re-bolted it.

At the top of the staircase he turned left. There were three doors along this stretch of corridor, one on the right, two on the left.

He opened the door on the right and stepped back to let me past without a word.

Parthian decor obviously extended to the bedrooms: the place was kitted out like a five-star cathouse. The only discordant note was the bed itself and the floor area immediately beside it. The bed had been stripped and the side mats were missing. No prizes for guessing why: if Zariadres's throat had been slit there would've been a lot of blood splashed around.

The room opened out on to a balcony overlooking the city. I went over and checked it out. Scrub that idea, then: anyone trying to get in this way, from any direction including above, would've had to have had monkeys in his ancestry.

'Nice view,' I said.

'It's the only bedroom on this side that has one.' Osroes was still standing by the door. 'That's why we don't use the other two.'

'Did you see the body yourself?'

Oops: mistake. The guy's nostrils flared, and he took his

time answering. Finally, he said, 'No, Valerius Corvinus, I did not. Not, I may say, from any squeamishness on my part. Magians are forbidden even to look at a corpse. I understand your High Priest of Jupiter is subject to the same restriction.'

'Yeah. Yeah, that's right.' Fair enough. Add it to the collection. Well, there wasn't much to be seen here, especially since the room had been cleaned to within an inch of its life. 'Let's go back down, shall we?'

'Certainly. You won't, I hope, want to look inside our private rooms?'

'No, that's okay,' I said. Then, as diffidently as I could: 'Uh, who has which, by the way?'

'I'll show you the corridor.' We went back to the landing. 'All of them are on the left along the outside of the house overlooking the city. Callion's is the first, then mine and finally Peucestas's.'

I glanced along the passage. Sure enough, there were three doors, plus another two – presumably more unused bedrooms – on the right, with a blank wall beyond. 'And no one, uh, heard any movement during the night? No creaking floorboards?'

'You asked that before.'

'Yeah,' I said. 'Yeah, I did.' I turned round just to check that from where I was standing, at the junction of the second corridor and the top of the stairs, I could see the door of Zariadres's room. I could, just. Then I stepped aside and let Osroes lead the way back downstairs.

Vitellius was talking when we came back into the atrium, but when he saw me he clammed up. The other two stared at me expressionlessly. I walked over to the couch I'd had before and lay down.

'So,' I said. 'Why?'

'Why what?' That was Callion.

'Why was he killed?'

'Who can say?' Osroes raised his shoulders. 'If we were in Parthia the answer would be easy: traitors die, and Artabanus would not hesitate to kill someone he viewed as a traitor, as he would view any of us. Also, no doubt there he would have his private enemies. But here in Rome? Who is there in Rome, apart from us?'

Three pairs of eyes – Vitellius's included – locked on to him, and the room was suddenly very quiet. I'd lay good money that that was the first time the thought had been put into words, although the suspect shortlist must've been obvious to all of them from the outset. It was interesting that Osroes had brought it up. He'd done it deliberately, that was for sure, and I wondered why.

'I had no reason, personally, to kill Zariadres,' Peucestas said softly. 'I swear it.'

'Nor did I.' Callion sipped his wine.

'And I didn't kill him either.' Osroes smiled; on that face it was like a razor drawn across where his mouth should be. 'There, Corvinus, that's done. You have three sworn denials. Of course, one of us may be given over to the Dark Lord, in which case a lie would come easily to him. Still, there is your question of why to answer.' He paused, and then added carefully, 'Plus the question of the door and the drugged porter.'

'The obvious explanation for that is that someone killed Zariadres and then slipped out,' I said.

'No,' Callion said, quietly but firmly. 'I told you, Corvinus, and I'll swear to it. There was no one in the house last night who shouldn't have been here and who was unaccounted for when Peucestas found Zariadres this morning.'

'To your knowledge.'

'To my certain knowledge.' He smiled. 'I'm afraid that you will have to think again.'

'So why the drugged door-slave and the open door?'

No one answered. Suddenly, I felt angry; so angry that for two pins I'd've chucked the whole boiling, gone straight round to Isidorus's and told him in words of one syllable just what he could do with himself . . .

Just for a moment. It was a close thing, though.

I gritted my teeth, unclenched my fists and tried to keep my voice a notch this side of civil. 'Okay,' I said. 'So tell me. Who drugged the porter and unbolted the door, and why?'

No response. Well, I hadn't really expected one, although that's not to say I didn't believe that at least one of the slippery bastards could've provided it; in fact, the belief was practically a certainty. I stood up.

'Thank you for your time, gentlemen,' I said. 'And your help.' And fuck you all, all three of you.

We left.

9

The litter was waiting for us outside. I let Vitellius get in first, then joined him. I was still fuming. Even so, I took the time to look left and right, up and down the road outside the house. Opposite, a blank wall stretched unbroken in both directions. There wasn't any cover – no doorways or over-hanging trees – on the house side, either. Interesting.

'Bastards!' I said as the litter guys headed off.

'They're Parthians,' Vitellius said equably. 'Even Callion, for all he's a Greek. Of course they're bastards.'

'I've met straighter snakes.'

'You were warned.' He settled back among the cushions. 'Well?'

'That business with the door. You didn't know it was open?'

'No.' Vitellius was frowning.

'And you're sure your men were on duty?'

He stirred uncomfortably. 'Not from personal knowledge. Corvinus, what are you getting at?'

It was just an idea, and I hated peaching, but we had to cover all the angles here. 'I was just thinking,' I said. 'These guys are only human, like the rest of us. We had a rip-snorter of a rainstorm last night. There isn't any shelter anywhere near the door. I just checked.'

Vitellius's little piggy eyes skewered me like knives. 'Ah,' he said. Just that: like I say, the guy was a lot smarter than he looked, although that wouldn't be hard. 'Good point, boy. I'll pass it on and get an answer for you. But I can tell you now, if the bugger out front wasn't in place then Isidorus will personally string him up somewhere high by his wollocks until he drops off.'

'Yeah,' I said. 'Yeah, that'll be really useful, pal. Shutting the stable door isn't in it.'

'It would certainly broaden the options, though.'

'Uh-huh,' I was looking out between the curtains. 'That's what I'm afraid of. Three more questions.'

'Go ahead.'

'One: Zariadres's death. How does it affect the negotiations?'

'How do you mean?'

'He was the delegation leader. Now he's gone, what authority do the others have?'

'The murder doesn't change anything at all. Zariadres was the leader, but he was first among equals. The delegation's principals gave all four of them carte blanche.'

'Yeah. Yeah, that's what I thought. Still, Osroes steps into Zariadres's shoes as prime dickerer, doesn't he? And Osroes is a different kettle of fish from Zariadres. The two didn't get on, to put it mildly. Or at least that's the impression I got. And he isn't too sweet on Phraates, either.'

Vitellius was looking at me for the first time with something approaching respect. 'You might have a bit of the diplomat in you after all, Corvinus,' he said slowly. 'No, you're right; he doesn't. Not that that changes things either.'

'Why not?'

'Because Phraates is Rome's choice for Great King. Osroes's personal feelings are neither here nor there.'

'But—' I stopped. Okay; leave it. There was the beginning of an idea there, but it was no more than that. I wasn't going to go out on no theoretical limbs, certainly not with Lucius Vitellius.

'But what?'

'Nothing. That was question two. Third question.'

'You've got the floor, boy.'

'Peucestas. He's the only one of the three I didn't meet before Zariadres's death. How did he get on with the guy?'

'Ah.' Vitellius leaned back. 'Peucestas is . . . rather a complicated man. In some ways, anyway. As far as I can tell – and that's not going far, because the bugger's not all that forthcoming – he'd nothing against him. Certainly he's no Osroes.'

'He's capable of killing, though.'

Vitellius shot me a look. 'Now why would you think that?'

'Because he's the quiet, solid type. Osroes is all mouth and no action. Not any action that would threaten him personally, anyway. Callion thinks too much, and if he killed someone he'd plan it better. Eunuch or not, Peucestas is a soldier. If he thought Zariadres ought to die, for whatever reason, then he'd kill him. No fancy plans, just a death. And we've only his word for it that Zariadres was dead when he found him.'

'Peucestas swore he didn't kill him.'

'So?'

'He's a Zoroastrian, Corvinus. A good one, as far as I can tell, or if not then he's a bloody superb actor. That may not mean much to you, but believe me it's a clincher. Zoroastrians don't take oaths lightly, especially if they offer them freely with no arm-twisting. Breaking an oath is the worst thing they can do. Take it from me, whoever killed Zariadres it wasn't Peucestas.'

'Then who did kill him?'

Vitellius grinned. 'Shit knows.'

A fair assessment of the situation as it currently stood. 'Yeah,' I sighed. 'Yeah, right.'

*   *   *

Perilla was waiting for me.

'Well?' she said.

I unlimbered the mantle and settled down on the atrium couch with Bathyllus's cup of wine. 'We've got our corpse,' I said. 'Not Phraates after all. Zariadres.'

'*Who* is Zariadres?'

Oh; right; I'd forgotten she didn't know anything about this business yet, barring in its wider features. That we would have to remedy. The hell with Isidorus's strictures on confidentiality: I'd need the lady's not inconsiderable brain in on this one pdq. She's a lot more devious than me, for a start, and deviousness, I'd reckon, was going to be an important quality in this case.

I gave her a quick guide to the turf and generally filled her in on the background. Such of it as there was. I thought she'd be upset we were back to the gory nasties, but she was relieved rather than not.

'It was like waiting for the second boot to drop,' she said. 'At least it's a normal murder now. You know where you are with bodies. Or at least you do, dear.'

'Uh . . . right. Yeah.' I glanced at her sideways. Strange woman, Perilla, sometimes. Me, I blame the reading.

'So.' She straightened a fold on her mantle: Perilla doesn't lounge around the house like I do, and in what she was wearing she could've received the Chief Priestess of Juno. 'What are your thoughts so far?'

'On who did it? One of the three of them, at least I hope so. Currently I'd bet on the Magian, but that's just because he's the only one to have even the sniff of a motive and I don't like the bugger. It doesn't mean zilch.'

'But if the front door was open . . .'

'Yeah. Right. That's the puzzler. I can think of three possibilities, but there might be more.'

'Go on.'

'The first's the obvious one: that the killer was an outsider.' She opened her mouth to say something, and I held up my hand. 'Lady, I know! The door had to be unbolted from inside, there was supposed to be a watchman in the street all night, and Isidorus had all the entrances and exits to the place stitched up tighter than a Vestal's winter drawers. I've thought of all that.'

'Oh, good.'

'First of all, we don't know for sure about the watchman; the guy should've been there, granted, but Vitellius is checking for me, and if he wasn't then given other circumstances an outsider is a distinct possibility.'

'The door would still have to be open.'

'Perilla, will you wait? I said "given other circumstances"! Gods!'

She smiled and ducked her head. 'All right, dear. But you're not doing too well at present.'

I scowled into my wine cup. 'As far as an outside killer's lying doggo's concerned there's no hassle. If he did manage to get in somehow it could've been at any time. Osroes showed me round and the place has enough unused rooms and cubby-holes for a dozen murderers. He could just have stayed hidden and waited his chance.'

'So how did he get out again? It wasn't a simple case of unlocking the door and drawing the bolts; he'd have to arrange for the drugging of the door-slave. Also—'

'Sure he would. He had help.'

'What?'

'I'm not claiming he was a total outsider, Perilla. That wouldn't work, no way. He had to have an accomplice on the inside, someone who could get him in and make sure he was safely bedded down, then slip the door-slave his wobbler with no questions asked. Which brings us back to Osroes. Osroes is a natural: the porter was his slave, he could have arranged that easy. Another thing: if he wasn't kidding me about Magians and dead bodies then getting someone else to do the killing would make sense.'

'Hmm.' Perilla twisted her hair. 'What about the guard?'

'Jupiter in bloody spangles, lady! I told you, Vitellius is checking on that! The theory's dependent on there being no sodding guard! He was keeping his head dry somewhere round the corner!'

'But Osroes – or whoever – wouldn't know that at the time, would he? Certainly not in advance.'

Oh, shit; she'd got me there. I took another swallow of wine. 'Okay. Point taken. So there are flaws.'

'Flaws is right, dear. What's your second explanation?'

'That the killer was an insider all the time, and opening the door was a blind. Not much of one, sure, especially with the guard there, but as good as he could manage. At least it would muddy the waters.'

'Very well. That seems reasonable. Three?'

'The door was never opened at all. Or not until the next morning, anyway.'

'But, Marcus, that doesn't make sense! The door-slave—'

'Listen. We're round to Osroes again. We only have his word for what happened, and the timings involved. He was the one who found the door unlocked and the porter asleep. And he had the poor bastard killed before we could get his side of the story. Like I say, an open door muddies the waters. Without it, it had to be an inside job; this way at least there's a doubt. We don't even know for sure that the guy *was* asleep, let alone drugged. Osroes could've made that up too.'

Perilla was quiet for a long time. Then she said, 'Osroes is Zoroastrian, isn't he?'

'Yeah, of course he's Zoroastrian! What has that got to do with—'

'Didn't your friend Isidorus – or Lucius Vitellius – tell you about Zoroastrians? Strict ones? They have a deep-seated aversion to lying. And Magians are very, very strict.'

'Gods, Perilla! Don't tell me that if—'

'No, wait, dear. This is important. He may be lying, of course, but it's extremely unlikely, especially if the lie was as direct as you say. Telling a direct lie, particularly for personal gain, is the worst thing a Magian can do. They believe it puts the soul in terrible danger, and Magians believe in the soul completely. I'm sorry, Marcus, and I'm no expert on Parthians, but I really do not think your third explanation will work.'

Bugger. Well, I bowed to the lady's superior knowledge; and Vitellius, I remembered, had said something similar about Peucestas, so that just about nailed the lid on. 'Then we'll just have to assume the fucking door was open then, won't we?' I snarled.

'Yes, we will. And please don't swear, dear. Even if you are disappointed.'

'Disappointed' wasn't the word I'd've used; what I felt was frustrated.

'It's not as simple as that, lady,' I said. 'I just don't know where I am here generally. The problem's getting inside these bastards' minds. They're foreigners, even the ones who've been brought up in Rome; I don't understand how they work. What makes them tick.'

'Much the same as with anyone else, I'd expect. Power. Money. Past grudges. That sort of thing.'

'Fine. Okay. But this Osroes is a case in point. Perilla, he was disgusted when I suggested Zariadres should be cremated. Genuinely disgusted. His idea of a good funeral is leaving the corpse out for the crows. And he'll quite happily torture a slave to death when he knows perfectly well that the poor bugger hasn't any information to give him. How the hell can you expect to understand people like that?'

'I don't know.' She smiled. 'What you need, Marcus, is an expert. A *real* expert.'

'I've got a fu—' I stopped myself. 'I've got a real expert. Two. One of them's a bureaucrat's bureaucrat and the other one thinks I'm an idiot.'

'No. I mean a non-technical expert, as it were. Another Parthian, for preference, one who isn't involved in the case. There must be someone like that in Rome you can talk to.'

I sat back. Yeah; now *there* was an idea! Also, it'd give me a different angle to work from, and that I needed badly. Some background on the Roman Parthians, Phraates and Tiridates – not the political stuff but something more personal – would be useful. Or potentially so, anyway. Not to mention Mithradates. Whether I liked it or not – and I didn't, much above half – that bastard would be relevant somewhere along the line, I'd bet my last copper piece on it.

So. What we wanted here was someone from the expat community these guys belonged to, someone not connected with the case but who might be able to dish any dirt there was going on the unofficial side . . .

'Caelius Crispus,' I said.

'*Crispus?*' Perilla frowned. 'Crispus isn't a Parthian, dear. Not even close. And he's scarcely been outside Rome.'

'Yeah, I know that. But the sort of person I'm looking for is right up his street. If anyone can suggest a name, it's that slimy bugger.'

'Ah.' She sniffed. 'I see. Well, if you put it that way . . . '

I grinned; Perilla didn't approve of Caelius Crispus. To be fair, it was mutual: given the choice between being visited by her or by a plague of boils Crispus would've taken the boils every time. Me – well, I'd known him since pre-Perilla days, and if we weren't friends by a long chalk we were on firm exchanging-insults terms. Certainly on my part I had a sneaking respect for the guy: anyone who's made it his business for years to rake through high society's dirty linen basket for profit and still isn't at the bottom of the river wearing concrete sandals has to have something going for him.

'Is he still with the foreign judge's office?'

'Yeah, I assume so,' I said. It was one of life's little ironies that Crispus was currently a praetor's rep; largely, I suspected, because he knew things about his boss that'd hand the guy a one-way ticket to an island if they ever got out. 'Unless he's managed to get something on someone higher up and weaselled his way into an even better job.'

'Then you'd better see him first thing tomorrow morning.'

Ah. Right; good point. I'd forgotten about the Augustalia. It started in two days' time, and, although it wasn't a major festival and places tend to stay open throughout, the government offices would be closed on day one. Given that Crispus wasn't exactly a conscientious civil servant where working hours were concerned he'd probably slope off early the afternoon before.

'Incidentally, Marcus, now we're on the subject and before I forget' – Perilla ducked her head and tugged at a fold in her mantle – 'there's a performance of the *Medea* on the festival's first day. I thought we might go.'

I froze, the wine cup an inch from my lips. Damn. 'Forget', nothing: she'd slipped that in deliberately. Not unexpected, mind: plays – Greek plays especially – are obligatory at the Augustalia. Unlike Perilla, who's a sucker for anyone in a mask, I'm no theatre-goer; light comedies I can just about take apart from the godawful plots, but tragedy bores the pants off me. Still, I could always sleep through it. Perilla doesn't mind, so long as I don't snore, which I try not to because the lady packs a wicked elbow-jab.

'Great. Great,' I said, and took a substantial swig. Well, now, *that* was something to look forward to, wasn't it?

She leaned over and kissed me. 'What I like about you, Marcus Valerius Corvinus,' she said, 'is that you are so enthusiastic.'

'Yeah. Right.'

Bathyllus shimmied in, and coughed.

'What is it, little guy?' I said.

'Dinner will be early this evening, sir. If that's convenient.'

'Yeah, that's fine, Bathyllus. What's on offer?'

'The chef is serving meatballs, sir.'

Meatballs? Bugger; I'd forgotten about the Great Lamprey Mystery. However, it'd been a hard day, and I just didn't feel up to any more sleuthing on the domestic front, especially if Meton was involved. We'd just have to grin and bear it for the present. 'Great,' I said. 'Meatballs are a favourite.'

'Yes, sir.' He didn't look convinced, which wasn't all that surprising. 'You have time for a bath, if you wish one. The furnace is hot.'

Good idea. Cut my losses. Bath, early dinner and early night. Then tomorrow morning I could beard Caelius Crispus bright and chirpy.

IO

I was over to the Capitol fairly early the next morning. I checked with the desk slave at the praetor's office that Crispus was still unhanged and on the payroll, got directions to his room – a different one from the last time I'd been here – and knocked on the appropriate door. This I was looking forward to.

'Come!'

Snappy and just bristling with authority. Evidently the guy was still on his way up. I grinned to myself and turned the knob.

He was sitting behind a desk dictating to a secretary on a stool next to him.

'Oh, fuck,' he murmured.

'Hi, Crispus,' I said. 'How's it going, pal?'

His gaze didn't shift but his hand fluttered against the secretary's chest. 'Off you trot, Menelaus. We'll finish up later.' The secretary uncurled himself from his stool, shot me an interested look, tucked his pen behind his ear and drifted out, closing the door behind him. 'Now. What is it this time?'

'Nice office.' I pulled up a visitor's chair and sat down. Crispus would never make consul, sure – he wasn't on that particular ladder, and even the Roman hierarchy has its standards – but he was clearly well on his way to being a grey eminence. I doubted if the praetor himself rated much better. Even the in-out trays were cedarwood.

'Come on, Corvinus. Just tell me what you want.'

'Perilla sends her regards.'

'Lovely. Now let's just get this over with, shall we? I've got work to do.'

'Yeah. I can see that.' There was only one wax tablet in the in tray; the other tray was empty. 'It's a hard life being a bureaucrat.'

'Bugger off. Or come to the point. I'm due in a meeting in half an hour.'

'Fair enough. The Parthian expat community.'

His eyes shifted. 'What? There isn't one.'

'Okay. The closest you can get. Armenian, Arab, you name it. You know what I mean.'

'You said Parthian. What's your interest in the Parthians?'

'Maybe I'm just broadening my cultural horizons.'

'And my great-grandmother was Cleopatra. There wouldn't be a connection with a certain group of easterners currently visiting Rome, would there? Also with an attack on a certain long-term resident's litter a few days back?'

Uh-huh. Well, Crispus was no fool; he kept his ear close to the ground, he could put two and two together, and information was his business. Still, what he guessed and what I actually told him were different things. And he clearly didn't know about Zariadres or he'd've slipped that in too.

'It's possible,' I said.

His expression had gone hard. 'In that case if I were you whatever you're up to in that direction, Corvinus, I'd back off before you get your knuckles rapped. Seriously rapped.'

'Fine. Advice noted. Now give, pal. I'm not asking for much.'

'Really? You going solo on this?' Then when I hesitated: 'Look, you nosey bastard, that's important. If you are just sniffing around for your own private reasons and the authorities find out that I've given you so much as the time of day then I could find myself processing tax returns for fucking Lusitania. So level.'

Well, he had a point. 'It's official, Crispus,' I said. 'That's all I can tell you.'

'You swear it?'

'Yeah, I swear it. Happy?'

He fizzed for a bit, but it was just for form's sake. Crispus would cheerfully piss in my urn, sure, but by this point in our relationship we could judge each other to a tee. I wouldn't mess him around with an oath, and he knew it. 'Okay,' he said. 'But if you're lying then I will come after you with a rusty pruning-hook. That's a promise. Deal?'

'Deal.'

'So long as we understand each other.' He leaned forward. 'Now. Just exactly what are you looking for?'

'I told you. Someone from the other side of the eastern borders who knows how these bastards think and knows the ins and outs of the expat community in Rome. Preferably someone who isn't too friendly disposed to his fellow expats and wouldn't mind dishing a little dirt on them.'

'Hang on, Corvinus.' He was frowning. 'You sure this is official? Cast-iron, spit on your grandmother's grave sure?'

'Believe me, pal, the authorisation comes right from the top. I'm not exaggerating, either.'

I'd impressed him, I could see that, but he still wasn't happy. His podgy, ring-covered fingers drummed on the desk. 'Okay. So let me think for a moment.'

I sat back and waited. It took him a good two minutes. Finally, he said, 'You remember the old Happy Bachelors?'

Sure I did: the chichi all-male club up on the Pincian that Perilla and me had got him thrown out of years ago for letting a woman into. I nodded warily. 'Yeah. Yeah, I remember that one.'

'It's changed hands now. Changed name, too, to the

Acanthus Leaf.' I said nothing. 'The guy you want to talk to is called Nicanor. He's the son of an Armenian businessman by the name of Anacus, and he spends a lot of time there. Don't tell him I sent you.' He reached for the tablet in his in tray. 'That's the best I can do. Now piss off and let me earn my salary in peace.'

'You get your membership card renewed, then?'

That landed me a disgusted snort. 'Bugger that! I wouldn't bother applying. The place was raided a year or so back and it isn't nearly as much fun any more. I spend my free time elsewhere.'

'Yeah? Where would that be, now?'

'Go away, Corvinus. Just go away, all right?'

'Fine. No problem, pal.' I got up. 'Thanks a lot.'

'And see if you can't arrange to be knocked down by a fucking cart en route.'

I left, grinning.

There wasn't any point in going to the Bachelors, aka the Acanthus Leaf, straight away, because it wouldn't open until after sunset. Home, then, for the moment. Not directly, though; while I was in this part of town I might as well drop in by the Velabrum pastry shops and pick up a few bits and pieces for Bathyllus and the lads as festival presents. After that I could fill in another hour or so very pleasantly at a wineshop, with maybe half a jug of Massic, a crusty roll and a plate of cheese and olives. Not a bad prospect.

I crossed Market Square – not easy; that time in the morning the square was heaving – turned right into Tuscan Street and headed for the Velabrum intersection. At least the weather had cleared up, with not a cloud in the sky. I'd had enough of litters. If that was how real diplomats got around then they could keep it.

I was just passing the mouth of an alleyway not all that far from Renatius's when a big guy in a labourer's tunic who'd been walking on my outside suddenly swerved sideways, catching me hard in a shoulder-charge with the full weight of his body behind it and bouncing me through the gap like a feather ball.

'Hey, pal, what do you think—' I stopped. Yeah, right; that answered *that* question. There were three of them now, the other two just as big as the first, blocking the Tuscan-side exit to the alley, and apologetic was something they didn't look. Before I could react, the guy in the centre gave me another shove in the chest that sent me staggering back further in. They kept on coming, closing the distance to nothing, and the guy shoved me again. We were deep in the alleyway now, behind a pile of assorted garbage.

Muggers, obviously; although what the hell they were thinking of going for someone on Tuscan in broad daylight I didn't know. This time I moved back with the shove, lifted my foot and drove at the middle guy's groin. Without so much as a check, he caught it in both hands and twisted. I went down hard, sprawling sideways on to my face and getting a fair-sized mouthful of the alley floor. Whatever had been living down there, it hadn't been house-trained. I spat the stuff out . . .

Just as a seriously hobnailed boot crashed into my ribs and made oral hygiene the last thing on my mind. Then a second boot came from the other side, closely followed by a third to the head. My knees came up into the hollow of my chest in an involuntary spasm as the fourth kick connected with my spine . . .

'That's enough, lads. I don't want him crippled. Let him up now.'

A huge hand gripped the neck-seam of my tunic and lifted me like I was a baby. The whole left side of my head was on fire, my ear felt like it was five times its size, and I'd got what sounded like a whole swarm of very angry bees inside my skull. Breathing wasn't too easy, either.

'Nothing to be alarmed about, Corvinus. Just settling a small debt.'

I focused with difficulty. One of the gorillas was holding me up while the other two stood by watching. Behind them was Mithradates.

I fought for breath. It was like someone had filled my lungs with razors and the bees were still there in earnest. 'You bastard!' I whispered. 'I'm a fucking Roman citizen! I could have you crucified!'

'No, you couldn't.' Mithradates grinned. 'Believe me. And I wouldn't advise you to try, not unless you've got a great deal more clout than I think you have. Besides, the punishment's over. Like I say, consider it just the settlement of a debt. You owed me that for two nights ago, and I always collect.' He turned his attention to the gorilla holding me. 'Let him loose.' The grip on my tunic relaxed. 'Now. That aside, I want you to listen to me very carefully, Valerius Corvinus. This business with the delegation. It's none of your concern. I'm asking you, very politely, to drop it. Isidorus will fully understand. All right?'

'Go and screw yourself!'

He gave a shrug. 'Well, you have been warned and you can't say otherwise. It was a pleasure meeting you again. Come on, gentlemen. Fun's over.'

He turned and walked back down the alleyway. I would've followed, but one of the gorillas stayed behind to see that I didn't, and in my current state I couldn't've taken him if he'd been an eight-year-old midget. A female one, at that. Then he left too.

I hobbled back on to Tuscan, getting leery stares as I

emerged from two passing large-bellied plain-mantles and a guy with a poleful of chickens. The whole business had taken no more than two or three minutes, max.

Shit.

Luckily, Renatius's wineshop wasn't all that far. I could have a quick wash and brush up there and repair such of the damage as I could before going back to face Perilla. That I wasn't looking forward to.

'Marcus, what on *earth* happened to you?'

'Uh . . . runaway bull from a butcher's shop near Cattlemarket Square.' I took the jug and cup from the goggling Bathyllus, poured myself a belt and swallowed it. 'I was standing between it and where it wanted to go.'

'Don't be silly. You know there aren't any slaughterhouses near Cattlemarket Square nowadays. Juno, your face is a mess! Bathyllus, send someone for Sarpedon!'

Sarpedon was our family doctor and – long in the past – one of my father's slaves. He was currently worth about five times what I was, and the chances of getting him to make a house call at this short notice were zilch. 'Perilla, I'm fine, okay? Just a bit bruised.' I lowered myself gingerly on to the couch. I was pretty sure my ribs weren't cracked, but I wasn't going to be dancing on any tables for the next few days. Bathyllus scuttled out. The little guy could scent trouble brewing, and I didn't blame him.

Perilla had sat down too. She was white as a sheet, and her mouth was a hard line. 'Just tell me exactly what happened,' she said. 'And this time don't lie.'

'I was mugged. In an alleyway off Tuscan.'

'Rubbish. In the middle of the day? And you've still got your purse. I can see it on your belt from here.'

'Ah . . . I fought them off.'

'Marcus Valerius Corvinus!'

Oh, bugger. I held up my hands, palm out. 'Okay. Okay. It was Mithradates and three hired gorillas. But this is as far as it goes, right? He was peeved about—' I stopped; I hadn't told Perilla about Mithradates. Or about the girl in the juggling troupe.

'About what? And who's Mithradates?'

'An Iberian prince. We, er, had a bit of a disagreement at the Parthians' dinner.'

She stood up. 'You'll lodge a charge of assault with the praetor's office.'

'No I won't.'

'*Marcus!*'

'Perilla, it's over. Don't make waves.'

We glared at each other. Then she came over and laid her face on my shoulder.

'I want you to give it up,' she said quietly.

'I, uh, can't do that.'

'Marcus.' Her voice was muffled, and it wasn't just from the wool of my tunic. 'I told you in the beginning. I have a very, *very* bad feeling about this. The next time you could be killed.'

'That's—'

'No. It isn't nonsense. All you have to do is go to Isidorus and tell him to find someone else. He'll understand.'

He'll understand. That was what Mithradates had said . . .

'No.'

Her face lifted. 'Then you're a fool!'

She meant it, too. 'Yeah. Yeah, maybe I am, at that.'

There wasn't much more to be said.

She pulled away and turned her back. 'There was a message for you. When you were out.'

'Yeah?'

'From Isidorus. You were right. He's checked with the guard, and the man admitted that he was sheltering during the worst of the storm under a tree out of sight of the front door.'

'Uh . . . good. Good.'

'I'm glad you think so.'

Hell.

I I

I broke my habit and took the carriage to the Pincian. I hate litters, sure – if Perilla didn't use the thing I'd get rid of ours and pension off the lardballs we use as bearers – but carriages are okay. You can think in a carriage. Besides, it was cushioned; even after a long, hot bath and a rub I still hurt like hell, and the Happy Bachelors was well out in the sticks, beyond Lucullus Gardens. It'd have to've been, in the old days; in any sort of moral climate short of the torrid and tropical the Bachelors would've been raided and closed down long before the authorities actually blew the whistle, if it hadn't been too far from the centre for the element of surprise to work; plus the fact that a raid on any night you cared to mention would've netted a fair percentage of Rome's great and good, who would no doubt have taken serious umbrage. Any local Watch commander silly enough to try it on without very specific orders from above would've found himself so far up shit creek that even a paddle wouldn't've helped.

That was in the old days. What the place was like now, in its new guise of the Acanthus Leaf, I didn't know. I got Lysias the coachman to drop me at the door and told him and the strongarm boys who were acting as escort torchbearers to wait for me.

I knocked, and the spy-hatch slid open. Well, that much hadn't changed, anyway.

'Yes, sir?' the slave behind it said.

'Just let me in, sunshine.'

'Are you a member, sir?'

'No, but—'

'Temporary membership is one gold piece. There is also an entrance fee of fifty silver pieces.'

Hell. 'Look, I just want to talk to a guy by the name of Nicanor. If he's in there maybe you can tell him that—'

The spy-hole snapped shut. Bugger, this looked like costing me an arm and a leg. I would *kill* Crispus. I knocked again. The spy-hole slid open.

'Okay, pal, you win.' I fumbled in my belt-pouch and handed over the money: one and a half big ones. 'Here you are. Now open up.'

He did, and I got an eyeful of the surroundings.

The last time I'd been through this door with Perilla the door-slave had been wearing a frizzed gilded wig and a tutu. This guy looked reassuringly normal. Seriously under-dressed and definitely on the effete side, sure, but normal. Yeah, well; judging by first impressions I'd bet that different name or not the proclivities of the Bachelors' clientele hadn't changed, anyway.

Nor had the decor. It was still way OTT, with enough marble veneer and gilt to leave the most nouveau of nouveaux-riches Market Square execs crying their little eyes out in envy. There were more bronzes scattered around the hallway than you could shake a stick at: Adonises, Harmodius-and-Aristogeitons, Olympic athletes, you name it, so long as it was young, male, well-muscled and stripped for action. The murals . . .

I took one look at the murals and decided I didn't even want to *see* them. The old Bachelors had been tame in comparison.

This was the place *after* a raid?

'Now, sir.' The door-slave was smiling at me. Some

would-be aesthete had gilded his teeth and gums. 'Were you wanting some company, or had you made your own arrangements? We have—'

'Uh . . . that's okay, pal,' I said quickly. 'No company. Like I told you, I'm looking for a guy called Nicanor. He around this evening?'

I was keeping my fingers crossed. I didn't know how long temporary membership lasted, but half a gold piece was a pretty stiff entrance fee on its own and I didn't fancy paying it more than once.

'He's in the lounge, sir. Was he expecting you?'

'No. He, ah, doesn't know me. But we've got a mutual fr—' I stopped myself. 'Acquaintance.'

'A club member? What would the gentleman's name be, sir?'

'Just give him mine, sunshine. It's Corvinus. Marcus Valerius Corvinus.'

'Very well. I'll tell him that you're here.' He shimmied off between a set of Egyptian columns painted and gilded within an inch of their lives. Well, I couldn't complain about the standard of service. Given that the guy was only wearing a spangled cache-sexe and diamond nipple-covers he could've buttled with the best of them. Jupiter knew where he'd put the entrance money. I twiddled my thumbs and tried not to look at the murals.

He was back in two minutes. 'If you'd care to follow me, sir,' he said.

The lounge was just that: a big room with a pool and fountain in the centre round which couches and tables had been placed at discreet intervals. Half hidden by potted plants, a Greek lyre-player was going through his Lydian-mode repertoire, and the air was delicately perfumed with the scent of roses. Most of the couches were occupied, doubly so. The door-slave pointed me towards a couch in the corner with only a single occupant. The youngster – he couldn't've been any more than very early twenties, max – was staring at me from over the lip of his wine cup, and even from this distance I could see he was in the process of getting quietly stewed.

'Would you care for a drink, sir?' the door-slave murmured.

'Hmm?'

'A drink. The first is complimentary, of course.'

'Uh . . . yeah.' The stare above the wine cup was so unblinkingly hostile it was beginning to unnerve me. 'You have any Caecuban?'

'Naturally, sir. Which year?'

Oh, shit! 'Look, just bring me a very large belt of the stuff, okay, pal? Chilled, if possible, but I'm not fussy.'

He sniffed and left. I had the distinct impression my street-cred with the staff had sunk as close to zero as made no difference, but some thorns on the primrose path of life you can live with. I went over to the youngster's couch, trying not to look at what was going on either side of me; not that any of the occupants seemed concerned.

'Ah . . . the name's Corvinus,' I said. 'Valerius Corvinus.'

'So Myron told me.' He had an accent you could've hammered nails into, and it made the aggressive attitude even more noticeable. 'What happened to your face?'

'I test boxing gloves for a living.'

Not a twitch; he stared back at me expressionlessly. Then he said, 'All right. So what do you want?'

There was a stool next to the table that looked like it might've been liberated from the palace at Alexandria. I pulled it over and sat down. 'Not what you think, for a start,' I said.

This time he laughed: a quick, sharp bark with no humour in it. 'No? Well, that's something. Who's the mutual friend?'

'Acquaintance. He said not to give you his name, and it doesn't matter anyway.'

Nicanor took another gulp of wine, set the cup down and drew the back of his hand slowly across his mouth. His eyes hadn't left mine. 'Okay,' he said. 'We'll leave it at that. You've told me what you don't want. Now tell me what you do.'

'Just to talk. I asked this . . . acquaintance . . . if he could put me in touch with someone who knows about Parthians. Local Parthians. Yours was the name he came up with.'

'Easy. They're five-star bastards, all of them. That enough for you?' His lips stretched in a toothed, drunken, humourless grin. 'There. Mission accomplished. You can go away now and leave me in peace. Test a few more boxing gloves.'

A slave – not Myron, a kid about eight or nine done up to look like Ganymede – brought my wine. 'Can I get you another?' I said. They didn't seem to believe in half jugs here, which didn't augur too well for the prices.

'It's your money.' I nodded to Ganymede and the kid went off. 'Fine. So you've bought yourself some talking time. What's your interest in Parthians?'

I wanted to ask him a few questions myself, nothing to do with the case; like what the hell his parents were doing letting him waste his life in a hole like the Acanthus Leaf. Certainly, from first impressions he didn't seem all that thrilled to be here, nor did he exactly blend in with the rest of the clientele. However, it wasn't my business, and all it would probably have got me was a raised finger. Quite rightly, too. 'Uh . . . you mind if I don't answer that one, friend?' I said. 'Or would you prefer it if I lied?'

That netted the first really straight, interested look I'd had from him.

'Yes,' he said. 'Let's have the lie.'

Jupiter on wheels! This wasn't supposed to happen! 'Ah . . . right. Okay. Uh . . . I own a trading company and I was thinking of expanding. I'm looking for a partner in Rome who's got connections over the Syrian border.'

He laughed; a genuine laugh this time, not the sour bark we'd had before. 'That's it?' he said. 'If that's the best lie you can manage then trying it'd've put you out on your fucking ear. My dad's a merchant and I've lived and breathed the eastern trade all my life. You wouldn't pass for two seconds.'

'Yeah?'

'Name three cities on the spice road east of Bactra; the northern route to Turfan, not the southern. How many camel loads equal one waggon load? How do you tell prime from second-grade cassia?'

'Uh . . .'

'You see? You're not even good enough to be a poor ringer.'

I sipped my wine. It was good Caecuban, chilled to perfection. 'Right. Granted. So you're left with the first alternative. Does that make a difference?'

He shrugged. 'Not one I can't live with. So what do you want to know?'

'Anything and everything. But we'll start with three names. Phraates, Tiridates and Mithradates.'

He stared at me for a long time over the top of his wine cup. Finally he said quietly, too quietly, 'Mithradates isn't Parthian. He's an Iberian.'

'So I lied again.'

'"Lied".' He drained his cup at a gulp and scowled. 'You know what the Parthians say about lying, Corvinus? It's the straightest way to hell. That's their general word for evil: the Lie. *Druj*, in Parthian. The joke is, they're the biggest fucking liars in existence.'

'Is that so, now?'

'Sure it's so. Forget the Greeks, the Cretans, they're amateurs. Parthians lie for the fun of it, or twist the truth so many ways from nothing you don't know whether you're on your feet or your head. Never believe a Parthian. Any Parthian. Especially when he claims he's telling the truth.'

Interesting. The Ganymede lookalike drifted over and swapped the empty cup for the new full one. Nicanor took a swig of the fresh wine and belched softly.

'So how about my three names?' I said.

'Phraates is the Grand Old Man of the Parthian contingent. He's been in Rome for ever, got a big, fancy place on the Janiculan. The others call him the Geriatric. They despise him.'

'You know Phraates?'

'No. I've met him, but that's all. We've talked once or twice. He's okay, for a Parthian, and no fool, whatever they say.'

Yeah, well; the guy was pushing seventy. I couldn't expect a twenty-year-old to be too interested or knowledgeable in that direction. 'What about his son Damon?'

It was like I'd pulled a string directly connected with Nicanor's brain. He set his wine cup down carefully, like it was made of eggshell.

'Oh, yes,' he said. 'I know Damon.'

There was something in his voice that stirred the hairs on the back of my neck. He'd spoken calmly enough, but I felt, suddenly, like I was standing on a piece of ground that the next moment just wouldn't be there any more.

'But you're, uh, not a friend of his,' I said cautiously.

Silence. Then, finally: 'No.'

'Want to give me a reason?'

'No,' he said again. He reached for his cup and took a long swallow. 'He lives with his father in that fancy place over on the Janiculan I mentioned. Not that that's out of choice, mind.'

'They don't get on?'

That got me the short, barking laugh again. 'No. But then there's nothing unusual in that, is there?'

Yeah, well; I could see where he was coming from. I hadn't got on with my own father, to put it mildly, and we were living in separate houses. For a man in his late thirties living with parents couldn't be easy. Also, maybe I was wrong but I'd guess from the sourness in Nicanor's voice that his own circumstances weren't all that far different. If he hung out in joints like the Acanthus Leaf then everything couldn't be exactly sweetness and light in his family, either. I sipped my wine. 'So what sort of a guy is he?'

'He's a bastard.' Nicanor reached for his cup and took another swig. 'Oh, yes, I know I said that all Parthians are bastards, but he's a bastard even by Parthian standards.'

'Yeah? In what way exactly?'

'How long have you got, Corvinus? This place closes at dawn.' He paused. 'You ever hear of the Immortals?'

The name rang a faint bell, sure – you can't live with a lady who's a history nut for upwards of fifteen years without something rubbing off – but I didn't think it was the right kind of bell. 'They were, uh, some sort of crack Parthian legion in the old days, weren't they?'

'Persian, not Parthian. Before Alexander. Yes, they were, but it's not what I meant. These Immortals are a frat. Damon's one of the founder members and Tiridates is the other. He chose the name.'

Uh-huh; I knew where he was now. Fraternities – 'brother-hoods' – are pretty common in Rome and getting commoner. They're exclusive gangs formed by rich wide-boys out for kicks of an evening: lots of hard drinking, heavy spending, night-time tours of the city's cathouses, that sort of thing. It'd be good innocent fun that harmed no one if it didn't usually involve some not so innocent breaking and entering, vandalism and mugging, sometimes even murder. Frats are the Watch's bane, because even when the young buggers are caught in the act Daddy's influence and Daddy's money tend to get things hushed up.

'Mithradates a member as well?' I asked. My ribs gave a twinge.

It'd been a guess, but Nicanor's brows came down. 'Sure. He's the group leader. Has been ever since he came to Rome two or three years back.'

Yeah, that made sense. Whatever group that bastard chose to join, even on our short acquaintance I'd've betted he'd be the leader automatically, straight off. And frats would be just right up his street. 'That so? You aren't involved with them yourself?'

'I used to be.' His eyes were clearly warning me off. 'Once. Not any more.'

'Now you just hang around this place instead.'

I'd deliberately kept my voice neutral, but he half flared up all the same. 'I've got my reasons. Not just the obvious one either.'

Right. 'Your, uh, father know where you go of an evening?'

He grinned; not a pleasant grin. 'Oh, yes!'

'And he doesn't mind?'

'He minds like hell. That's one of my reasons.'

I winced. It wasn't just the words, it was the way they came out: flat, matter-of-fact. Passionless. 'You an only son?' I said. 'Or have you got any brothers or sisters?'

It was a natural question, and I didn't expect the reaction it got. Nicanor's face suddenly flushed a deep purple. 'Fuck off, Corvinus!' he snapped; so loud that the couple on the nearest couch stopped what they were doing and gaped at us. 'You just fuck off! Leave my family out of it! Stick to your bloody Parthians!'

Jupiter! I held up both my hands, palm out. 'Okay. Okay! Forget I asked!'

He was glaring at me, and I could see that it was touch and go whether he'd answer or call Ganymede to have me thrown out. Finally, though, he raised his shoulders and took another slug of wine. 'Fine,' he said quietly. 'I'm sorry. Just keep your distance, agreed?'

'Agreed.' I took a sip of my own wine to give him some space and set the cup down. 'Tell me more about these Immortals.'

'Like I said, Mithradates is the leader, the ideas man. Tiridates and Damon tag along on his coat-tails. Mostly it's just wineshops and brothels, but Mithradates and Damon have a taste for trouble. The evening usually ends up in a fight, somewhere or other.'

'What about Tiridates?'

Nicanor grinned. 'He's a coward. He blows hard enough, sure, but he keeps clear of any real action. The same goes Damon, for that matter, but if he can be sure of winning he's right in there. That's why he's a bastard. Mithradates I can take; he's just a thug.' He swallowed the last of the wine in his cup. 'A clever thug, mind. Mithradates is smart.'

Yeah; I'd bet he was. That was why he'd reminded me so strongly of Sejanus. There was another smart thug who'd used brawn and brain to reach the top of the ladder. 'He's been in Rome two, three years, you say?'

'Uh-huh. His brother's king of Iberia. Mithradates got up his nose once too often and had to clear out in a hurry.'

I turned round, caught Ganymede's eye and pointed to Nicanor's cup. Ganymede nodded. 'Where does he get his money from?'

'Fuck knows. Not his brother, certainly. He's not short of a gold piece or two, though, that's for sure. Probably Tiridates subs him. He's rich enough, and he follows Mithradates around like a pet dog.'

'These Immortals ever get into trouble? Real trouble?'

'You kidding?' Nicanor laughed. 'A Parthian prince, a prince's son and one of the Iberian royals? No way! Or nothing they can't buy their way out of without missing the cash. Besides, when he's in Rome Prince Gaius is an honorary member. No one's going to mess with him.'

My spine went cold. 'Gaius?'

'Sure. He's chummed with them for years. Hand in glove.'

Oh, shit; this was a complication I didn't need. If Gaius was a friend of Mithradates then I'd made a dangerous enemy. Seriously dangerous. It explained why he hadn't been all that worried about possible repercussions, too. If he had Rome's crown prince in his pocket then a complaint of assault to the praetor would be about as effective as a sunshade in an avalanche. That was one nugget of information I definitely wouldn't be passing on to Perilla.

Ganymede came over with the fresh cup. I waited until he'd gone.

'Just one more question, pal,' I said, 'and then I'll leave you in peace. Tiridates ever say anything about wanting to be Great King?'

Nicanor snorted into his wine cup so hard the wine splashed into his face. He mopped it off with the sleeve of his tunic. 'You obviously haven't met many Parthian princes, Corvinus. Getting to be Great King is all he thinks about, twenty-four hours a day.'

'What about Phraates?'

'I told you. Tiridates despises him, calls him the Geriatric.'

Yeah. Right; that was more or less what I'd thought. And Nicanor had started up enough new hares to be going on with. I drank the last of my Caecuban and stood up. 'Okay. Thanks for the chat, friend. Enjoy your evening.'

He looked at me in surprise. 'You're going?'

'Sure. You've been very helpful.'

'The place is just warming up. They've got some good entertainment booked.'

'Uh . . . no. No, I have to get back home.'

Nicanor grinned. 'You're a real prude, underneath, aren't you, Corvinus? Fair enough, suit yourself. I'll see you around. If you want another chat some time you know where to find me.'

'Right. Right.'

On my way out I paid for the three cups of wine I'd ordered. What with the entrance money that left my belt-pouch pretty empty. Yeah, well, it'd been worth it; I didn't know where Crispus had dug Nicanor up from, or why he'd chosen him, but I couldn't've asked for a better choice.

I took the carriage home.

12

The next day was the start of the Augustalia.
Unlike in the Greek towns to the south, where they go in for that sort of thing, as a festival it's never been all that popular at Rome, not where ordinary punters like me are concerned, anyway; scarcely surprising, because instead of the usual healthy Roman diet of racing meets and all-day sword-fights what you get at the Augustalia is a non-stop orgy of culture. Which was why instead of being happily out sleuthing or relaxing in a wineshop I spent the morning sitting through a lyre recital followed by readings from the Greek lyric poets before going home for a quick bath, a change of mantle and the trip out to Marcellus Theatre for Euripides's bloody *Medea*.

I *hate* the Augustalia.

I grizzled like hell. Not that it had any effect.

'I contracted for a play, lady,' I said as we piled into the litter for the lyre concert. '*Just* a play. Where did these extras suddenly spring from?'

She kissed me. 'Stop grumbling, dear. If I'd told you beforehand you would've made other arrangements, and you didn't. You hardly ever go with me to these things. A bit of culture is good for you. Besides, it'll give your mind a rest from murder and politics.'

Well, at least she was back to her feisty self after the wobbler of two days back. Still, 'rest' wasn't exactly the term I would've used: by theatre time I'd had Alcaean glyconics up to the eyebrows, my brain was a wrung-out dishrag, and I was really, *really* looking forward to the Euripides: concert halls are tricky, sure, but you can sleep in a theatre.

Not that I was missing much because the big E's *Medea* isn't exactly a laugh a minute (*pace* Perilla, it's not entirely free of murder and politics, either, but that's by the way). I woke up just after the screen had revolved to show the slaughtered kids and the queen getting ready to fly off in her dragon-chariot. Perfect timing, in other words. As we made our way towards the exit through the drift of nutshells and apple cores I was feeling pretty smug.

Not so Perilla.

'Marcus, I'm ashamed of you!' she snapped. 'That was an extremely good production!'

'Yeah. The effects were nice. I liked the effects. Especially the—'

'No one else in our row was sleeping! I looked!'

'Yeah, well, maybe the poor buggers don't have understanding wives.' Smarm, smarm. 'In any case—'

Someone shouted my name. I looked down the rows, towards the VIP seats at the very front. An old man in a fancy embroidered mantle was waving to me. When he saw he'd got my attention he pointed towards the exit door on his level. I waved back and gave him the thumbs-up.

'Who was that, dear?' Perilla said.

'Uh . . . Prince Phraates. I think he wants us to meet him outside.'

She frowned. 'Marcus, *no*! We are going straight home to dinner! You are *not* getting involved with—'

'Oh, come on, lady!' I grinned. 'I've had six solid hours of culture today, four of which I didn't bargain for. You're a weasel, and you owe me. Besides, the guy probably only wants to say hello.'

'Corvinus, I will kill you!'

Before she could object any more I grabbed her arm and steered her to the exit. Sure enough, Phraates was waiting for us beside a snazzy carriage in the open space between the theatre and Apollo's temple. How he'd arranged the carriage – it was just after sunset, and he would've had to get it there in violation of the bylaws – I didn't know, but there it was. Parthian princes can get away with these things.

'Ah, Corvinus,' he said. 'Did you enjoy the play? What did you think of Jason? Wasn't he superb?'

'Yeah. Yeah, he was all right.' Beside me, Perilla snorted. I ignored her.

'And this must be your wife, Rufia Perilla.' Phraates smiled at her and got a stare in return that was straight off a December Alp. Oops; this might be embarrassing. 'You're the poet Ovid's stepdaughter, are you not, my dear? I had the honour of sitting next to him at a dinner party once. A very long time ago now, of course, but I've never forgotten. He was quite the most intelligent, civilised and humane man I had ever met. I'm delighted to make his daughter's acquaintance.'

Gods! Talk about smarm! I glanced at Perilla. Forget the frozen stare: the lady was thawing so fast you could hear the crackle. 'Ah . . . really?' she said faintly.

Phraates gave her another smile and turned to me. 'I was wondering,' he said, 'if you and your wife might care to join me for dinner tonight. Nothing special, but it would give us a chance to talk a little in private.'

Uh-oh. I shot Perilla a quick sideways glance. 'Yeah, well, I'm afraid tonight's a bit difficult. You see—'

'Also, Rufia Perilla' – Phraates turned back to her – 'I do have something a literary scholar like yourself might be interested in seeing, which you could perhaps examine while Corvinus and I have our talk. The manuscript of Euripides's *Helen*.'

Pause; *long* pause. Perilla's ears had gone pink. Finally, she said, 'The . . . ah . . . *original* manuscript?'

Ladies don't drool, but I could see she was coming pretty close.

'Oh, yes. It's quite authentic. I bought it in Athens some years ago from a direct descendant, and it has some fascinating marginal notes in the poet's own hand. But of course if you've made other arrangements for this evening then—'

'No! Oh, no!' I don't think I'd ever heard the lady squeak. She did it now. 'No arrangements! None at all! Certainly not! No!'

'Well, that's excellent.' Phraates beamed. 'We can all go in my carriage, naturally – it isn't far, just the other side of the Agrippan Bridge – and you can use it to return home. Corvinus, perhaps you'd care to leave your wife here while you instruct your litter-slaves.'

'We'll instruct them together.' I was grinning from ear to ear. I wasn't going to miss this; no *way* was I going to miss this! I took Perilla's arm and pulled. 'Come on, lady. Instructing the slaves time. Back in five minutes, Phraates.'

I hustled her towards where we'd left the litter and accompanying lardballs parked, further round the curve of the theatre.

'What happened to the "straight home to dinner", then?' I said.

Perilla sniffed, but her ears were still pink and it spoiled the effect. 'Don't be silly, dear. Your Prince Phraates is perfectly charming and it was a very gracious invitation. How could we refuse?'

'Easy, lady. I was just about to. You were the one who sold out, and you did it in spades. For a bit of smarm and a look at a second-hand book-roll. I'm ashamed of you.'

She looked at me like I'd suddenly come out in purple

blotches and sprouted feathers. 'Marcus, that is an original manuscript of a Euripides play! Do you know how many of these are extant?'

'No.'

'Well, neither do I. But I've never seen one, nor am I ever likely to otherwise. I am *not* passing up the opportunity.'

I shrugged. 'Fine. So you explain things to Meton. He's been slaving over a hot stove all afternoon and when we roll in at two in the morning the guy is not going to be greatly chuffed.'

She stopped. Her eyes widened and she put a hand to her mouth. 'Oh, gods!' she said. 'I'd forgotten all about Meton!'

'Right. Your job, lady. I'm staying out of this one.'

'He'll be absolutely furious!'

'Yeah. Blazing.' I kept my face straight.

'He's probably . . . making . . . the sauce . . . right at this minute.'

Our eyes met. I don't know which of us actually started laughing first, but ten seconds later we were hugging each other helplessly and getting scandalised looks from the other theatre-going punters.

'It's not really funny, you know,' Perilla said at last, when she could breathe.

'Uh-uh. Not in the slightest. We'll be living on boiled cabbage for a month. Still, it's done now.'

'Let's hope Phraates gives us a good dinner, then.'

We instructed the litter-slobs to carry the glad news to the Caelian and went back to where Phraates was waiting.

On the way to the Janiculan we postmortemed the *Medea*, or at least Phraates and Perilla did. Me, I looked out of the window and thought.

I was impressed with Phraates, seriously impressed: slice it how you will, in comparison with just having yourself made

Great King of Parthia bringing Perilla all the way round from freezing-daggers-drawn to pink-eared-and-squeaking in thirty seconds flat takes some doing. Phraates had managed it without breaking sweat. It hadn't been a spur-of-the moment thing, either: he'd obviously done his homework in advance, finding out the lady's full name and family background and choosing just the right bait to hook her. Which was interesting. Me, I wouldn't bet the guy hadn't set the whole accidental meeting up from the start, including the business of the handy carriage; and that took careful planning. Geriatric, nothing: Phraates was a very smart cookie indeed. In which case—

'Wouldn't you agree, Corvinus?'

I turned round. 'Hmm?'

Phraates smiled. 'Forgive me. I've broken your train of thought. I was just saying to your wife that for me the intriguing thing about the *Medea* is how it manages to oppose so successfully two very different but equally cogent moral systems.'

'Yeah? I thought it was just about a witch who murdered her own kids.'

'Marcus!' Perilla snapped.

Well, maybe it had sounded a bit crass at that, and we were his guests after all. He was only trying to bring me into the conversation. 'I'm, uh, afraid I don't know much about literature,' I said. 'And plays aren't really my bag.'

'Indeed?' The old guy didn't seem all that put out, or maybe it was just good manners. 'A pity. I always think, myself, that the theatre can teach us a lot about life. Certainly as much as true history or philosophy. I'm quite a devotee myself.'

'Never mind Marcus,' Perilla said. 'Do carry on, Prince.' The lady sounded almost gooey. Jupiter! This was *Perilla*?

He turned back to her. 'Well, if you're sure. You see, where your sympathies lie in the *Medea* depends on your choice of standpoint.'

'In what way?'

'According to his own moral code, Jason is completely justified in what he does. On the other hand, Medea is also correct, morally, in condemning him because in terms of her code his marriage to Creon's daughter is a total betrayal of herself.' He was still smiling. 'So which of them is right in the end?'

'Surely they both are,' Perilla said. 'That's the essence of the tragedy. But by murdering her own children Medea sets herself beyond the pale.'

'To the Greek mind, yes. Although the Greeks themselves put a high value on revenge. And to even the score the poet is careful to dignify Medea's chain of reasoning. Myself, I feel that Euripides was trying very hard to send his audience home a little more open-minded than when they sat down.'

'Oh, come on, pal!' I said. 'The bitch was a murderess!'

Phraates shook his head. 'No, Corvinus. I'm sorry, you've misunderstood. I'm not justifying her actions totally, and I don't believe that Euripides was, either. However, I do think that the play's intention was to make us think . . . less in blacks and whites, as it were. Jason and Medea come from completely different backgrounds and, as I say, they follow different moral codes. The instinctive reaction is to favour Jason's and regard Medea's with horror. However – and this is the point – that does not make hers any less viable. Nor does it make her – judged by her own standards – a less moral being than Jason is.' He shrugged. 'Well. Perhaps we're getting a little too serious here for a pre-dinner chat. That's the Agrippan Bridge ahead. I'll apologise in advance for the meal; I eat quite simply when I'm at home, and I'm afraid you'll have to take pot luck. It'll be nothing like the banquet poor Zariadres put on for us a few days ago.'

I didn't answer, just settled back against the cushions. I may not be a literary buff, but I'm not stupid, either. And I'd bet a barrel of oysters to a pickled walnut that whatever the devious, smart-as-paint old bugger had been talking about there it hadn't been Euripides.

I don't get over to the Janiculan a lot. Not many city guys do, for much the same reasons: barring the heavily built-up tenement area in the bulge west of the Sublician where the city proper has spilled across the river, most of it's either commercial ground heavy on warehousing and storage or – on the slopes of the hill itself – real up-market residential; what the property marketeers call urban villas. Mega-rich country, in other words, although most of the money's new: businessmen, entrepreneurs, grain- or oil-trade speculators, that sort of thing. The old families tend to stick with their ancestral mansions built in the days when the other side of the Tiber was nothing but fields and virgin woodland, along the Sacred Way or on the slopes of the Quirinal or the Viminal. Getting the Fabii or the Cornelii to pile their bits and pieces on to a mover's cart and shift west of the river after three or four hundred years would take a major earthquake, at the least.

Even for the Janiculan, Phraates's place was certainly something, taking up quite a slice of east-facing slope. Once through the gates the carriageway led up through parkland and stretches of formal garden that wouldn't've disgraced Maecenas Gardens itself, and the villa, when we finally reached it, covered the best part of half an acre. Serious stuff. As the carriage came to a halt slaves rushed out with torches and a major-domo who could've done Creon in the play we'd just seen without changing costume opened the door and bowed.

'Tell the chef we've two more for dinner, Hermogenes,'

Phraates said, getting down. 'We'll eat in the blue dining-room.'

'Yes, lord,' the major-domo murmured. I glanced at Perilla. Not a batted eyelid. Right; well: some people seemed to manage it okay. Me, if I told Bathyllus we had two surprise mouths for the nosebag I'd have a sniff and a kitchen rebellion on my hands.

Phraates dismissed the carriage and bodyguard – we'd been flanked from Marcellus Theatre by what seemed like half a cohort of mean-looking heavies armed with clubs; clearly the guy wasn't taking any chances of a second attack – and led the way up the marble steps.

'Come in, please,' he said.

I'd been expecting something pretty up-market, sure, but even so I was gobsmacked. For size the formal atrium would've done justice to a city-centre public hall, and the decor left most art galleries in the shade. To provide that amount of statues and wall paintings must've taken an army of artists. Not second-raters working from catalogues and skimping on materials, either.

'We'll go somewhere more amenable, I think.' Phraates had taken off his embroidered mantle and handed it to a bowing slave in exchange for a silk dressing-gown. The major-domo was waiting respectfully. 'The east sitting-room, Hermogenes. See that the wine is taken there, will you? And some fruit juice for the lady Rufia Perilla. That suit you, my dear?'

Perilla dimpled and blushed. Sickening. 'Oh, yes,' she said. 'Yes. Certainly.'

'This way, then.' We carried on through the atrium towards the panelled doors at the far end. 'The wine will be Greek, Corvinus. I hope you don't mind.'

'Uh . . . no. Not at all.'

'I prefer Greek wine to Italian myself, although I'd value

your opinion. This one's a rather nice Samian I laid down about forty years back, and it's at its best. I don't drink much these days, but I do find a cup or two of it is very pleasant before dinner. If you'd rather have a Caecuban or something similar then please do say. Hermogenes would be delighted to look out a decent jar for you.'

'Right. Right.'

The major-domo moved ahead of us and opened the doors, then stepped back and bowed again. Beyond was another pillared hall in flecked-pink marble, with a fountain spilling water into a broad pool at its centre. Phraates led the way down a cedar-panelled corridor and opened another door.

'Here we are,' he said. 'Make yourselves at home. If you'll excuse me for a moment I'll just go and get the manuscript I promised. Then, Corvinus, perhaps we can have our little chat.'

He left.

The room was a lot smaller and a lot less formal than the atrium, but the decor was just as pricey. The three couches were antiques, wood inlaid with ivory and upholstered in red satin with a matching table, and although there weren't any statues or wall paintings the walls, like those of the corridor, were panelled in fine-grained wood. The floor was covered with carpets, in the Parthian style. I noticed there was another door, presumably leading to a side room.

'Nice,' I said.

Perilla settled herself on one of the couches. 'I like him,' she said. 'Phraates, I mean.'

'Yeah, lady. I noticed. I think the word is "dripping".'

'Stop it, dear. You know what I mean. He's not at all what I expected.'

I lay down on one of the other couches. 'Well, he's lived in Rome all his life. That makes him a Roman, practically.'

She frowned. 'No, I don't think it does,' she said slowly. 'Or not quite. He's not Roman. Something somewhere in the middle of Roman, Greek and Parthian, perhaps.' She paused. 'He isn't married, is he?'

'Uh-uh.' I stretched out. 'As far as I know, he has a long-term live-in Greek mistress. And a son, of course. Damon.' I'd been wondering about the dining arrangements. The mistress, sure, I doubted if she'd be joining us – social niceties aside, the Greeks are like the Parthians: barring the ordinary domestic side of things men and women tend to lead their own lives, and the villa would have separate women's quarters – but Damon was another matter. After my talk with Nicanor I'd've liked the chance to see Damon at first hand.

'That's curious, isn't it?' Perilla said.

'What's curious?'

'Damon's not a Parthian name. It's Greek.'

'He's illegitimate, lady. And his mother's Greek.'

'Yes, I know. But Phraates recognises him, or I assume that he does. I'd've expected him to have a Parthian name, myself.'

'I don't know how these things work. Maybe—'

The door opened and a slave came in with the wine tray, cups and two jugs. He set it on the table, poured a cup and handed it to me, then did the same with Perilla's fruit juice.

'Thanks, pal,' I said. The slave bowed – still without a word – and left. I sipped . . .

Forget Euripides; this was real Greek poetry.

'How's the fruit juice?' I said.

'It's apple, and chilled. Absolutely delicious.'

There was a plate of dried fruit and nuts beside the jug. I was helping myself when Phraates came back in.

'Good,' he said. 'They've brought the wine.' He poured himself a cup. 'What do you think, Corvinus?'

'Best Samian I've ever tasted.' It was, too, by a mile. I'm

not generally taken with Greek wines – they tend to be on the heavy, sweet side – but this one was superb.

'I'm glad. I thought it was rather nice.' Phraates was holding a book-roll canister. 'Here we are, Rufia Perilla. My part of the bargain.' I swear he winked at me as he handed it over. Like I say, Phraates was a seriously smart cookie. The lady took it like it was spun glass. 'We'll go into the adjoining room so we don't disturb you.'

13

The next room – the one through the door I'd noticed – was a smaller version of the one we'd just left, with hardly enough space for a reading couch, a chair and a twelve-lamp candelabrum. Like in the sitting-room, there were lamps already in place and lit.

'You have the couch, Corvinus,' Phraates said, closing the door. 'I prefer a chair in any case.'

I lay down, cradling my wine cup. Okay, maybe I was being picky, but before we got seriously down to things a scrap more honesty might be in order.

'None of this is accidental, is it?' I said.

The blank look I got back was perfectly judged; but then given the level of Phraates's other accomplishments that wasn't surprising.

'I'm sorry,' he said. 'I'm not with you.'

'This whole evening was a fix from the start. The meeting at the theatre. The dinner invitation. The carriage. The Euripides original that hooked Perilla then got rid of her. You set everything up in advance, including this room.'

'Indeed?' The blank look had disappeared; Phraates didn't look too pleased, to put it mildly. 'And what leads you to that conclusion?'

'Come on, pal! I may not know my Jason from my Theseus but I'm not stupid.' I indicated the oil lamps. 'As far as these're concerned, it's obvious. Even someone as rich as you are doesn't keep every room in the place lit on the off-chance it'll be used. Your major-domo had his instructions long before we got here. Now tell me I'm wrong.'

I thought for a moment I'd gone too far – guys like Phraates don't like being told to their face that they've been sussed – but suddenly his expression cleared and he laughed. 'Oh, dear,' he said. 'I really have grossly underestimated you, Corvinus, and believe me that is something I very seldom do. You're quite right, of course, I did arrange things. From the best possible motives, naturally. And you will, despite what I said, have an excellent dinner. That I guarantee absolutely.'

Well, he couldn't say fairer than that. 'How did you know we were going to Marcellus Theatre?'

'Oh, that was simple. I had one of my slaves strike up a conversation with your coachman yesterday. One of my female slaves. Quite a good-looking girl, so don't be too hard on the poor man, will you?'

I found myself grinning back. Yeah, that'd do it: Lysias had always had an eye for the girls, and a trip to the theatre isn't exactly classified information. Simple but effective. 'Fair enough. So tell me about the motives.'

Phraates sat down. 'They're straightforward too. We had to talk privately, and this was the . . . well, the pleasantest, least overt and most convenient way I could think of. You're not upset, I hope?'

'Uh-uh.' I sipped the wine. It went down like liquid velvet. 'Not at all. So far. My congratulations.'

'Thank you.' He smiled. 'Well, then. I'll leave the governance of the conversation up to you. Where do we start?'

'With a question. Why me?'

The eyes flickered, just for an instant: that he hadn't been expecting. 'I beg your pardon?'

Yeah, well, it was nice that I could still do something to throw the slick old bugger off balance. I didn't flatter myself that now he'd been caught out he was levelling. All it meant was that he was using a different approach. 'I asked Isidorus the same thing, and got his answer. Now I'd like to hear yours, that's all.'

'Then I'm afraid I must disappoint you. I insisted on an independent investigator, yes, but I named no names. How could I? You were Tiberius's personal appointee, and that being the case like Isidorus himself I had no further choice in the matter. Surely Isidorus told you that?' I didn't answer. 'That said, now that I know you personally I have no complaints in retrospect. None at all. You think in a straight line, you don't start with any preconceived ideas, you've no personal or political axe to grind, in the career sense or otherwise. You're gauche, insensitive – forgive me – and you call a spade a spade, even when you know you shouldn't and the result will be that someone clouts you with it. You are basically very simple.' He smiled. 'Does that answer your question?'

'Uh . . . yeah.' Jupiter in rompers! Well, I'd asked, and honesty goes both ways. 'More or less.'

'On the other hand – or rather, also, because I don't believe these are negative qualities, far from it – I'm reliably informed that you can be discreet where discretion is important, and you have a strong sense of justice, even where the justice in question may, shall we say, go rather against the natural grain, your own included. Happy?'

'Delirious.' I took a swig of the wine. 'Thanks a bunch.'

'You're welcome. And I was being complimentary. Believe me.'

'Yeah. Right. So let's move on. Tell me about Tiridates.'

The smile disappeared completely. 'In what way?'

'Maybe this is one of the spades you mentioned. If so, then tough, you can clout me if you like. I get the distinct impression that Tiridates and his pal the Iberian don't exactly support you for Great King. Also, that there's at least one guy in the embassy – Osroes – who'd agree with them.'

Phraates was staring at me. Suddenly, he laughed again and shook his head. 'Corvinus,' he said, 'I really am very glad that Tiberius appointed you. Do you know how long it would've taken someone like Lucius Vitellius to say all that to my face?'

'No. I don't really care, either. So how about an answer?'

He set his wine cup down beside the chair. 'Before I give you that I have to explain a little of the background. I'm sorry, but that's essential. Under Parthian law, both my nephew Tiridates and I are eligible candidates for the kingship; *equally* eligible candidates. There is no such thing as primogeniture. Just because I am the elder doesn't mean to say that my claim is any stronger than his. And, incidentally, we are both more eligible than is Artabanus, who is only royal through his mother. You understand?'

'Yeah, sure, but—'

'Of course, eligibility isn't everything, which is why Artabanus is presently Great King and I am not. My strength is that I have the support of Rome and – consequent on this but not wholly so – the support of the anti-Artabanus faction at Ctesiphon. As long as this continues, my claim is stronger than my nephew's; but *only* as long as it continues. If it were to be withdrawn – or naturally if I were to die – then Tiridates would be next in line.'

Right. Now we were getting somewhere. 'If you were to die,' I said neutrally.

Phraates smiled. 'I know what you're thinking, and you're quite right. Tiridates would love to see me dead, and he would not be averse to . . . shall we say giving fate a nudge. I'm not surprised, nor do I blame him. Murdering relatives has always been endemic in our family. My stepmother – an ex-slave, incidentally, given as a gift to my father by the Divine Augustus – poisoned my father to gain the throne for her own son, whom she then married and later killed. For us royals this is quite normal behaviour.' He must've noticed my expression. 'Oh, yes. Brother-and-sister marriages, and less commonly mother-son ones, are completely acceptable to Parthian custom, in certain quarters. Our friend Osroes, being a Magian, would certainly approve. But that's by the bye. As I say, we Parthian royals have always murdered our kin, or tried to, if they were obstacles. It's become a sort of game.'

'"Game",' I said.

'Oh, yes, indeed. More or less. The attempt, anyway.' His eyebrows lifted in amusement. 'I've shocked you, haven't I?'

'Yeah. Yeah, actually you have.' Sweet gods, Perilla was right: the guy wasn't Roman, no way, never, not unless you were comparing him with Romans like that old bitch Livia. And even Livia wouldn't've called bumping off your relatives a game. If you can't take murder seriously then what's left?

'Then I'm sorry. But the fact remains: of course Tiridates would like to see me dead, especially under the present circumstances. The important question is, is he working actively to that end? Was he responsible for the attack on my litter? I don't know, and that is what I need you to find out.'

'Was that why you had your food tasted at the dinner?'

Phraates chuckled. 'Ah, so you noticed? Partly, although I doubt if he could've engineered anything. He was a guest himself. No, that was just standard practice. The etiquette, if you like, of the Great King's table, and I was very concerned to show myself the Great King that evening. It may've caused a little temporary indignation, but these formalities are important. Now. If you don't mind, let's move on to the next point.'

'Okay.' I took a steadying sip of my wine. 'Mithradates. He's got your nephew under his thumb, and my bet is he doesn't like you either.'

'Oh, it's quite mutual.' Phraates sipped at his own wine cup. 'I did enjoy your little spat, by the way. Very embarrassing for me politically, of course, and he knew exactly what he was doing all the time, but I still enjoyed putting him down. It does no harm for a future Great King to show that he has teeth and isn't afraid to use them. And you're absolutely right again: Mithradates has my nephew completely infatuated. Which says just as much about Tiridates as it does about the Iberian. Kings – good ones – can't afford to allow other people to exert too much influence over them. Tiridates would make a very poor Great King.' He set the wine cup down. 'Mithradates, by the way, could well be a danger to me. He's ambitious, quite ruthless, and he has a very powerful personality. Fortunately, he's also intelligent.'

'Fortunately?'

'Because he'll always choose the winning side, and he's clever enough to work out which that will be. Oh, yes; he, too, would love to see me dead and Tiridates on his way to Parthia with a Roman army behind him. On the other hand, he knows that neither Rome nor the anti-Artabanus faction wants a puppet king.' He smiled. 'At least, not a king who's someone else's puppet. At present, he has the promise of Armenia, which is enough for anyone. He'd be a fool to sacrifice a bird in the hand for two very doubtful ones in the bush, and Mithradates whatever else he may be is no fool.'

Yeah, okay, I'd accept that, especially his final assessment. Still, I wasn't entirely convinced that Phraates was right this time. Personally, I wouldn't lay any hefty bets that Mithradates wouldn't go for the two birds option after all, only it'd turn out that the bastard had already limed the twigs.

'Incidentally,' I said, 'we had a sort of brush yesterday, the two of us. Maybe I should mention that, just in case it's relevant.'

Phraates gave me a sharp look. '"Brush"? What kind of brush?'

I indicated the bruise on the side of my face. It wasn't so noticeable now as it had been, but it was still pretty obvious. 'Down an alleyway off Tuscan Street. He had three hired gorillas with him.'

'He attacked you?'

'Yeah. No bones broken, but he didn't seem too pleased that I was taking an interest in the case.'

Phraates's chin lifted, nostrils flared and lips set in a straight line. The expression was pure outraged eastern royalty. 'What happened?' he said quietly. 'Tell me. Exactly.'

I told him. His face didn't change. If anything it hardened.

When I'd finished, he said, 'You have my apologies, Corvinus. And my thanks. There will be no repetition, I can promise you that. Be very, very sure. I'll have a word with our Iberian friend personally.'

'Yeah. Yeah, right.' Well, the point had been made and taken on board, and like I'd said there'd been no bones broken. 'Okay. We'll leave it at that. Last name, then. Damon.'

Phraates reached for his cup and sipped again before he answered. His expression had gone blank again.

'Ah,' he said. 'I was wondering when you'd ask me about Damon.'

'He's your son. A descendant in the male line. Doesn't that make him a candidate for the kingship too? At least a sort of one?'

'His mother and I aren't married, under either Roman or Parthian law. If we had been then yes, it would. Or it might, in the first case. The fact that she's Greek, and a former courtesan, wouldn't be all that important. As it is' – he shrugged – 'no, not at all. Simply being my son doesn't qualify him.'

'In your eyes or in his?'

Phraates looked straight at me for a long time, toying with the stem of his wine cup. 'You're very perceptive, Corvinus,' he said at last. 'However, your answer is, in my eyes, in Parthia's and in Rome's. Those are the only three factors that matter. I've been very careful all his life to give Damon no reason to think otherwise.'

Uh-huh. The answer was clear enough, sure, but I hadn't missed the fact that he'd pussyfooted. Interesting. 'You, uh, don't have any other children? Legitimate ones?'

Again, I thought he wasn't going to answer, but finally he did. 'Yes. And a wife. Or I used to have. Two sons and a daughter. They died of a summer fever, all four of them, along with most of my house staff.'

My skin prickled. There hasn't been a major outbreak of plague in the city for a long, long time, sure, but localised killer diseases that destroy whole families or even whole neighbourhoods and then vanish as suddenly as they came aren't too uncommon. Some people survive, some die, some never catch the disease at all; there doesn't seem to be any logic behind it, and as far as doctors are concerned you can forget the buggers because they don't have a clue either. 'When was this?' I said.

'Over twenty years ago. They died within days of each other. I wasn't touched.'

Twenty years. The guy would only've been in his mid- to late forties. No big deal: lots of men married and had kids at that age, even non-widowers. 'You didn't think of re-marrying?'

'No. There was little point. I was my father's youngest son and at that time my brothers were still alive. I'm not a particularly religious or superstitious man, but I did feel that in taking away my whole family perhaps the gods were telling me I wasn't fated to have legitimate issue. Besides, I already had . . . let's call it my unofficial *ménage*; which, let me say, my wife knew of, if she didn't actually approve. That predated my marriage by several years. It would've been a terrible insult to Polyclea if I'd simply taken another, younger wife after being with her for over a quarter of a century and fathering her child.'

Polyclea. I hadn't even known his mistress's name. 'But you didn't marry her.'

'I offered. She refused.' He smiled. 'Polyclea always has been a woman of probity and very strong conviction. She said, as I remember, that while she knew my late wife hadn't minded her sharing my bed as a mistress she'd certainly disapprove if she shared it as wife. I took her point. Still, it was another reason to marry no one else.'

'So at this time Damon would be what, mid- to late teens?'

'Eighteen, yes. Two years older than my dead elder son.'

'How did he feel about the situation?'

Phraates set his cup down. 'Corvinus, I'm sorry, but this is getting rather too personal for my comfort. What Damon feels or felt isn't relevant. If I had married his mother after my wife's death then, yes, under Parthian law it would have made him legitimate retrospectively, but that would have been a technicality. He could never have been a serious candidate for the Great Kingship. Besides, the question of his legitimacy is academic. Even if Damon were of pure royal blood through the male and female line he would, now, still be ineligible. He knows this himself.'

'Yeah? Why's that?'

'Another rule governing the choice of a Great King is that the candidate must be whole and unblemished. Two months ago Damon got himself involved in a silly knife-fight and lost most of a finger.' Phraates's lips tightened. 'As I say, being maimed makes no real difference to his prospects, but it does put the seal on things. No; Damon is not eligible for the kingship; not even – now – in his own mind. He knows that as well as I do. Now I'd be grateful if you'd leave him, please. We have plenty of other things to discuss.'

'In a moment. Just one more question?'

I was working on the edge here, and I knew it. Phraates had stiffened. 'If you must,' he said. 'But only one.'

'He was at the dinner party. If he doesn't have . . . let's call it an official status then why was he there?'

'Not by my doing. Nor by Zariadres's, for reasons you'll appreciate. Tiridates – and Mithradates – asked for him to be invited as a personal favour. The three of them are good friends.'

'The Immortals?'

His eyebrows lifted, and the stiffness with them. He almost smiled. 'You've heard the name? Corvinus, you have been busy! Yes. I don't approve, and Damon knows that I don't, but he has a right to lead his own life as he sees fit. It's just youthful high spirits. They don't cause any real trouble – lasting trouble, I mean – and giving the boy money to spend is the least I can do for him.'

Right; I'd heard all that before, a million times. The usual father's justification, with a large helping of guilt behind it and the blinkers firmly in place. It came strange from Phraates, but still . . .

'He's hardly a boy,' I said.

I'd gone too far this time: Phraates's smile disappeared. 'Corvinus,' he said, 'I've spoken enough about Damon. You will drop the subject. Now, please.'

Yeah, well; even a Great King's human and has his weak points. And I'd got what I wanted in any case. I moved on. 'Okay,' I said. 'Let's talk about Zariadres's murder. You think it's linked to the attack on your litter?'

The hesitation was fractional, but it was there all the same.

'Probably,' he said. 'Almost certainly. But the "how" is another matter entirely.'

'Yeah. That's what I want to ask you about. You have any theories?'

'No. Zariadres was a representative, not a principal, as are the other ambassadors. His death makes no difference at all, politically. At most, it's an embarrassment to Rome, but since the embassy is by its nature unofficial even that's a minor issue.'

Uh-huh; that was more or less what Vitellius had said. Still, the political angle was too obvious a one to be dismissed out of hand. 'Fine,' I said. 'Even so, do you mind if we work it through?'

'Not at all. Carry on.'

'Okay. There are two possibilities I can see. The first and simplest, because it comes with its own motive, is that the guy was killed by an agent of Artabanus.'

Phraates leaned back in his chair. 'Indeed.'

'One problem with that is that Isidorus says there are no Parthian agents in Rome. Me, I'm pretty sceptical on that point, but then he's the expert and we'll take it as fact until we know otherwise.' I paused, but Phraates's expression stayed bland. 'The other problem's more serious. Zariadres was either killed by someone already in the house or his murderer was let in to do the job. Whichever way you play it, someone on the inside was involved. Fine. So we put all that together, the positive and the negative. The logical conclusion is that the embassy brought Artabanus's agent with them.'

Silence. Total silence. I really had Phraates's attention now.

14

Phraates had gone very still. You could've heard an ant cough.

'You think, Corvinus,' he said slowly, finally, 'that one of the embassy themselves is a traitor. A secret supporter of Artabanus.'

'It's one possibility, sure. And like I say, given the first premise, it's the simplest solution.'

'Why not one of the servants?'

'Again it's possible. Me, I'd assume all the servants had been carefully vetted at the start, but then I'm no Parthian. What do you think?'

'Oh, I agree. Absolutely.' The guy wasn't smiling now, and the hardness – the concentration – was back in spades. I could see how he'd make a king. 'In fact, I can guarantee it. The servants are all the personal property of the several ambassadors, and every one has proved his or her loyalty beyond question over many years. Loyalty to a master is important in Parthia, even more so than it is here. A good slave will literally die before he betrays his master. No, you can discount the servants. The masters are far more likely. So. Who is it to be?'

I shrugged. 'I'd be guessing. I don't know them well enough, I don't know their pasts and I don't know what makes them tick. That's where you come in.'

'All right. Let's take them one by one. Osroes.'

Yeah, that bastard made a logical starting point, and it was interesting that Phraates had plumped for him first as well. 'He hated Zariadres. Or maybe that's putting it too strongly.'

'Perhaps a little strongly, but not by much. On the other hand, hatred isn't too strong a term to describe his feelings for Artabanus. Osroes is a Magian, a zealot. When he hates, he hates. Artabanus, to him, is the arch-hypocrite. He pays lip-service to Zoroastrian beliefs but only for political reasons. He is given over completely to what Osroes would call the Lie. Osroes may dislike me as being too Romanised, but at least I'm no hypocrite; I don't pretend to be a practising Zoroastrian myself. Artabanus does, and that is what damns him in Osroes's eyes. Literally. Most important of all, Osroes lives up to his own principles. He would no more work for Artabanus, especially if it entailed prolonged deceit, than he would spit into an open fire.'

Uh-huh. Well, I'd asked. And if Phraates was that certain then there wasn't much more to be said. 'Okay. Callion.'

'Callion is Greek. His family is one of the oldest in Seleucia, and to him his city, his family and his Greek roots are the most important things in life. Artabanus is currently engaged in the destruction of Greek influence and culture within his borders. If I were made Great King, I would reverse Artabanus's policies, or at least aim for a working balance. Callion, therefore, supports me absolutely, because I'm the only person who can rescue Greek civilisation east of the Euphrates from extinction without bloodshed.'

Shit; I was getting a bad feeling about this. 'Peucestas,' I said.

'You know, I think, Peucestas's story, in outline, at least. His family is Mihran, from Rhagae. They – and he – supported my brother's attempt on the kingship twenty-five years ago. After his defeat Artabanus had Peucestas's immediate family put to death. How do you think Peucestas views Artabanus? Generously enough to act as his agent in Rome?'

The silence lengthened. 'It has to be one of them,' I said.

'Yes. If the theory holds. So which?'

Bugger. 'You like to choose, pal? Pick a name?'

He shook his head. 'No. I would not. You said you had another theory. Perhaps we should hear that.'

I took a deep breath. He wasn't going to like it, I knew that now. 'Yeah. Okay. The problem with that one is that it doesn't explain the open door; in fact, it doesn't make much sense all round. Sure, we don't know for absolute certain if the door *was* open, but after what you said about Osroes I'm willing to give the guy the benefit of the doubt, so I'll take it as fact.'

'Go on.'

'Let's say someone – call him X – doesn't want you going to Parthia as Great King.'

'I assume you don't mean Artabanus? Or one of his agents?'

'Uh . . . no.'

'Then perhaps we should waive anonymity and call him Tiridates.'

'Ah . . . right. Yeah, that was the general idea. With an option on his Iberian friend providing the brains.'

Phraates laughed. 'Use both of them if you like, Corvinus. Separately or together. I don't see anything particularly fanciful in the theory so far. Although it may run into difficulties later.'

'Oh, I'm fully aware of that, believe me.' I took a swallow of wine. 'Okay. So first Tiridates – or whoever – tries outright assassination, the attack on your litter. The problem there is once he's made his move the guy's stymied because you're alert now and you're not going to give him a second chance.' Phraates put the tips of his fingers together against his lips. I waited, but he didn't comment. 'So. He has to find another way of screwing you. If he can't kill you he might be able to do something from the other side. You said yourself, the only edge you have over him is that you've got the vote of the anti-Artabanus faction in Parthia and the Roman government. Fine. So the first step is to change the odds there. Putting Zariadres out of the way leaves Osroes as the embassy's dominant voice, and Osroes isn't too keen on you to start with. He hates Artabanus, sure, but he doesn't actually favour you as such. True?'

Phraates lowered his hands. 'Corvinus, I'm sorry to interrupt but we've been over this already. Zariadres's death has had and will have no effect on the negotiations. The embassy aren't empowered to choose between Tiridates and myself; their instructions were to ask for me specifically.'

'Yeah, I know. But only because you were Rome's candidate, the guy with the army at your back. What if you weren't? Or if they were given a genuine choice?'

'Carry on.'

'Who decides imperial policy these days?'

'The emperor, naturally.'

'All the time? One hundred per cent off his own bat? You like to bet on that, maybe?'

I could tell he saw where I was heading. His mouth hardened. 'Tiberius would never allow Prince Gaius to formulate major state policy.'

'Yeah, I realise that, but he's placed close enough to give it a few nudges. After all, the situation isn't clear-cut to begin with. You're both eligible candidates for the kingship, so that part balances. On the other hand, and I'm sorry to have to say this, Rome has to think of her returns. Just getting to Parthia'll be no pleasure trip for you, and then there's the military campaign. You're nearly seventy, and Tiridates isn't half that. Plus, Gaius knows the guy well, they've been pals for years, and whether Tiberius likes it or not Gaius is Rome's next emperor, probably not that long distant. Me, if I was Tiberius, I'd at least give the idea house-room. Especially if the Parthian embassy weighed in on Tiridates's side.'

I thought I'd gone too far. The room was so quiet you could've heard paint dry, and Phraates's expression looked like it had been carved with a chisel.

Finally, he relaxed. I could see, though, that it took an effort.

'That, Corvinus,' he said, 'was definitely one of the spades I mentioned. You don't mince words, do you?' I kept my mouth shut. He laughed quietly. 'Well, I shouldn't complain, should I? Not when I complimented you on precisely that quality. You're right again, of course, up to a point. All I can put against it is what I said earlier: whatever his personal aspirations in that direction may be, judged by both Parthian and Roman standards Tiridates would make an appallingly bad Great King. And neither the Romans nor the Parthians are stupid.' He tried a smile that didn't quite work this time. 'I'm afraid as a working hypothesis, in its present form at least, your second theory has certain practical flaws that outweigh its attractions. Do you have a third?'

Sure I did, or rather a strand that would tie in with what I'd been saying, but I was keeping that to myself at present: if he hadn't liked the last offering he'd be even less chuffed if I trotted that little gem out into the open. He might be a smart cookie, one of the smartest I'd ever met, but he was only human after all. He had his own blindnesses. And his own areas of weakness.

'Uh . . . not at the moment,' I said. 'Not as such.'

'Then we'll rejoin your wife and see how dinner is progressing.' Phraates stood up. 'I've enjoyed our talk very much.'

I didn't move. No; I couldn't leave it there, not and square it with my conscience, even if he didn't like it. 'One more thing, Prince.'

'Say it.'

'Bodyguards are fine, but me, I'd take it further. I'd watch myself at home as well.'

Pause; long pause. I thought for a moment he was going to bite my head off, and I would've deserved it, but in the end he only nodded. 'Yes, Corvinus,' he said. 'Oh, yes. I had thought of that possibility myself, thank you.' A half smile, this time with no humour to it at all. 'Incidentally, you would, I think, make an excellent Parthian royal yourself. In some respects, at any rate.'

I didn't answer. I'd made my point, and both of us knew it. Maybe Phraates wasn't totally blind to certain aspects of the situation after all.

'That was marvellous.' Perilla snuggled down among the carriage's plump silk cushions. 'We should get out more often.'

'Yeah.' I was feeling comfortably full. The old guy hadn't been kidding about the quality of the dinner: only the three of us or not, his chef couldn't've pulled out more stops for a twenty-plate banquet. You didn't get to taste wine like that every day, either.

'And the spices he gave me will be the perfect peace offering for Meton. It's almost as if he knew we'd need something or other.' The lady giggled to herself. She'd broken her usual rule and had a cup of Phraates's eighty-year-old Falernian. Now she could let her metaphorical hair down the effects were beginning to show. 'He really is a very charming man.'

I grinned. 'You're smitten, aren't you?'

'Slightly.' She poked me with the toe of her sandal. 'I'm also, as you've probably noticed, slightly drunk, and that doesn't happen very often. But then, he does set out to charm. I'm not surprised he's going to be Great King. How was your little chat?'

'Okay.' I glanced out of the carriage window. We hadn't got Phraates's full complement of bodyguard, just the usual four torchbearers, but then we didn't need them. We weren't Parthian royals. 'I think his son Damon might be out to kill him. Or at least involved somewhere along the line.'

Perilla's eyes widened and she sat up. 'Oh, no!' she said. 'Oh, Marcus!'

'It's only a theory, lady, but it makes sense. Where his father's concerned he's got a chip on his shoulder the size of a log. He's a prince but not a prince, and it's all Phraates's doing. The old guy didn't say so in as many words, but I'd guess that when he swans off to be Great King of Parthia his only son'll be left kicking his heels in Rome, and that'll've gone down like a lead balloon. On the other hand, Damon's in thick with Tiridates and Mithradates, and one gets you ten those bastards have something on the boil. As an insider he'd be the perfect accomplice.'

'But he's the man's son!'

'That's no bar. In fact for a Parthian royal – which is what I'd bet Damon sees himself as – it's practically an invitation. The guy can't expect to have a crack at the kingship himself, sure, but if he throws in with Tiridates and the bugger makes Great King then he's sitting pretty for a major provincial governor's job, at least. And in Parthia that practically amounts to a kingship anyway. Not bad in exchange for helping to kill a father you hate.'

'Marcus, you have no proof.'

I shrugged. 'No. But like I say, it fits. Damon would've known where his father was going the night of the attack, maybe even the route the litter-bearers would take on the way home. And it explains his invite to the embassy dinner. That was pure ego-feeding. Tiridates had got the guy his rights for once. If it'd been left to Phraates he'd still be waiting in the wings when hell froze over.'

'All right,' Perilla said. 'How do you think it works?'

'It's a two-pronged plot. Separately, each prong could do the job, just, in theory at least. Together they support each other and make the thing certain. On the one side, they kill off Phraates. That's where Damon comes in, and it clears the field. On the other, they work on the mood of the embassy – that's why Zariadres had to die – and engineer a Roman policy change so we support Tiridates. That's—'

'Marcus.'

'Yeah?'

'I may be slightly drunk but there's nothing wrong with my cognitive processes.'

'Uh . . . right. Right.'

'Listen to yourself, dear. Policy is policy. It's decided at imperial level.'

'Yeah.' I shifted uncomfortably. 'Sure it is. Only for this to work – have a chance of working – there has to be a fourth member of the team.'

'And who might that be?'

'Uh . . . Prince Gaius.' Her mouth opened. I went on quickly. 'Look, lady, it's just an idea, okay? But Gaius is definitely a crony of the three of them and—'

'Marcus, I've said this before! That incident with Mithradates was bad enough. If there is any – *any* – possibility of Gaius being mixed up personally in this then orders from Tiberius or not I think you should drop the case forthwith. I am serious.'

Bugger. Still, it was my own fault. I should've kept my theories to myself. 'Yeah, well . . . '

'I'm not prepared to discuss the matter. We'll talk about it further in the morning.'

She threw herself back against the cushions tight-lipped with fury and closed her eyes. Hell. Women. Nice going, Corvinus; straight in again with both feet, and only myself to blame this time. I sighed.

My brain hurt; enough for one day. I shut my eyes and dozed.

15

Perilla was still fast asleep when I came down to breakfast the next morning, and when she finally surfaced I was already almost finished. Seeing her coming with a definite preoccupied expression on her·face, I steeled myself for round two as promised, but as she passed my couch she leaned down and kissed me.

'You haven't had a shave this morning,' she murmured.

We breathe again. Evidently for reasons of her own the lady had decided on a truce, at least temporarily. I mopped up the last of my honey with a crust. 'I, uh, thought I'd go down to Market Square for a change,' I said. 'Have one there.'

Bathyllus was hovering with a tray of rolls. Perilla lowered herself on to the facing couch like she was afraid her head would fall off if she moved it too much. Yeah, right; *that* explained things! I offered up a silent prayer of thanks to whatever god protected peabrain husbands who couldn't keep their mouths shut in carriages.

'I don't think I'll bother with breakfast this morning, Bathyllus,' she said. 'Perhaps just a camomile tisane. Or preferably something a little more fatal.'

'Yes, madam. I will consult with the chef.'

I grinned. 'You should stay off the booze, lady. You aren't used to it.'

That got me a level, bleary-eyed stare and a set to the lips you could've drawn lines with. 'I'm feeling quite recriminatory enough for both of us at the moment, thank you,

Marcus,' she said tartly. 'And the next time one of your cronies asks me to try his sixty-year-old Falernian just say "Phraates" to me. Is that clear?'

'Yeah. Yeah, sure. And it was eighty-year-old.'

'Fine. Good. That makes me a lot happier. Now I'm sorry, dear, but I don't feel capable of breakfast conversation at present, especially if it takes the form of smart repartee. If you're going out then go and leave me to die in peace.'

'Okay,' I said, getting up and dabbing my lips with the napkin. 'I'll see you later.'

'Marcus.'

'Yeah?'

'You will be careful, won't you? You know what I mean.'

'Yeah. I know what you mean. I'll be careful. Promise.' I bent down and kissed her. Sure I would. If Gaius was involved in this business I'd go as careful as a flea in party slippers.

It was a beautiful day: the weather had cleared completely, the sky above the city was a pure cloudless blue and there was a stiffish breeze from the east. Good walking weather, and after the previous night I needed the cobwebs blowing away. I turned up Head of Africa in the direction of Suburan Street.

The shave'd been a good idea. A Market Square barber's stool is almost as good as a wineshop for thinking, so long as you choose your barber carefully and avoid the chat merchants, and thinking was something I needed to do. There'd been no word yet from Lippillus over at Public Pond re the knife gang, which was a pity since it was still the most promising avenue. On the other hand, I'd had enough of theorising to be going on with. What we needed here were a few more hard facts. It was time, perhaps, to chase up a loose end or two.

Such as the puzzle of the dinner party juggling troupe.

Maybe it meant nothing, but the woman's fluffed catch had nagged at me because it'd been the only one she'd made, it'd come right at the start of the act, and as far as I could tell there was no reason for it. Professionals – and she'd been a top-notch professional, pick of the bunch – didn't slip up like that. Oh, sure; the explanation was obvious: that she'd seen someone – or something – she hadn't been expecting to see, and it'd thrown her. But who or what was it?

I replayed the scene in my head. The woman had run through the door on the right to the other side of the stage, then turned and reached for that first baton, the one she'd missed . . .

Yeah; that was the key moment. When she fluffed the catch she'd been facing towards the audience on the far right-hand side of the room – her left – seeing them for the first time. So who had we got? Who had she seen? Top table nearest the door was Osroes and Peucestas; next pair Mithradates and Tiridates . . .

Right. Those two were the obvious bets, especially my pal the Iberian. If I wasn't mistaken and Mithradates had set the whole thing up then for it to work he'd have to know in advance that the girl would be sticky about co-operating and that her brother – or whoever the guy with the muscles had been – would back her up. He couldn't assume that, quite the reverse: pleasing the customer after the show's over is how most girls in the entertainment business make enough to pay the rent, and their relatives or boyfriends just have to grin and bear it. So if Mithradates *did* know, then it meant he'd tried it on before and could be certain of the outcome; and that suggested familiarity on both sides. Not an amicable familiarity, either. My bet would be that the older woman – the girl's mother – hadn't known he'd be there until she turned and saw him sitting ten feet away, and it put her off her stride.

It could still be nothing, but like I say it was a loose end that might lead somewhere and worth checking out. So how did I go about it?

I was down Suburan Incline and on the edges of the Subura itself when I remembered Aegle, the girl who'd helped me out back when the young Vestal had got herself murdered. She was a flute-player not a tumbler, sure, but the entertainment business in Rome's a small world and if she didn't know the troupe herself she'd probably be able to put me in touch with someone who did. The shave could wait: Aegle's flat was in one of the older tenements near the Shrine of Picus, along Suburan Street in the other direction from Market Square. She could've moved, sure, but it wasn't far out of my way and it might save a lot of hassle. I was pretty hopeful about finding her in, too: this being the Augustalia she'd be playing evening gigs herself, which meant she'd be sleeping late. I might get a stool thrown at my head for disturbing her, mind, because from what I remembered of the girl she was no respecter of persons.

Apropos of which. Most of the good bookshops are in the Argiletum, but I'd seen one tucked down an alleyway near the Shrine where I could buy a peace offering. Aegle wasn't your typical good-time girl, and books were a passion, drama especially. I rooted through the guy's limited stock and came up with a copy of Menander's *Curmudgeon*. Second-hand, but it was all there as far as I could tell, the rollers and the pages themselves were all in good condition and the copyist wasn't one of the spider-in-the-inkwell brigade. Perfect.

I found the tenement – not one of the most salubrious, even for Suburan Street – climbed the stairs to the fourth floor avoiding the occasional pool of bodily fluids and knocked. No answer. Bugger. I knocked again, louder this time.

Feet padded to the other side of the door and a voice said, 'Yeah? Who is it?'

Aegle, and sarky as hell. Maybe this hadn't been such a smart idea after all. Well, at least she was in. 'Uh . . . Marcus Corvinus,' I said.

The bar on the inside was lifted and the door opened. I'd been right about her sleeping late. Her strawberry-birthmarked face was puffy and her tunic was sleep-creased. Still, she was smiling, which was a good sign.

'Corvinus! Don't you purple-stripers keep decent hours? What the hell brings you here?'

'Ah . . . I'm sorry, lady,' I said. 'Can I come in?'

'Sure. Feel free.' She stepped aside. 'Just give me a minute to wake up. And close your eyes to the mess, okay? Me and the room. I didn't know I'd be entertaining.'

I followed her through the tiny lobby into the flat itself. 'Flat' was dignifying it, which is par for the course at top-floor tenement level: rents go down in these places the further up you are, and so do facilities and floor space. Here, right under the tiles, there was just the one room with a shuttered window and gaps between the ceiling joists stuffed with straw to keep the worst of the wind and rain out.

Aegle padded barefoot over to the window and opened the shutters. Light streamed in, showing a mattress on the floor, a clothes chest, a couple of shelves with two or three book-rolls plus a few knick-knacks, a flute-case leaning against the wall and nothing else except for the flowering plants on the windowsill.

'Here,' I said, giving her the Menander. 'Add this to your collection.'

She glanced at the title tag. 'Hey! Great!'

'Maybe under the circumstances breakfast would've been better.'

'Uh-uh. They fed us at the gig last night, and I have to watch my figure.'

It was a good figure to watch. The huge birthmark

covering half her face might've spoiled things in that part of the looks department, but what else there was of her made up for it. That and her personality.

I stepped over the mattress and sat down on the clothes chest. 'So. How're things going?' I said.

'Workwise? Okay. I'm booked up all through the festival, which is pretty unusual, I can tell you.' She laid Menander carefully beside the other rolls on the shelf. 'You weren't wanting a slot yourself, were you? Because if so—'

'Uh . . . no. No, it isn't that.'

'Fine.' She grinned and settled down cross-legged on the mattress facing me. 'I couldn't've fitted you in anyway. Although I could recommend two or three other girls who'd be grateful for the work. So. If he isn't fixing up a gig then what's a purple-striper doing slumming it in the Subura?'

'Looking for information.'

'That's news?' The grin widened. 'On what, for example?'

'I'm trying to trace a family of jugglers.'

'You have their names?'

I shook my head. 'They were booked for' – I hesitated – 'for a foreigners' dinner party a few nights ago. On the Palatine.'

Aegle leaned back and whistled through her teeth. 'Oh, Corvinus, you do move in high circles, don't you? Are we talking imperial here?'

'Uh-uh,' I said. 'And I'm sorry, lady, but I can't tell you any more, not even the address, okay?'

'Is that so, now?' She gave me a long, considering look, then shrugged. 'Well, you've got your reasons, no doubt, but I can't work on nothing. Were you there yourself?'

'Yeah. Yeah, I was there.'

'So you remember their act.'

'Yeah. There were four of them, looked like a family. The youngsters – a girl and a boy built like the Rhodes colossus – had this thing where he held her by the legs and spun her.'

Aegle clicked her tongue. 'Jarhades and Erato. The older couple, that is. They've been around for years, and that used to be their speciality. They must've passed it on to their kids.'

'Jarhades? What sort of name's that?'

'He's Syrian. Or Armenian, maybe, I'm not sure. Erato as well, for all the Greek name.'

'That right, now?' Still, it'd make sense; certainly from what I could remember about the troupe they'd all had that eastern look to them. 'You know where I can find them?'

'Sorry, there I can't help. You could try the jugglers' and tumblers' guildhouse – that's in the Remuria near Four Ways Fountain – but I'll tell you now they're not keen on giving out addresses. The guildhouse takes a cut from every gig, and some punters try to reach a private arrangement.'

'Hell.' The Remuria was way the other side of Rome. And from what Aegle was saying a trip down there might prove to be a wild-goose chase anyway. 'That the best you can do?'

'I could ask around, sure. That'd find them for certain, but it'd take time. You in a hurry?'

'Marginally.'

'Wait a minute, then. Let me think.' Her brow creased. 'There's a wineshop that the easterners hang out in near Cattlemarket Square. I can't say for certain, but you might find Jarhades there, or at least someone who knows him. That do you?'

'Sure.' Cattlemarket Square'd be a lot closer, and I could go down there after my postponed shave. 'You know the name?'

'Mano's.'

'Got you. I'll find it.' I stood up. 'Thanks, lady, you've been a great help. I'll let you get back to bed now.'

'Oh, I would've had to've been up and around soon anyway. You're welcome, any time. Come back if it doesn't work out.' She got to her feet. 'By the way. When you get to Mano's try not to breathe too much.'

'What?'

'Never mind. Just remember, okay? And thanks for the Menander.'

I left.

Market Square was heaving, especially the bit under the porticoes of the Julian Hall where the barbers and tooth-pullers plied their trade, and I had to wait twiddling my thumbs for almost half an hour before I got to the head of the queue and a place in one of the chairs. Luckily, though, the guy I got was one of my regulars and after the briefest of exchanges he shut up and left me as usual to my thoughts. Not that these were all that earth-shaking, mind. He'd done the important scraping and was down to trimming my sideburns preparatory to sprinkling on the talc when I had an idea.

'Uh . . . you're Syrian, aren't you, pal?' I said after the razor was well clear of my cheekbone. Most of the Market Square barbers are Syrians or Asiatics. There ain't no other profession that combines the eastern loves of personal titillation, chatting and the world of the cars better than barbering.

'That's right. Apamea.'

'You happen to know somewhere called Mano's? Down Cattlemarket Square way?'

'Oh, yeah. Sure. I know Mano's.'

'Where is it exactly?'

He'd been shaking talc from a perforated cylinder on to his hand. Now he paused. 'You got a reason for asking, sir?'

'Yeah. I was hoping to meet someone there.'

The guy almost dropped the talc-shaker. 'At *Mano's*?'

I was beginning to have a funny feeling about this. 'Uh . . . it's just a wineshop, right? Not a male brothel or some sort of pick-up joint?'

'Nah! Nothing like that.' He was grinning as he applied the talc. 'It's just very . . . eastern, is Mano's. You won't see no Romans there, certainly no purple-stripers.'

'Suits me, friend. No purple-stripers is a recommendation. So where is it exactly?'

'On the waterfront past Hercules's temple, just before the granaries. There's a narrow alley between two warehouses. Blink and you'd miss it.'

'Fine. Thanks, pal.' I paid, gave up my seat to the next punter and headed back towards the Temple of the Twin Gods and the alleyway through to Tuscan Street.

I hadn't got five yards when someone put a hand on my shoulder.

'Valerius Corvinus!'

I turned, feeling the ice form in my gut. Shit: Mithradates, not togged out in his Asiatic gear this time but wearing a sharp-looking plain mantle over a blue tunic embroidered in gold at the neck. The bastard was smiling. Not that that made him look any pleasanter. You get smiles like that floating down the Nile an inch clear of the water, with a pair of eyes sitting just behind them.

At least there were no hit-men with him. And Twin Gods' Alley was a major thoroughfare.

'Yeah. That's me,' I said, carefully taking his hand off my shoulder. He had more rings than fingers.

'You have time for a cup of wine?' he said. 'My treat. Just to show there's no hard feelings.'

Nice as pie. You'd never think that the bugger had stood by and watched me being beaten up, would you? I wondered for a moment if Phraates had already had his little talk with the guy, but that was unlikely.

'You know,' I said slowly, 'I don't think I do. Besides, I'm careful who I drink with.'

If I'd expected him to flush or get angry I was disappointed.

The smile didn't waver. 'Pity. Oh, by the way: did you and your wife – Perilla, isn't it, or am I wrong? – enjoy your meal last night with Phraates?'

The ice in my gut sent another shaft of cold up my spine. 'Yeah,' I said. I wasn't going to give him the satisfaction of asking how he knew; the fact that he did was worrying enough. I didn't like the mention of Perilla, either; that hadn't been accidental. 'Yeah, it was okay.'

'And your talk? Interesting, was it?' This time I didn't answer. Carefully, deliberately, he put his hand back on my shoulder and pulled me closer. He wasn't smiling now, and his breath smelled of some sort of expensive spice; cinnamon, maybe. 'Listen, Corvinus, because I'm not messing around here with silly warnings. You back off, boy. You back right off, before you get in too deep to haul yourself out, or I'll see you broken. Not just kicked around a little, but broken. That's a promise. You understand? And if you're *really* persistent I might just extend the same courtesy to that wife of yours, if—'

He hadn't been expecting it. Nor had I, for that matter, nor the three or four respectable punters who were passing at the time and kept on passing at about twice their original speed. My hands moved of themselves, grabbing the bugger's fancy tunic, ramming him backwards so hard against the alley wall that he almost made a dent and holding him there.

'Now you just listen to me, *pal*,' I said softly. 'You so much as think in that direction and tame gorillas or not, Gaius or not, I swear I'll cut out your fucking liver and feed it to you in slices. Now do you understand *that*, or shall I draw you a fucking picture in crayon?'

Our eyes locked. He smiled, and the shoulder above where my right fist gripped the material lifted.

'Oh, Corvinus,' he said. 'You shouldn't have done that. You really should not have done it.'

I let him drop. He winced as his back scraped against the wall, a stretch of rough brickwork that Augustus must've missed when he was swapping the stuff for marble. 'That's my look out, friend,' I said. 'Just don't forget, right?'

'I won't forget. You can be very sure of that.'

I stepped aside. He flicked a smear of brick dust from the front of the tunic then reached up and, carefully, gave my bruised cheek a friendly pat. Then he smiled again, turned away without another word and walked off back towards Market Square, leaving me staring after him.

Fuck.

Well, there wasn't much I could do about that little problem for the moment; what had happened had happened, and I didn't regret it because I'd meant every word. Still, I wasn't going to tell Perilla; no *way* was I going to tell Perilla, ever.

I carried on down the alley between the Julian Hall and the temple, pushed through the jostling crowds on to Tuscan Street and made my way to Cattlemarket Square.

16

Cattlemarket Square was heaving, too: everywhere was, this second day of the festival. Still, it was a more cheerful kind of bustle. The hucksters were out with their trays, and the whole place smelled of grilling meat, hot poppy-seed bread rings and roasted nuts. At the vegetable market side of the square a troupe of actors had set up a makeshift stage and were putting on one of the old Atellan farces. I hung around watching for ten minutes or so – long enough for the guy with the bag to get a handful of coppers out of me – but I've never found Atellan humour particularly funny. Unlike, strangely enough, Perilla: culture vulture the lady may be, but I've seen her double up at jokes that had beards when Romulus had his first shave.

I finally managed to push my way through the mob and into the comparative quiet of the alleyway that led past the side of Hercules's temple and down to the river. Okay; so where was this Mano's, then?

If it hadn't been for my friendly Syrian barber I'd've missed it altogether. 'Alley' was pushing things: all there was to see was a gap barely more than a body's-width between two huge warehouses. I made my way down it.

The gap only went in for a few yards before it ended up in a wooden staircase so steep it was practically a ladder. Yeah, right, that explained things: the place must be part of one of the warehouses, probably a floored-off section up among the roof-beams. Interesting. And not your typical wineshop, by any means.

I climbed to the top of the stair. Sure enough, there was a door leading into the right-hand warehouse just below the tiled roof, and I could hear a murmur of voices.

I pushed the door open. The first thing I noticed was the smell that wafted out, a sort of sweet, herby smell like someone was burning leaves from an aromatic plant. I half expected to be stopped, but I wasn't. In fact, most of the punters paid me no attention.

I'd been right about the set-up. Whether or not it accounted for the whole top of the warehouse, the room was pretty big, with a ceiling so low I had to duck under some of the beams. It was packed, too, even at this time of the day; not that that would've mattered, because although there were shuttered windows opening out on the city side half of them were closed and the darker areas were lit with tapers. They weren't what was causing the smell, mind: I noticed that besides the usual jugs and wine cups most of the punters had tiny metal dishes in front of them hardly bigger than walnut-shell halves, that were smoking gently. Every so often a guy would pick up his dish, hold it to his nose and inhale.

Uh-huh. I knew where I was now, although I'd never been in one of these places before; not that there could be many around, in Rome at least. *Try not to breathe too much*, Aegle had said. Oh, ha-ha. I wasn't surprised that my Syrian barber had said I wouldn't find any Romans here, either. We've got a lot of vices, sure, but *qef* isn't one of them. We leave it to the degenerate easterners, along with depilatories and male cosmetics.

A man was coming towards me carrying a tray of the little bowls and a censer of glowing charcoal.

'Uh . . . excuse me, pal,' I said.

He stopped. 'Yeah?'

'You wouldn't happen to know if there's anyone here by the name of Jarhades, would you?'

'The juggler?' He nodded with his chin towards one of the tables at the back. 'That's him over there, the man in the dark green tunic.' Hey! Right! 'What can I get you, sir?'

'Uh . . . you have any wine?'

His mouth split in a gap-toothed grin. 'Sure. I wouldn't recommend it myself, mind.'

It's always good to find someone who's honest about his wine, especially when it's rotgut. 'It'll do,' I said. 'Oh, and if I'm going to barge in on the guy you'd better bring another of what he's having as well.'

'*Qef*. You've got it.'

I paid upfront – the *qef* was a lot cheaper than the wine, although that wasn't much – and made my way over.

'Uh . . . excuse me, friend,' I said. 'You're Jarhades?'

At least I'd got the right guy, because he was definitely the juggler from the dinner party. He'd seen me coming, too, and his eyes were on the purple stripe on my tunic – I wasn't wearing a mantle – that showed under the cloak.

'That's me,' he said cautiously.

'You mind if I sit here?'

'Suit yourself.'

I pulled up a stool. 'The name's Corvinus. Marcus Corvinus. And we've met before, in a way.'

'Yeah? And when'd that be, now?'

'Four days ago. I saw your act at a dinner party on the Palatine.'

He was scowling. 'Those fucking Parthians?'

'Yeah. Those, uh . . . them. I was really impressed.'

He'd been studying my face. Suddenly his expression cleared and he beamed. 'You're the purple-striper who shoved his oar in over Calliste, right?'

'Ah . . . right.'

'That's different.' He turned round and yelled, 'Mano!'

My waiter – he must be the actual proprietor – was already on his way with the order.

'Yeah?' he said.

'Bring my friend here some proper wine. Not that piss, the Syrian stuff you keep below the counter. Put it on my bill.' He turned back to me. 'Unless you'd like some *qef*.'

'Uh-uh,' I said. 'Wine'd be great.' I was trying to follow Aegle's advice, impossible though it was. Just breathing normally was beginning to make me slightly dizzy. Jarhades seemed fine, but I supposed you got used to it.

'So . . . what did you say your name was?'

'Corvinus. Marcus Corvinus.'

'Well, Marcus Corvinus, you put it there.' He held out a hand, and we shook. 'I owe you one. You want a free show, you've got it, any time, any place, even if I have to make a cancellation to fit you in. Erato'll say the same.' He chuckled. 'Sweet holy Baal! I never thought I'd see that bastard's nose rubbed in the dirt, but you did it proper!'

'You know him? I mean . . .'

'Mithradates? Sure, we've played for him and his pals a few times. The last time, though, I swore never again. Erato too. Calliste's virgin, and she's only thirteen. Batis held him back while we ran for it. We never saw his money, but the hell with that; we do all right without.'

'Batis is the big young guy?'

'That's him. My son. Adopted son, rather. He's Erato's, by her old master.' His voice was matter-of-fact. Yeah, well; it wasn't an unusual scenario.

'Uh . . . she's a freedwoman?'

'In a way. Her mistress wanted to sell her. She did a runner and we met in Antioch. You know Antioch?'

I tried to keep my expression neutral: admitting that your

wife's a runaway slave, especially to a stranger, isn't too hot an idea. The authorities get very *intense* over runaway slaves, and there ain't no moratorium, either. 'Ah . . . sure,' I said. 'I've been to it. Nice place.'

'Best city in the world. We'd still be there, but Erato wanted to come to Rome. Calliste was born here.' Mano came back with the wine and the *qef* bowl. He set the coins I'd given him down on the table. Jarhades gestured to them. 'Put these back in your pouch, Corvinus, and try the wine.'

I sipped. Good, sure, far above bulk-produced Campanian and Gallic, but not up to top Latian standard. Still, I appreciated the guy's patriotism. 'So. Tell me more about Mithradates.'

Jarhades picked up his *qef* bowl and inhaled deeply before setting it down. 'That's why you're here? To ask me about Mithradates?'

'Yeah.' I waited for the next, logical question, but it didn't come. 'You mind?'

'No. You'll have your reasons, no doubt, but the hell with that. You're no friend of his, and nor am I. I said: he's a bastard. If I'd known he was the one who'd hired us for the evening I'd've spat in the agent's face.'

I put down my wine cup. '*Mithradates* hired you?'

'Sure. For double the fee, paid up front. Plus some more, probably, that our slimy bugger of an agent didn't mention. Not that we knew at the time. All we knew about was the venue. When Erato saw him sitting there she nearly blew the act.'

'Yeah,' I said. 'Yeah, I noticed that.'

'I don't blame her. She hates Mithradates like poison. Still, we had to carry on whether he was there or not. You have to, don't you?' He pushed over the *qef* bowl. 'You want to try this, by the way?'

'No. No, I'll pass,' I said. I took a swallow of the wine. 'You ever been to Parthia?'

'Certainly. Been all over, when I was on my own. Not after Erato, though: her being a runaway slave Parthia was too dangerous for us.' Things clicked. So she'd been a *Parthian* slave! That explained why Jarhades had been so upfront about her. If she'd run from a master on the other side of the Roman border it would've made a difference, but escaped Parthian slaves are no concern of Rome's. 'Like I say, when we teamed up we came straight here. She was fourteen at the time, just past Calliste's age.'

I took a swallow of wine. 'So, where's she from?'

'Hecatompylus. That's a Greek town just south of the Caspian. Her family sold her when she was two.' Yeah; that wasn't unusual, even in the empire, especially with girls. When food runs short in the poorest families selling off the youngest mouth makes sense. It's not always a bad thing for the kid, either: leave her where she is and she'd probably starve to death anyway, and at least a slave, being property, is well cared for. 'The guy who bought her was a merchant based in Ecbatana. Then like I say when she was thirteen her master got her pregnant and his wife didn't want her in the house. She didn't wait to be sold. She ran instead. The gods know how she got across the border and all the way to Antioch with the kid, but she managed it. I found her on the dockside trying to get a passage to Rome. That was twenty-odd years back. We've been together ever since.'

'Where did she learn juggling?'

'I taught her. But she was a natural, all the same, much better than me almost from the start. And Calliste's better than both of us.'

'How about . . . what did you say your son was called?'

'Batis. No, Batis is too slow and heavy for a juggler or a tumbler. He makes a good anchor-man, though, he's got a great sense of timing and he works well with Calliste. She trusts him, and that's important in our business.' He indicated my wine cup. 'You want another?'

'Yeah, sure.' I turned to catch Mano's eye. 'Let me get this one.'

'No. I was going to say, if you're finished I'm sure Erato'd like to thank you as well. We're just round the corner. Unless you're busy, of course.'

You've had it yourself, no doubt. I didn't particularly want to be cast as the wineshop crony the man of the house had brought back with him, and this particular loose end looked like being played out. On the other hand, to refuse – or to lie – wouldn't be polite, especially since the guy seemed so keen for me to come, and he obviously liked to talk.

Besides, the atmosphere in the place was seriously beginning to get to me.

'No,' I said. 'No, I'm not busy. That'd be great.'

'Fine.' He stood up.

'Just round the corner' was pushing things, but it wasn't all that far, one of the tenement blocks in the Velabrum, more up-market than Aegle's but still a long way from the top bracket. We climbed the stair to the second floor and Jarhades pushed the door open.

'Hey, Erato!' he called. Inside, I could hear the murmur of voices. Jarhades frowned; evidently this didn't happen very often. 'She's got company.'

'Maybe another day, then.'

'No. She'd be sorry to miss you.' He hung his cloak on one of the pegs in the small entrance hall. 'Come on through.'

There were four people in the room, sitting around a central table. Three of them I'd been expecting: the woman, her daughter and the big guy I now knew was Batis.

The fourth I hadn't expected at all. The fourth was Peucestas.

17

We stared at each other. The Parthian cleared his throat. 'So, Corvinus.'

I glanced at Jarhades. He was standing like he'd been cemented up from the inside, and he didn't look too friendly, either. Obviously I wasn't the only one to be surprised.

'What's going on here?' he said.

Erato got up quickly, crossed over to him and gripped his arm. No spangle and glitter now; she was wearing a respectable matron's tunic, her hair was in a tight bun and without the make-up she'd had on at the dinner party she looked her age.

'It's all right,' she said.

'Is it fuck.' Jarhades was still glaring at Peucestas. 'Who's he, and what's he doing here?'

'I came to see my son,' Peucestas said quietly.

Everything went very still. Then Jarhades moved.

'Dad, *no!*' Batis might not be quick enough on his feet for an acrobat, but he was across the room in a second, between Jarhades and the Parthian, and the solid bulk of his shoulder slammed against Jarhades's chest so hard I could hear the ribs grind. Jarhades gasped; it must've felt like hitting a stone wall, and the effect was just the same.

Oh, shit, I was definitely one too many here. Obviously a bad time to come calling. I remembered what Jarhades had said in the *qef* shop, about Erato's master getting her pregnant and her doing a runner to avoid being sold. And now you saw the two of them together – Batis and Peucestas – and knew who they were the resemblance was clear enough. Add twenty-five years to one, or take it off the other, and physically they'd be dead ringers. Apart from in one major respect, of course . . .

For a moment, the tableau held, like something out of the play they'd been putting on in the square. Jarhades stood clutching his ribs, half leaning on the young man's shoulder. Erato was white as a sheet, one hand over her mouth, and the daughter's eyes were out like doorstops.

Peucestas might not've moved, but I had the impression from the look in his eyes that even if Batis hadn't been there he could've handled the situation, no sweat.

'Sit down,' he said to Jarhades. 'It isn't the way you think.'

'Do what he says, love,' Erato said in the ghost of a voice. 'Please.'

Batis moved aside. Jarhades stood swaying for a moment, his fists balled. Then he pulled up a stool and sat on it, glaring.

'Batis is my son, yes,' Peucestas said, 'but Erato isn't his mother.'

Whatever the guy had been expecting, it obviously wasn't that. He stared at Erato, his head moving from side to side like a stunned bull's.

'I couldn't tell you,' Erato whispered. 'First it was too dangerous, then it was too late. And by that time the truth didn't matter.' She glanced sideways at Peucestas.

'She was my slave,' he said. He was still speaking very quietly, and his eyes hadn't left Jarhades's face. 'That part's true enough. But she was only the boy's nurse. And she ran because I told her to, taking the child with her. Up until the dinner I didn't know that either of them were still alive.'

'They would have killed him.' Erato reached over to touch Jarhades, but her hand stopped short. 'The way they killed the others.'

'Batis's mother was my chief wife,' Peucestas said, in a matter-of-fact voice. 'Artabanus ordered her and my children impaled.'

Oh, shit.

Jarhades grunted. Some of the stiffness went out of him. 'So,' he said to Erato, 'there was no merchant in Ecbatana after all?'

'No.' Erato had got some of her colour back, and like Peucestas's her tone was matter-of-fact. 'The family had a house there, so I knew it well enough, but we lived most of the time in Rhagae. I had to lie to you about that, too. I'm sorry.'

'The king's men came before dawn one morning, when we weren't expecting them,' Peucestas said; his eyes still hadn't wavered. 'I'd no time to do anything but give Erato her orders and what little money I had by me and send her out the back way. I'd have saved the others if I could, but that wasn't possible. A young girl with a baby she could pass off as her own had at least a chance, but I never thought I'd see either of them again in any case. I should have died with the others. Instead Artabanus was merciful. I was castrated, then carried into the courtyard to watch my wife and children die. As a lesson in obedience.' His gaze shifted to me. 'If you didn't know my reasons before for supporting Phraates, Corvinus, you know them now. When that animal is captured my price is his skin, taken from him living.'

There was a long silence. Finally, Jarhades turned to Peucestas. 'So,' he said tonelessly. 'Thank you for explaining, at least.' Peucestas didn't answer. 'You're taking the boy with you? Back to Parthia?'

I glanced at Batis. Neither he nor the girl had moved. He was frowning; she was still staring wide-eyed, like a kid at a puppet show.

'Oh, no.' Peucestas shook his head. 'No. That would be

stupid. If Phraates becomes king then yes, of course, in time: Batis is my heir, the only one I have or can ever have now. For the present he's safer where he is.' He looked at me again. 'Corvinus, I'd be grateful if you didn't pass the information on to your Palatine friends, as I have kept it secret from my colleagues. My family – what there is left of it – is still important in Parthia. If Rome knew that they held the heir then . . . ' He smiled briefly. 'Well, you know how it is yourself. However this turns out, I've no desire to see him used as a bargaining token. You'll do that for me? Please?'

'Yeah,' I said. 'Yeah, sure. No problem.' I swallowed. Jupiter!

'Good. Thank you. Money is another matter. Of course my son will need—'

'We don't want your money,' Jarhades said.

Peucestas stood up. 'I won't quarrel,' he said gently. 'Especially today. I owe you and Erato too much for that. The money will be there whether you use it or not. I'll make the necessary arrangements.' He held out his hand. After a pause, Jarhades took it. 'Now. We have a meeting scheduled for this afternoon, and I have to be getting back before I'm missed. Also' – he smiled again – 'no doubt you'll have a lot to talk about after I've gone. We'll meet again before I leave.' He made a move towards Batis, then seemed to change his mind. Instead, he simply gave him a brief nod, walked past me towards the door, opened it and left without another word.

There was an awkward silence.

Gods alive!

'Uh . . . maybe I should be going as well,' I said.

'No.' Jarhades was still frowning. 'Erato; wine for our guest.' She got up without a word and disappeared into the next room.

Batis sat down on the bench. 'Dad, I swear to you,' he said softly. 'I didn't know.'

Jarhades shook his head. 'Forget it, lad, it's not your fault. It's no one's fault.'

'Does that mean Batis is a prince?' Calliste said.

I turned to look at her properly for the first time. The name fitted: she was a little stunner, even without the make-up and the skimpy costume. But thirteen or not, the question and the tone had been a four-year-old's. The hairs rose on the back of my neck.

Jarhades's frown had lifted. He reached over and stroked her hair. 'More or less,' he said.

'Oh.' That was all. The girl turned her big, vacant eyes on me. 'You were at the dinner party, weren't you?'

'Yeah, that's right,' I said. 'Corvinus. Marcus Corvinus. You're a very talented girl, Calliste.'

'Yes, I know.'

It should've sounded arrogant, or precious, but it didn't: it came out simply, in the same childish voice that was way too young for the body. I glanced at Jarhades.

'Leave us to talk,' he said gently. She got up and left the room. With a muttered excuse Batis followed her. Jarhades waited until they were gone and then said to me, 'You can see now why I didn't want that bastard touching her.'

'Yeah,' I said. 'Yeah, I can.'

'It's nothing serious.' He was looking down at his hands. 'She's just a bit slow. But as a juggler and tumbler she's first-rate.'

I didn't answer. *Just a bit slow*. Yeah, sure. Well, they seemed happy enough. And he was right: she was good at what she did. That was all that mattered.

'Batis worships her, and it's mutual.' He looked up. 'Still, that's a problem for the future, isn't it?' Erato came in with a tray: two cups of wine and a plate of cheese and olives. 'Here's the wine. It's Syrian, as good as Mano's or better.'

Erato was avoiding his eye. She set the tray on the table then sat down on the bench opposite.

'I'm sorry,' she said. 'I'd've told you if I could.'

I got up quickly. 'Look, you can do without me, right? You don't need—'

'Sit down. It's all right.' Jarhades half smiled and ducked his head. 'Though I won't say it hasn't been a shock.' He turned to Erato. 'You've nothing to be ashamed of, girl, quite the reverse. Now. We have a guest. I told him you'd want to thank him for what he did at the dinner. Was I wrong?'

'No.' Erato wiped her nose on her tunic sleeve, her expression the stiffly formal one you get sometimes with peasant women when they're doing what they see as their duty. 'You're very welcome here, Marcus Corvinus. And I'm grateful, very grateful. We all are.'

I took a swallow of the wine. It was good stuff, and after that little scene with Peucestas I needed it. 'All the guy really wanted was to make trouble,' I said.

Jarhades nodded; he didn't seem all that surprised. 'Yes. That I'd believe. That's him all over. You get people like Mithradates; they meddle for the sake of meddling, then sit back and watch the fun.'

'And at least this time no one got hurt,' Erato said.

' "This time"?' I said.

Jarhades scowled and pushed the plate of cheese and olives over towards me. 'What these flash young society bastards do to each other at their parties, girl, is up to them,' he said. 'They deserve all they get, and you won't catch me crying.'

The hairs on the back of my neck were lifting gently. I reached for a piece of cheese.

'Uh . . . what specific flash young society bastards would we be talking about here exactly?' I said.

'You'll've seen one of them at the dinner.' Jarhades sipped his wine. 'Damon. Prince Phraates's son.'

Something cold touched my spine. 'Mithradates had a spat at a party with Damon?'

'No. Not him; you said it yourself, he just stirs things up. The other lad went by the name of Nicanor. He—'

'*Nicanor?*'

'That's right.' Jarhades shot me a sharp look 'You know him? Father's an Armenian merchant, very big in the spice trade.' He turned to Erato. 'What's his name again? Aratus?'

'Anacus,' Erato said. 'His wife's from Antioch. They've got that fancy house near the Caelimontanan Gate, the one with the—'

'Uh . . . this party,' I interrupted. 'You care to tell me about it? The whole story, from the beginning?'

'That was the one I was telling you about at Mano's,' Jarhades said. 'When Mithradates made his pass at Calliste. Quite a big affair, a birthday bash. It'd be, what, two or three months ago now?' He looked at Erato. She nodded. 'The host had booked us along with another couple of acts. We weren't there ourselves when the trouble started – we'd had the business over Calliste by then – but we got the story from one of the others. It was young Nicanor's fault, sure, but Mithradates began it, setting Damon on at him.'

'Damon was always needling the other boy,' Erato said. 'If you've met him you'll know why. He's soft as new-pressed goat's cheese.'

Yeah, well; that was a verdict on Nicanor I wouldn't entirely agree with, but it didn't really matter and I kept my mouth shut.

'Anyway.' Jarhades stoned an olive. 'Then seemingly Nicanor shouts out something about Damon having fooled with his sister – Nicanor's sister – and goes for him with a knife. When they pull the two apart Damon's lost a finger.'

'The sister had died,' Erato put in. 'Two or three months before that. I forget her name.'

There was something about her tone that set the prickles in my neck going again. '"Died"?' I said.

'Of a fever. That was the official version, anyway. Rumour was, though, they buried her hand separate. And with what her brother claimed you don't have to look far for the reason.'

Right; a pregnancy and suicide. Oh, shit. Not that I thought the story had any relevance, apart from explaining how Damon had come by the wound that put him out of the running for the Great Kingship, even if he was only eligible by his own reckoning. 'The girl killed herself because she was pregnant by Damon?'

'So people said at the time. And there was no trouble later about the finger.'

I sat back. Yeah, gossip aside – and the lady was clearly a born gossiper – that last was pretty surprising. Damon might be illegitimate, sure, but he was still a Parthian prince's son, and in Rome you don't carve bits off sprigs of the nobility and get away with it unless you've got serious clout. Or, of course, for an equally good reason. Hushing up a pregnancy and a suicide – especially if the girl's father was a big wheel in the city's merchant community – was as good an explanation as any, even if Phraates was a prince of the blood. It explained why Nicanor hated Damon's guts, for a start, and why he wanted nothing more to do with him or his cronies. Also why he'd been so touchy on the subject of his family. I tucked the little nugget away for future reference.

'What's your interest, anyway?' Erato had picked up Jarhades's wine cup and was sipping at it. The distraction seemed to have done her good. If I hadn't seen her onstage in a spangled bra and fringed panties I would've placed her as a Suburan housewife swapping scandal with a neighbour over the shelled peas. 'In Damon and his friends, I mean?'

The born gossip's question; I should've been expecting it. Erato was no fool, either.

'Uh . . . 'I said.

'Now, now, girl,' Jarhades grunted. 'That's none of our business. Let the man drink his wine in peace.'

Well, she knew about the Parthian delegation anyway, or at least that the guys were in Rome and that they were Parthians, if not the whys and wherefores. Also, she and Jarhades had been pretty helpful, and maybe there was more where that came from. 'No, that's okay,' I said. 'I'm looking into a murder. One of the people at the dinner, name of Zariadres.'

I hadn't been expecting what happened next. The lady set the cup down sharply, and it caught the edge of Jarhades's hand, tipped, and splashed wine on to the tabletop.

'*Who?*' she whispered. The colour had left her face.

Jarhades and I were both staring at her. 'Zariadres,' I said. 'You know him?'

She shook her head numbly. 'No. I . . . at least, not that . . . no.' She stood up. 'I'm sorry. I'll get a cloth.'

I watched her go. Shit; she was lying, sure, that stood out clear as a pig in a swimming pool. The only question was what I was going to do about it.

'What was that in aid of?' Jarhades said. He looked as mystified as I felt.

'You don't know either?'

'It seems there's a lot of things I don't know, Corvinus. What happened exactly, with this Zariadres?'

I told him. It took a while, even though I kept strictly to the facts, and I had one eye on the door all the time, but Erato didn't reappear. Finally, when she did, she came straight over to the table, eyes lowered, and began to wipe up the spilled wine while Jarhades and I watched in silence.

When she'd finished, she put the cloth down and turned to me. 'He was a Suren, wasn't he?' she said.

'What?'

'This Zariadres. He'd be from the Suren family.'

'How—' Jarhades began. I laid a hand on his wrist, and he stopped.

'He must've been named after his father. Or maybe an uncle.' Erato sat down, and her voice was as expressionless as her face. 'The Surens and the Mihrans – Lord Peucestas is a Mihran – are enemies. They always have been. It was a Suren that Artabanus sent that day to castrate the master and execute his family. His name was Zariadres, too.'

18

It was well past noon when they let me go. I was grateful to be out in the street again. The unexpected connection between Zariadres and Peucestas had come as a real facer, and I needed peace and quiet to think it over.

Peace and quiet and a wineshop. Sure, I'd had the two cups of Syrian, but that was pleasure, not business. If I was going to think, I needed a wineshop wall at my back, half a jug within easy reach and the soporific drone of barflies slagging off the city admin dole-queue clerks, analysing the last set of races in the Circus or explaining at alcoholic length to the barman how their wives-stroke-girlfriends didn't understand them and what bastards their bosses were. The usual, in other words. I headed back in the direction of Iugarius and Renatius's place.

So; Peucestas might come across as pretty straight, but he had motive in spades. Plus, of course, a prime opportunity: he'd been the one to find the body, and I only had his word for it that Zariadres had been dead before he got there. Sure, the real villain of the piece had been the other Zariadres, his father or uncle, and he was probably long gone – Erato had said, later, when I asked her, that he'd been pushing sixty when Peucestas's wife and kids had been executed – but for easterners, like our backwoods Sicilians, guilt's an inherited thing and revenge doesn't stop with the guy immediately responsible. Having a close relative a corridor's length away, practically unguarded, in a foreign city where the authorities would chew their own legs off before getting involved would be practically an open invitation to murder.

The question was, of course, how the situation had been allowed to arise in the first place. I might not know Parthians, or the diplomatic world in general, but common sense told me that sending two men on an embassy, one of whom was related to someone who'd been responsible for lopping the bollocks off the other and sticking his family on pointed stakes wasn't too bright an idea; especially if – as had to be the case – both parties were aware of the link. No doubt Isidorus would say that sort of thing happened all the time in diplomatic circles, but to me it made no sense at all. If Peucestas was the killer then it'd been a crime just waiting to happen.

Having the motive and the opportunity were one thing; being guilty of the actual murder was another. Besides, from what I'd seen of him I liked Peucestas, and if he'd slit Zariadres's throat I couldn't altogether blame him. This case was turning into a real bugger.

Then, naturally, there was the other important question that Erato's little scrap of information had raised . . .

I was on Iugarius now. As usual this time of day it was packed to the gunnels, both sides and the middle. Not that Renatius's would be crowded: most of the punters you see around the Market Square district are sharp city types, plain-mantles and above, and Renatius's is definitely spit-and-sawdust tunic territory. He serves good honest wine, though, better than the overpriced stuff you get in the chichi places in this area that cater for the upwardly mobile set. And give me droning barflies over pushy execs doing private deals and knifing their absent colleagues in the back over jugs of second-rate Alban any time.

I'd just passed one of the chichi-est wineshops – there're quite a few on that stretch, which is another reason why

Renatius's isn't heaving – when someone called my name. I turned. Nicanor was coming out of the door with two other youngsters of about the same age. All three were wearing party mantles and looking, among the respectable whites of the pedestrian traffic, like louche peacocks in a duck-run. One of his pals was carrying a wine jug, the other had an arm round his shoulder, and all that was holding the two of them up was hope.

'Hey, Corvinus! How are things?' The words were slightly slurred: Nicanor mightn't be as far gone as his mates, or if he was he carried it a lot better, but he'd still've given a newt a close run for its money. 'Still chasing Parthians, are you?'

The lad with the wine jug whispered something into his pal's ear and they giggled together.

'Yeah, more or less,' I said easily, ignoring the looks we were getting from disgruntled mantles forced to edge round the sudden pavement-jam. City-centre mantles are the starchiest in Rome. 'You're pretty late back from your night out, aren't you, pal?'

Nicanor raised his shoulders. The garland slipped down over one eye, and he absently pushed it back. 'A going-away party. Quintus here's cousin' – he nodded at the kid with the jug – 'is off to join his legion this morning.' He glanced up at the sun. 'Oh, shit! Is that the time?'

A large narrow-striper clutching a precarious bundle of wax tablets in the fold of his mantle glared at us and stepped carefully round, muttering. Quintus blew a raspberry after him. I grinned: those kids weren't all bad. 'Yeah. I'm afraid so,' I said. 'Maybe you'd best get home.'

He shook his head, almost dislodging the garland again. 'No hurry. And I owe you a cup of wine.'

'You don't think maybe you've had enough?'

'What's that got to do with it?' He leaned against the wall and forced himself upright. 'Not here, though. The bugger

who runs the place threw us out. We'll go further up the
street.'

'What about your friends?'

Both of them were out of things. Quintus – the guy with
the wine jug – had sat down and was grinning into space. The
other one had his back to the bricks and looked like he was
seriously considering throwing up.

'They'll be okay. They're used to it.' Nicanor took my arm.
'Come on, Corvinus. I owe you a drink, and I pay my debts.'

Yeah, well; I couldn't just leave him, that was sure.
And after my conversation with Jarhades and Erato I had
questions to ask. 'Fine,' I said. 'Just the one. But I choose the
wineshop, right?'

'Deal.'

We left Quintus and his pal – I'd bet the missing bits of
their names figured pretty high on the social roll –
communing with nature and carried on up Iugarius, drawing
disapproving stares and tuts all the way from passing punters.
At least Renatius's would be safe: I could have a quiet word
with Renatius himself to make sure that the one cup didn't
turn into five or six, and slip one of the regulars a silver piece
or two to see him safe home at the end of it. I owed his parents
that much.

'So where was the party?' I said.

'The Quirinal. Or at least that's where it started. Quintus
had a friend near the old Flaminian Racetrack. We were
going to drop in on him when it finished.'

'Iugarius isn't on the way to Flaminius Circus from the
Quirinal.'

'Yeah, I know, but we took a detour. Decimus wanted to
make a speech on the rostrum. We never did reach Quintus's
friend's. We were pretty drunk.'

Were pretty drunk! Bacchus on skates! They'd been lucky
the Watch hadn't lifted them, or worse: the city streets are no

picnic area after dark, especially for three legless youngsters with more money than brains. Which in their case wouldn't be difficult. 'You've been out all night?'

'Sure. We slept in the portico of the Julian Hall until the slaves turned up at dawn and threw us out.' He sounded like it happened most nights of the month. Maybe it did.

'So how about this morning?'

'It seemed a shame to go home. Flavius's serves a good breakfast, the wine's good and one thing led to another. We'd've been all right if that bastard Quintus hadn't been sick over the guy at the next table. He turned out to be a praetor with no sense of humour.' He glanced at me owlishly. 'How far's this place of yours, then?'

'We're at it.' I pushed open Renatius's door and went in.

Half a dozen pairs of eyes swivelled towards us, the same number of eyebrows climbed towards the ceiling and there were a couple of whistles. Then the punters went back to their drinks. As far as reaction went, that was it: as a whole, Renatius's customers tend to keep themselves to themselves, at least until the newcomer's bought his own wine and if he doesn't look a soft touch.

Nicanor was looking around the bare wooden tables and benches and the plain walls. 'You drink *here*?' he said.

One of the tunics in the corner next to us sniggered into his cup and I sighed. Yeah, well, at least Charax the loud-mouthed cowboy builder wasn't in evidence today. The mileage that smart bugger could've got out of a spoilt-brat kid dressed up in a fancy party mantle just didn't bear thinking of. 'My choice, remember?' I said. 'And I happen to like it. Sit down and I'll get the drinks.'

'No, it's my treat. I'll get the—'

'Shut up.'

For a wonder, he did. While he parked himself none too steadily at an empty table I went over to the bar. Renatius was rinsing cups, and from the sour look on his face he'd heard the kid's initial comment.

'Afternoon, Corvinus,' he said. 'Who's your fancy friend? Or are you nursemaiding?'

'Just make it two cups of the usual, pal,' I said. 'No added smartass comments. And some bread, cheese, sausage and olives.' It was past lunchtime, I was getting peckish and no doubt Nicanor could do with something to soak up the booze.

Renatius's eyebrows rose for the second time. *'Cups?'*

'Cups. And don't come over asking if we want refills, either.'

'Suit yourself.' Renatius cast a professional eye over my shoulder. 'He looks like he's had as much as he can take for one afternoon, anyway.'

'Right. Exactly.' I opened my belt-pouch to pay, adding a few silver pieces on the side. 'And see if you can get one of the lads to scare up a litter and watchdog him home when we've finished.'

Renatius poured the wine. 'This another of your cases?' he asked.

'Could be.'

'You certainly pick them, don't you?'

'He's okay. Or he will be in a few years when he comes out the end of it. If he lives that long.'

I carried the wine and the plate of food over to the table. Now he was off his feet, Nicanor had taken on a sort of boiled-fish look: stiff and slightly glazed. I put a wine cup in front of him, laid the plate between us and sat down opposite.

'Cheers,' he said, taking a swig. 'Hey, this isn't bad.'

I took a mouthful from my own cup. 'Renatius's Spoletian is about the best in Rome,' I said. 'He gets it from his cousin's farm. Same goes for the cheese and sausage. Tell me about Damon and your sister.'

I'd been wondering how to broach the subject, and I'd decided the in-your-face approach was best. For the next five seconds, I thought I'd made a mistake. It was as if I'd thrown a bucket of ice-water over him. Nicanor set his cup down slowly, staring at me and reddening, all the signs of drunkenness gone.

'How do you know about Sebasta?' he said.

So that was the girl's name. 'One of the jugglers at the dinner party when you cut off the guy's finger told me.' Deliberately, I avoided his eyes and reached for a slice of sausage. 'He got her pregnant, didn't he?'

'That's none of your fucking business!'

'No, it isn't,' I agreed.

He took another swallow of wine. 'She was sixteen. Three years younger than me. Yes, Damon got her pregnant. When she found out she killed herself.'

'She had an affair with him?'

'Sebasta wouldn't've looked twice at that piece of filth. He raped her.'

Uh-huh. Yeah, well, it was possible, but only just: families in Rome keep a close eye on their daughters of marriageable age, and under these circumstances rape isn't all that common. More often than not, a pregnancy comes about because the girl has made at least some of the running and has been seeing the lad concerned behind her parents' backs. That was more likely, in this situation too. Besides, Nicanor had been fond of the girl – more than fond from his reaction – and any account I got from him was bound to be biased.

Nicanor had been watching me, scowling. He got to his feet, lurching slightly. 'You don't believe me, do you?' he said. 'Well, Corvinus, you can just—'

I grabbed his arm across the table and pulled him down. Although I had my back to the room, I could feel the other punters' sudden interest. You don't often get a floor show in Renatius's, and the customers tend to make the most of it.

'Sit down,' I said. 'Sure I believe you. Why not? Besides, like you say it's none of my business.'

Nicanor sat. The effort seemed to have taken all the energy he had, because he slumped like a sack of grain. 'My fucking father had been throwing her at Tiridates,' he said. 'Tiridates wasn't interested. Damon was, though, but not in marriage. The two of them – and that bastard Iberian – cooked it up between them. They got her on her own one day and Damon raped her. Satisfied?'

So. It made some sort of cock-eyed sense, anyway. Maybe I might believe the story after all. 'You want to tell me the whole thing from the beginning?' I said quietly.

Nicanor reached for his wine cup and drank most of what was left at a gulp. 'You don't know my family, Corvinus,' he said. 'My mother's okay, most of the time, but she wants to get on in society and she does whatever my father tells her. He's a real bastard. He'd swim through shit to get his feet on the ladder. Any ladder. Marrying his daughter to a Parthian prince would've done that, and to hell with what she thought herself. He could've been a pimp and Sebasta one of his whores. Mother wasn't much better. We had some real screaming matches.' He swallowed the last of the wine. 'Trouble was, it was all the one way, wasn't it? Tiridates wasn't interested. Why should he be? He's fucking royalty. You know what that means?'

I nodded, but didn't interrupt; the guy was off and running with the grudge between his teeth, and all he wanted now was a sympathetic audience.

'He wouldn't've had Sebasta as even a secondary wife, not the daughter of an Armenian merchant and a low-class

Syrian who hadn't so much as looks going for her. He strung Dad along, sure, but only for what he could get. Snob or not, Dad's stinking rich, that's one thing you can say for him, and he threw money at Tiridates like he was Croesus. I know that crowd. They were just playing games, all of them. I told Dad they were laughing at him up their sleeves and he was wasting his time, but he wouldn't believe me. It was just a joke to them, a mean, evil, sordid joke.' He lifted the empty cup to his lips and set it down. Despite what I'd said, I was going to signal Renatius to bring him another, but he didn't seem too concerned so I left it. 'Then Tiridates asks him if he can take Sebasta out in his carriage for the day to Fidenae, with just her maid as chaperone. Dad agrees although Sebasta herself's against the idea, and that's it. She never reaches Fidenae. They take her to some mutual pal's fancy villa outside the city where Damon's waiting and he rapes her. Big laugh all round. Big joke. Who cares about a social-climbing Armenian merchant's daughter, anyway?'

He was scowling into the empty cup. I reached mine over and poured half the contents in, and he drained them at a swallow. It hung together, sure it did. Especially if you knew Damon and Tiridates. 'She didn't say anything? When she got back?'

'No. But then she wouldn't. Sebasta hated Dad as much as I do. Mum worse.'

'And she didn't tell you?'

'No. I knew something was wrong because she kept to her room most of the time after that, and Tiridates stopped coming. But I didn't know what, until she hanged herself a month later and left the note saying she was pregnant. Then I got the story from the maid. Finally. They'd paid the bitch to keep her mouth shut, and she was never Sebasta's anyway.'

'Your sister didn't say anything about Damon in the note?'

'No. Just that she was going to have a child and preferred to die first. My father thought – he still thinks – it was Tiridates's. He blamed her – blamed *her*! – because knowing she carried a Parthian prince's child she still killed herself when she could've had it and put him under an obligation to marry her, or at least taken her as a formal concubine. Bastard!'

Yeah, I'd tend to agree. Social climbers aren't nice people at the best of times, and Nicanor's papa Anacus sounded like the arse-end of the breed. Not that the story was unusual: I'd heard it a dozen times before. Or, if not the third-person-rape permutation exactly, its straightforward equivalent. Marriage brokering isn't always all sweetness and light, and the upper social stratum has things crawling around in it that'd disgrace a sewer. The people that really get hurt – like Nicanor's sister – are the poor kids caught in the middle.

'So you went after Damon?' I said.

He shook his head. 'Not at once. And not openly. I'm a coward, too, in my way, Corvinus, and his father could've made trouble, especially since no one was accusing him. I waited my chance. I didn't want to kill him. Killing wasn't bad enough.'

'You took the opportunity of a silly drunken brawl to cut off his finger. So even Damon would have to realise he'd never make Great King.'

'And live knowing it. Knowing who to thank and why. Right.' Nicanor bared his teeth in a grin. 'I don't want Damon to die. Not for a long, long time.'

'What about your parents? You didn't tell them? About it not being Tiridates who was responsible?'

'Why should I? They didn't care in the first place, and Sebasta's gone anyway. Besides, Dad's still pretty thick with him. And he's got a new prospect lined up to help him on his way.'

'Yeah? Who's that?'

'One of the consulars. A guy by the name of Lucius Vitellius.'

I nearly swallowed my wine cup.

19

I bundled Nicanor into the summoned litter – he was sober enough not to need watchdogging after all – and went back into Renatius's to have my postponed half jug and my think, the latter of which had added to itself considerably in the last half hour.

The kid hadn't had any details about his father's involvement with Vitellius, none at all, just the fact and the name, which was maddening but not altogether surprising given his current family circumstances. Sure, the likelihood was that it was a complete red herring: as far as I could tell, the whole business with Sebasta, nasty as it was, had nothing whatsoever to do with the case apart from shedding some barely needed light on the characters of Tiridates and Damon and explaining how Phraates's son had lost his finger. All the same, I didn't feel too happy about the coincidence, if it was a coincidence, of a name from the sharp end cropping up where it shouldn't.

I poured my first cup from the new half jug and made a start on the untouched bread and cheese. One aspect certainly posed no problems: as far as dodginess of character went, Lucius Vitellius had it in spades; I'd known that long before I'd got into this business. Also, although one end of the conundrum was flapping around loose the other was pretty firmly tied in. Vitellius, as the head of the senatorial commission to dicker with the Parthian delegation, had a definite, central connection with that side of things. On the other hand, slippery and devious as the bugger undoubtedly was by nature, he seemed to be toeing the official line like a good Roman public servant should. What he did in his private capacity – and even Roman public servants had their own private business to conduct in their own time – wasn't relevant. So long as the two didn't clash, it was all fine and dandy.

So long as the two didn't clash . . .

I sipped my wine. Yeah; that was the clincher, and it was where Vitellius's character came in. Me, I wouldn't've trusted the bastard an inch. If he saw some kind of personal advantage offer itself and felt safe to grab it then my bet was he'd take the chance with both hands. The question was, did it exist and if so what was it? That was something I'd have to find out.

Tiridates. That was the other puzzler. Nicanor had said that his father was still on good terms with the guy. Anacus might be a social climber and having once got his hooks into a Parthian prince he wouldn't want to let go in a hurry, but even if he were the double-dyed bastard his son described him as that took a lot of swallowing. By Nicanor's account again, he knew nothing about Damon being responsible for Sebasta's pregnancy, but even if he had in the circumstances it would've made things worse, not better. As far as Anacus knew, Tiridates had seduced the girl, got her pregnant and so caused her suicide. Even if he did put the blame for the last squarely on his daughter, to carry on treating the guy responsible as if he was still a bosom buddy just wasn't natural; or rather, given the bastard Anacus evidently was, it'd need a pretty hefty reason. Sebasta was dead; there was no question of a marriage alliance or whatever any longer. So what could the reason be?

The obvious answer was blackmail, or rather the prettied-up society version of blackmail. Tiridates had taken advantage of a girl from a rich, if not socially distinguished family, and as a result the girl had killed herself. Her death might not be directly his fault, sure, but under the rules of the social stratum he moved in he'd owe a debt; just how big a debt being decided by where exactly her family came in the social stakes. In actual fact, Anacus would be in a better position there than he knew, because what Tiridates would be paying for if the truth ever got out was something far worse than a simple seduction. He wouldn't be paying in money, mind, nothing so crude: that was where this high-class type of blackmail differed. Anacus was rich enough already, probably richer than Tiridates. His price – whatever it was – would be something else, and it wouldn't be cheap. That might bear thinking about, too.

On the other hand, I couldn't buy blackmail as an idea, or not altogether, anyway, not even the high-society version. Tiridates hadn't seemed all that bothered about possible repercussions when he'd set the rape up, and he certainly couldn't rely on the girl not peaching, either immediately or later. Also, he didn't strike me as the kind of guy who'd be blackmailed easily, not by the likes of Anacus, anyway: he was too arrogant, too sure he could do what he liked with other people beneath him socially, and to hell with the consequences. Like Nicanor had said, he and his pals had been laughing in their sleeves at the Anacus family all the time. Setting things up so Damon could rape Sebasta was nothing but a joke.

Fine. Great. The bugger of it was that if I scratched the blackmail angle and assumed that all this had some sort of relevance to the case I had to explain why despite everything Anacus and Tiridates were still an item. It might make some sort of sense – just – from Anacus's side, but what was in it for Tiridates? And – more important – how, if anywhere, did Lucius Vitellius fit in?

I sank a mouthful of wine and topped up my cup. Shit; I didn't know, I just didn't know. The whole thing was probably a mare's nest. All the same, I had a gut feeling about it; it was too much of a coincidence to be coincidental, if you like, and two members of the triangle being involved with the Parthian business was suspicious as hell. It was just lucky that when I'd asked Crispus to recommend a Parthian expert he'd put me on to young Nicanor. If he hadn't done that then I'd never have known . . .

I stopped as the implication hit me. Bugger. Crispus! Caelius fucking Crispus!

It hadn't been an accident, no way had it been an accident: the devious, muck-raking bastard had given me Nicanor's name deliberately. Why he'd done it – probably, knowing Crispus, for unsavoury reasons of his own – I didn't know; but I'd bet a year's income to a mouldy sprat that he had all the answers at his greasy fingertips.

The foreign judge's staff would be back after their festival break, and the afternoon still wasn't all that far gone. If I hurried I could catch him.

I got Renatius to put the rest of my half jug on the shelf, bolted the rest of the cheese and headed off for the Capitol.

He was in; just. And he wasn't too pleased to see me either. But then, what else was new?

'Hi, Crispus,' I said. 'Have a nice festival?'

I thought he was going to bite my head off. When I'd come in he'd been fastening a very pricey-looking dove-grey cloak round his shoulders while the secretary I'd seen last time adjusted the folds at the back. His hand paused on the buckle-pin like he was thinking of taking it off again, but he didn't. 'It's been a long hard day, Corvinus,' he said. 'You don't improve it.' He turned to the secretary. 'Tell the others I'll be along shortly, Menelaus. And don't forget the bathing cap.'

The secretary left with a sniff. I sat down in the visitor's chair. 'Uh . . . bathing cap?'

Crispus sighed, took the cloak off after all and went back behind his desk. 'What do you want this time? Make it quick, please.'

Shit, not a nibble; he was certainly coming on. Just a few months ago we'd've had threats and temper tantrums, but he'd got the busy executive manner down pat. Maybe it was the snazzy new office. Yeah, well, I shouldn't criticise: being a linchpin of the great wheel of government a whole six hours out of the twenty-four was a pretty gruelling job. 'What's Lucius Vitellius got cooking with the Armenian Anacus?' I said.

Pause. 'Who?'

'Come on, pal! You put me on to his son Nicanor. You mentioned the guy's name yourself.'

'Did I?' He was inspecting his nails, but I had the distinct impression of nervous smugness. 'Oh, yes. He's a spice merchant, isn't he? Now why on earth should Lucius Vitellius be involved with someone like that?'

It occurred to me that so far the bugger had asked more questions than I had. And I knew prevarication when I met it. I leaned forward and had the satisfaction of seeing him flinch.

'Crispus, you bastard,' I said evenly, 'you gave me Nicanor's name on purpose so I'd find out about the father and Vitellius having business together. And if you say "Did I?" again I'll wring your scraggy neck.'

'All right,' he said. 'Then I won't. That's not an admission, mind.'

'Sure it isn't. Perish the thought. So why did you do it?'

Crispus cleared his throat; he was nervous now more than smug. His shifty eyes shifted. 'Come on, Corvinus!' he said. 'You told me you were engaged in an official investigation.

As a conscientious public servant I was – I am – trying to help you. But splitting on senior members of the Senate, especially where their private business is concerned, is another matter. After all, I do have my professional reputation to consider.'

I laughed. 'Jupiter in a fucking hand-cart, pal! You've been dishing the dirt on guys like Vitellius for years! Why should now be any different?'

'There may be . . . complications.' Was it my imagination or was the bastard sweating slightly? 'Don't press me. Not this time.'

I didn't like the sound of this; I didn't like it at all. Crispus was a born dirt-disher; professional, sure – he wouldn't've got where he was without being shit-hot at finding out things Rome's administrative movers and shakers would rather keep buried and were willing to give him a discreet hand up so they stayed that way – but he enjoyed the game for its own sake. If he said that he didn't want to play any more, it meant whatever he'd dug up in the dirty laundry basket was a lot worse than just a set of soiled smalls. Maybe I should back off, at that. Give him a bit of room to slither, anyway.

'Okay,' I said. 'Just this once I'll compromise. All you've got to do is nod or shake your head. Does it have anything to do with Prince Tiridates?'

Crispus's naturally pasty face went even whiter, and he swallowed. 'Look, let's just—'

'Just nod or shake your head.'

Slowly, he nodded. Bull's-eye!

'Some sort of three-way scam, then? Tiridates, Vitellius and Anacus?'

Swallow. Nod.

'And Vitellius's bosses don't know about it?'

A hesitation; a nod, turned into a head-shake.

'They *do* know?'

No response; evidently that was all I was getting on that point. Odd. 'But it's political?'

Another hesitation, followed by a reluctant nod. The guy was sweating now in earnest. 'Corvinus, please—' he said.

'You're doing well. Don't give up now.'

'No.' He pushed his chair back and got up like someone had jerked him on strings. 'That's as much as I'm giving you. You're okay, you're an outsider, but I've got my job and my neck to consider. Work the rest out for yourself. And I swear if anything gets back to me over this, official or not, I'll hunt you down. I'm serious. Clear?'

Yeah, well; maybe I was expecting too much. The guy had played fair by his own lights, better than fair, and as a senior senator Vitellius would have major clout even if he wasn't directly concerned with the foreign judge's department. At least now I knew I wasn't chasing shadows; I'd just have to find a lead some other way. I stood up. 'Thanks, pal,' I said. 'You've been a big help. This time I mean it. Enjoy your evening.'

He didn't move. Then, when I had my hand on the door-knob, he said, 'Wait.'

I turned. 'Yeah?'

'Talk to a man in the spice market by the name of Gaius Praxa. Ask him about pepper.'

I didn't reply. I just opened the door and went out.

Pepper, eh?

Yeah. Right . . .

20

The spice market was on the east side of the Velabrum, near the end of Tuscan Street and facing the slopes of the Palatine. Not all that far, in other words, and I had a fair slice of the afternoon left. There was no time like the present.

I'm no traveller, me: boats make me sick, give me Roman cooking any day, and as for sightseeing you can drop it down a very deep hole and forget it. All the same, a walk through the spice market can send even my pulse racing. Rome's a pretty olfactory city, in places too olfactory: some bits down by the Tiber, near the big meat market where the slaughter-houses and tanneries are, or in the fullers' quarter, you breathe through your mouth because using your nose is a bad, bad idea. The spice market's the opposite. You walk through it with both nostrils wide open, taking in as much as you can get and begging for more. I didn't recognise many of the scents – you'd need a culinary nut like Meton for that – but even I picked out the hot, peppery tang of ginger and the rich aromatic smell of cinnamon. For most people, mind, a sniff's about as close as they come. Spices – any spices – are seriously pricey, some literally worth their weight in gold. Even the spiced-honey pastries you can buy from the hawkers at the market's edge cost as much as a cookshop takeaway.

I stopped at a likely looking stall run by an old girl wrapped to the eyeballs and clanking with enough gold bangles to fit out a cathouse. That's another thing about the spice trade: a lot of the people involved in it, including the stallholders themselves, are foreigners. Real foreigners, I mean, from outwith the Roman borders. This example with her brown-henna'd palms and dark, unfathomable brooding-vulture eyes could've been pure desert Arab from the empty quarter beyond Egypt where – so they say – the phoenix lives.

'Excuse me, Grandma,' I said. 'You happen to know where I can find a man by the name of Gaius Praxa?'

'End of Five Godlets Alley,' she snapped in an accent that was pure tenement-Aventine balcony-hanger. 'And watch who you're calling grandma, pal. My eldest's just turned six.'

So much for the mysteries of the east. Shit. Well, how was I supposed to tell under that lot? 'Right. Right,' I said. 'Sorry, lady. Ah . . . where would Five Godlets Alley be?'

'Carry on past the litter-rank and the urinal. It's on your left before the cookshop. You can't miss it, even with your eyesight.'

'Uh . . . yeah. Yeah, thanks.' I beat a hasty retreat.

She was right, though. The small wayside shrine that gave the alley its name was unmistakable. Who the godlets were, and why there were five of them, I didn't know – they weren't Roman, anyway – but from the little offerings of flowers, fruit and scraps of cloth they must've been pretty popular. I gave them a nod in passing and turned into the alleyway.

There wasn't a sign, but the place at the end was obviously what I was looking for: a fair-sized warehouse on a stone-built platform, currently open along its length but with heavy shutters folded back against the central and side pillars and stacked along the inside walls with linen bags, rushwork baskets and a few wooden chests. An elderly bearded man was sitting in a high-backed chair beside a set of bronze scales, engrossed in an open book-roll.

'Gaius Praxa?' I said.

He looked up and smiled. 'That's my name. What can I do for you, sir?'

Strong accent – it reminded me of Nicanor's – but an educated voice.

'I was told to ask you about pepper.'

Yeah, well, it did sound pretty silly, like one of these secret cabbalistic greetings that sad buggers like the Fellowship of the Golden Ox-Goad exchange, especially when they know some poor bloody non-initiate is listening. If Praxa was surprised, though, he didn't show it. Carefully, he rolled up the book – I noticed it wasn't written in Latin script – and stowed it away in its cylinder case.

'What kind of pepper?' he said.

'Uh . . . there's more than one kind?'

'Oh, yes. The simplest and crudest is long pepper. Such as is in that basket over there.' He nodded towards the rushwork basket to my left which was full of what looked like dried bean-pods. 'Then there's black and white pepper. Both are made from long pepper but their natures are different. Black pepper is stronger-tasting, more pungent, as well as being the most common. The white variety is milder.'

'That so, now?'

He got to his feet. He was taller than I'd expected, and stooped, with bushy eyebrows and washed-out grey eyes. 'You asked. I've answered,' he said. 'Now. At least I should know your name.'

'Corvinus. Valerius Corvinus.'

'So.' He nodded gravely. 'And you're interested in pepper, Valerius Corvinus.'

'Yeah. So it seems.'

'For any particular reason?'

'Uh-uh.' I grinned. 'Not that I know of at the moment.'

If he thought the answer was a bit odd – and I wouldn't've blamed him – he didn't show it.

He just grunted. 'Fair enough. Perhaps a reason will suggest itself. If not – well, I wasn't doing anything particularly vital at present anyway, and I'm not a stickler for reasons myself. Interest will suffice. Up you come and have a look round.'

I climbed the shallow steps to the platform. The scents from the open spice bags caught at my throat.

'Pepper comes from India, or from the south-facing slopes of the Caucasus. The pods grow on trees rather like myrtles but taller, and the corns inside resemble myrtle berries. In fact, before it started to be imported myrtle was the nearest equivalent. People have tried to grow pepper trees in Italy but the quality's very poor and it has never really caught on. Long pepper is simply the pod itself, dried whole.' He reached into a bag and brought out a handful of small, wrinkled seeds. 'This, now, is black pepper. To make it, the corns are taken from the pod and dried in the sun or over fires, while for white pepper they're soaked in water before drying to remove the outer husk. Then the pepper is loaded into sacks and transported along the trade route through Mesopotamia into Syria, or round to the north through Armenia. There is a sea route from Arabia to the Indus, but that takes much longer and it's expensive.' He smiled. 'Now. Have I bored you enough or is there anything else you'd like to know?'

I was examining the other bags. One of them was full of what looked like huge salt crystals. 'What's that?' I said.

'A curiosity. It doesn't have a Latin name that I know of; we simply call it reed honey. It's from India too. Taste it. Go ahead, it's quite pleasant.' I did. The thing was sweet, like honey but with a different flavour. 'It's a form of dried sap. Not culinary; I'm no doctor, so I don't know its uses exactly, but we sometimes sell it to the medical profession.'

I moved on to a wooden chest full of thin rolls of flaky

brown bark. This I knew: Meton put it into hot spiced wine.
'Cinnamon, right?' I said.

'Indeed.' He was watching me carefully.

'That from India as well?'

'From beyond Ethiopia. The Ethiopians buy it from the
cave-dwellers who live to the south of them.' Praxa picked up
a broken segment and rubbed it between his palms, scenting
the air between us. 'People used to believe the sticks were
twigs from harvested phoenix nests, but that isn't true. The
cave-dwellers bring them from much further still on rafts
without sails or oars or rudders.'

'Yeah? How do they do that?'

He shrugged. 'I don't know. I'm not a seaman, either. But
the round trip can take as long as five years and cost the lives
of half the crews. The sun is so close to the earth that it
chars them, the air is full of poisonous vapours and the
forests along the coast are inhabited by dwarfs who kill with
needles blown through hollow canes. Or so my traders tell
me.'

'All for a bit of scented bark, right?' I said. Bugger; no
wonder the stuff was so pricey. Curiosity satisfied. Back to
business. I turned away from the sacks. 'Uh . . . you
mentioned two possible land routes. For the India trade.'

'Through Mesopotamia and Armenia. Yes. The spice
road splits at Bisutun in Media, east of the Tigris. One
branch goes north to Nisibis into Armenia and then crosses
the Syrian border at Zeugma, the other carries on through
Parthia to Palmyra and over the Syrian desert.'

Well, I'd take his word for it. 'That's all there are? Just these
two?'

'Apart from the sea route I mentioned, but as I said that's
seasonal, time-consuming and more expensive, besides
being more dangerous. In the event that a war with Parthia
closed the Syrian borders then it might be relevant, yes, but

not otherwise. Even then it couldn't carry a quarter of the traffic the market needs.'

Uh-huh; I was beginning to see why Crispus had pointed me in Praxa's direction. I still didn't know where all this was leading us, but the guy certainly knew his stuff. 'Let me just get this clear, pal,' I said. 'What you're telling me is that the Parthians have almost total control over the empire's eastern spice imports, right?'

He was looking at me like I'd just asked him to confirm that I only had one head. 'But of course they do. They always have.'

'And the, uh, trade would be pretty profitable, would it?'

He laughed. 'Oh, yes. I don't know the exact figures but the overall profit for the luxury trade must be in the region of a hundred million a year. And spices – including pepper – account for a considerable slice of that.'

I almost choked. Holy immortal gods! A hundred million a year *profit*? That was more than the tax levy on a fair-sized province brought in, and even that was gross, not net. The back of my neck was beginning to itch. 'So any merchant who controlled the trade at both entry points into Syria – the Armenian and the Mesopotamian – would clean up?'

'If he controlled both, yes. It would have to be both. In practice that would be impossible because the situation could never arise. There are too many individual merchants, and too many vested interests, to produce that sort of monopoly. He would need two kings in his pocket, for a start: the Great King himself, or his Mesopotamian governor at least, and the king of Armenia. Not to mention a blind eye on the part of the Syrian authorities on the Roman side.'

Forget the itch; my brain had gone numb. Oh, shit. Impossible or not, it was too much of a coincidence to ignore: Anacus the spice merchant; Tiridates the Parthian prince and – if anything happened to Phraates – Rome's candidate for the Great Kingship; Tiridates's bosom buddy Mithradates, ditto for Armenia; and finally Lucius Vitellius who, unless I missed my guess, as a result of his Parthian duties would be next in line for the all-important Syrian governorship . . .

Coincidences happen, sure, but not that calibre of coincidence. It all fitted. *How* it fitted, and what the practicalities would be, I didn't know, but the whole thing smelled like a cartload of month-old fish.

'That's . . . ah . . . fascinating,' I said.

'Indeed?' Praxa was still watching me closely. 'You seem to have found a reason for your interest after all, Valerius Corvinus. If you'll forgive me for saying so.'

'Uh . . . yeah. Yeah, I have.' Gods! What was I into here? No wonder Crispus had preferred to keep his mouth shut. A business scam like that, massive as it was, wasn't technically illegal, sure, especially since any monopoly would only apply outside Roman jurisdiction so Vitellius wouldn't be breaking any laws, but still—

I skidded to a mental halt. Hang on, Corvinus, hang on! Mithradates, fine, no problem: he was the current choice for Armenian king nem. con. Vitellius – well, he was Rome's chief dickerer with the Parthians, any subsequent dealings with them would almost certainly involve him and so the Syrian governorship was practically a cert. But Tiridates wasn't in the running for Great King at all, was he? Unless, of course, Phraates died leaving him the only other candidate . . .

Damon. Phraates's son. He couldn't ever be Great King himself, and his father had made it clear that he couldn't expect any sort of position with him in charge. On the other hand, he was definitely persona grata with Tiridates, and if he were to take the kingship by stepping over Phraates's corpse there might be a key Parthian governorship – such as

Mesopotamia, for example – up for grabs. Especially if Damon had helped arrange for him to be the only living candidate . . .

That fitted, too. Oh, shit. Make that two cartloads of month-old fish.

Praxa was waiting politely, eyebrows raised. 'Ah . . . you ever come across a guy by the name of Anacus?' I asked.

'Yes, of course. I buy from him regularly. His family have been merchants and shippers in Antioch for generations. Is Anacus another interest of yours?'

'Yeah. You mind?'

'Should I?'

'It's a big company?'

'Very. One of the biggest in Syria.'

'What's he like? Anacus?'

'As a person? An excellent businessman. In fact, I might say business is his life.'

'Straight?'

'Certainly. I wouldn't deal with him if he weren't. He drives a good bargain, but his spices are top quality. He does his own shipping, as well, and that's as important for spices as it is for wine. I really must ask you, Corvinus. Natural curiosity is one thing, but we seem to have moved off pepper and on to areas a great deal more personal. Why do you want to know about Anacus?'

'He's pretty well-off, isn't he?'

'Yes. Although as I say business is his life and the money aspect is secondary. Now I don't wish to seem impolite, but I'll ask you again: what's your interest in Titus Anacus?'

'No particular reason. I know his son, that's all.'

'Nicanor?' Praxa frowned. 'A disappointment, that lad. Good business brain, as he would have coming from that family. But no interest, I'm afraid. Also, relations between him and his father are . . . somewhat strained.'

'Because of his sister's death?'

The eyebrows had gone up another notch. 'Perhaps. Because of that, and for other reasons. I don't know the details, nor do I wish to. They are none of my business. Nor, I would suggest, are they of yours.'

'Right. Right. I'm sorry.' Jupiter! I felt like crowing. Crispus had come up trumps after all. Now I needed space to think. 'Thanks for your help, friend. I've learned a lot.'

'About pepper?' The old man's tone was as dry as one of his peppercorns, and his grey eyes rested on me in a considering way. 'Don't mention it, Valerius Corvinus. I hope – whatever the reason for your interest may be – that I've managed to satisfy it.'

'Oh, yeah,' I said. 'Absolutely.'

That was putting it mildly; the old guy had given me cause to be grateful in spades. If hauling the top off an unexpected can of worms was a reason for gratitude.

I left. The sun was pretty far over now. It had been a long, long day and I should be heading back to the Caelian. Perhaps a chat with Perilla was in order.

21

I got back just in time for dinner. *Just* in time: Bathyllus had brought in the starters and Perilla was already parked on the dining-room couch.

'Marcus, where have you been?' She lifted her chin for the welcome-home kiss. 'You only went out for a shave. I was getting worried.'

'Yeah, well.' I lay down on the couch opposite and took a restorative swig from my wine cup. 'Things developed. You know how it is. How are you feeling, lady?'

'Better, thank you. And speaking of developments there has been one on the lamprey front.'

'What?'

'Meton, dear, and his missing basket of lampreys. You remember?'

Oh, gods! This I could do without. I took another swallow of wine. 'Okay,' I said. 'I'm anaesthetised. Tell me.'

Perilla sniffed. 'There's no need to dramatise, Marcus. I simply happened to bump into Titus Petillius this afternoon and I asked him if any of his household had seen anything.' Petillius was our next-door neighbour, a seriously large guy from Veii with widespread commercial interests in the dyeing and laundering field. 'He said that he'd check.'

'And?'

'One of his slaves was polishing the door brasses on the morning in question and saw the thief actually walk out carrying the basket.'

I stared at her. 'He did *what*! And he didn't stop him?'

'No. He never even thought of it. The man was decently dressed – the slave said he was wearing a freedman's cap – and didn't appear unduly furtive. Obviously a professional.'

Yeah, right. And the fact that the lampreys had been nicked wouldn't've come to light subsequently, either; not as far as Petillius's household were concerned. Perilla and me got on okay with the neighbours, sure – or as well as we'd ever done, the guy being a water-drinker who thought I was a dipso – but since the abortive love affair the year before between Bathyllus and the then-not-yet-Mrs Petillius relations between the two sets of bought help had been strained, to say the least. On reconsideration we were just lucky that the lamprey-napper hadn't had 'thief' embroidered on his tunic. If he had, Petillius's slave would probably have offered to help carry the basket.

'Would he recognise the guy again if he saw him?' I asked. 'The slave, I mean.'

'It's possible. But he certainly wasn't from around here. The man was very sure about that.'

Yeah, well; me, for reasons given above, I wouldn't rate that assurance particularly highly. Still, it'd been Petillius himself asking the questions and you don't buck the master, so perhaps I was maligning the bugger. I sighed. 'Well, that seems to stitch it up, lady. There's nothing we can do about it now. It's a shame, but there you go. File and forget.'

'Indeed.' She dipped a quail's egg. 'Now, Marcus. You were saying. About things developing.'

'Yeah.' I told her about the Peucestas business. 'At least we've got someone with a strong motive at last.'

'You think Peucestas was the killer?'

'It's a possibility.' I reached for the nearest plate of nibbles. 'Certainly one that makes sense. If the guy's uncle was responsible for the deaths of his wife and kids, not to mention his own castration, then he'd have reason in spades. Add that to opportunity and he's a prime candidate.'

'But?'

Yeah; there was always that 'but'. 'From what I've seen of him, Peucestas isn't the murdering type. Killing, yes, he's capable of that. But he wouldn't cover well, or if he is covering then he's pretty good at it. Added to which, if he was responsible then how does the Phraates side of things fit in? He hates Artabanus, he wants him gone, and if Phraates has Roman backing for a coup then what does he gain from screwing things up?'

'Perhaps your Phraates element doesn't fit in.' Perilla selected one of Meton's chickpea rissoles and dipped it in the fish sauce bowl. 'Does it have to? The two might be quite separate.'

'It's possible, sure. But it's messy.'

'Real life often is.'

'Maybe.' I took another swig of wine. 'Even so, there's an explanation that makes just as much sense and covers more ground.'

She paused, the rissole halfway to her mouth. 'And that is?'

'You're not going to like it. I can tell you that now.'

'Marcus, if you're going to advance one of your half-baked political theories—'

'It isn't half-baked. And it's only partly political.'

'Oh, marvellous! That makes me feel a lot happier.'

'I think Lucius Vitellius might be conspiring with Tiridates and his Iberian pal to sideline Prince Phraates for Great King.'

Perilla put the rissole down. 'Marcus,' she said. '*That* is political.'

'Only slightly. I haven't explained yet.'

'You don't have to. It's absolute nonsense. Lucius Vitellius is an ex-consul, a very respected member of the Senate in good standing with the emperor and, as far as I know, no one's fool. Why on *earth* would he do a stupid thing like that?'

'For money. Quite a lot of money. Or, of course, he could just be stringing his partners along for what he can get in the short term, because although he's a greedy pig like you say he's no fool. Which of the two I don't know yet, but the rest fits like a glove.'

'Really?'

'Really. Less of the sarcasm, lady. Just hold your fire and pin your ears back.'

I told her the rest of the day's news, from my conversation with Nicanor ('That boy needs a good shaking!') to what I'd learned about the spice trade from Gaius Praxa; minus, naturally, any reference to the little incident with Mithradates. That might go further than anything else to back the theory up, sure, but the less Perilla knew of that side of things the better.

'And that's it?' she said when I'd finished.

Bathyllus was serving the main course. I leaned sideways while he ladled pork stew with barley and fennel dumplings onto my plate: Meton was obviously in one of his hearty moods. 'Uh . . . yeah,' I said. 'More or less.'

'Then let me get this clear. You think that this man Acanus—'

'Anacus.'

'. . . is after some sort of monopoly of the spice trade—'

'Pepper. Probably just pepper. That was what Crispus implied anyw—'

'. . . between Parthia and Rome, and to get it he is conniving at the assassination of the Roman candidate for the Great Kingship, with the assistance of two eastern royals and a Roman consular. Correct?'

'Ah . . . yeah. Yeah, that just about—'

'And you're sure you didn't have any of that *qef* stuff your friend Jarhades was sniffing?'

Gods! I didn't deserve this! 'Look, lady, I told you. It all fits. How or why I don't know, certainly not in detail, but it does.'

She spooned a dumpling. 'All right. I'm not unreasonable.' Jupiter! Not so much as a blink! 'Convince me.'

Hell. Where did I start? 'Okay, let's begin with Anacus. He's the catalyst; without him, I doubt if any of this would be happening. His family have been in the spice trade for generations, and they're big but he wants them bigger. He—'

'That's guesswork, dear. You've never met the man. You don't know.'

'It's a reasonable assumption. Praxa said he was a career businessman. And are you going to give me a fair run at this or what, lady?'

'Probably what. But carry on in any case.'

Oh, whoopee; there's nothing like encouragement. I took a spoonful of pork. 'Okay. So Anacus hears – probably from Tiridates, who he's trying to hook for his daughter – that the thrones of both Parthia and Armenia are shortly going to be changing hands, and that Vitellius is odds-on favourite for the Syrian governorship. The guy's no fool; he realises that, Mithradates being a pal of his hoped-for son-in-law, or whatever, as far as personal contacts go he's sitting on potential control of the empire's eastern spice route. He—'

'Marcus, dear, I'm sorry for interrupting.'

'Then don't. Indulge yourself.'

'It's simply that before you go on I have a few queries. First of all, exactly how does this Anacus manage to corner the spice market? What are the mechanics of the process? Second, even if it's possible why should Tiridates and Mithradates help him do it? Even if Tiridates were to become king of Parthia, which he almost certainly won't?'

Bugger; both reasonable questions, and I wasn't absolutely sure I had the answers to either of them. Still, with Perilla you can't afford to show weakness. Where going for the throat in arguments is concerned, the lady could give a wolverine lessons.

'Yeah. Right.' I took a fortifying belt of wine. 'As far as the spice route business goes, I'm not sure, not as such. I'll give you that.' She opened her mouth. 'Come on, Perilla! I'm no merchant, and no economist, but it must be possible, okay?'

'That, dear, is what's termed a circular argument.'

'Look. The Parthians and the Armenians charge duty on any goods crossing their borders, in or out, just like we do, and any merchant trading with the empire has to have a licence. Right?'

'I don't know, Marcus. I'm no expert on trade either. But yes, I'd assume so.'

'Fine. So put the two together. We're talking preferential status here, with teeth. My guess is that Anacus – or his contracted suppliers – would skip the export duty so his over-heads were lower, while his royal pals would simply make it difficult for any major rival to operate. The two factors combined would give him all the edge he needed. You know how bureaucracy works, lady. If you've got enough clout there're a dozen ways to put even the most successful company on the ropes, and kings've got it in spades.'

'Hmm.' Perilla frowned. 'Very well, Marcus. I'll concede that it's possible. The likelihood of it happening, though, is completely another matter. Why should Mithradates and Tiridates – assuming he were king of Parthia, which as I say is an impossibility in itself – bother to give Anacus preferential status at all? What do they get out of the arrangement?'

'That's where Vitellius comes in. Anacus is the catalyst, remember? Tiridates wants to be Great King. He's eligible by birth, the only thing stopping him is that he isn't Rome's choice. That's his uncle.'

'Wait a moment. Not just Rome's. The Parthian nobles who sent the delegation want Phraates too.'

'Uh-uh.' I was on stronger ground here. 'All they want at root is no Artabanus. The only reason they're asking for Phraates is they know that at the end of the day he's the guy who'll have the Syrian legions at his back when he crosses the border, because Artabanus isn't going to go peaceably. If Rome were to switch to Tiridates then the odds are they'd be happy to tag along.'

'But, Marcus, the Roman authorities don't *want* Tiridates!'

'No. But say they didn't have the option. Say Phraates died before the deal was struck.'

'Oh.' That had got through. Perilla was staring at me wide-eyed. 'You mean if his nephew had him murdered?'

'Right. Sure, he might swing the changeover nem. con., no problem – after all, he's the only other Parthian prince on offer – but it'd be far better if he had some insurance: someone on the inside to smooth the way, deflect any awkward objections, argue his case.'

'Lucius Vitellius.'

'Lucius Vitellius. We're talking diplomacy here, and these political buggers are pragmatists through and through. Vitellius knows the ropes, he knows how to handle them. The choice isn't just between Phraates and Tiridates. Rome doesn't *need* another war with Parthia; the Wart's no Crassus or Antony out for glory. If he can persuade Artabanus to pull in his claws and knuckle down without a fight then he's happy. And the death of the main claimant would give both sides the chance for a bit of behind-the-scenes dickering. Only in that case Tiridates would be back out in the cold without the likelihood of another shot at the job.'

'What about Mithradates? How does he gain?'

'Mithradates is easy. Sure, whatever happens he's got Armenia, because the Wart won't back down on that one, so that side of things isn't relevant. All the same, if Phraates becomes Great King he'll have a sharp and very powerful cookie next door to him who doesn't like him at all and certainly doesn't trust him the length of his arm. If Tiridates wins out all that's changed. They're old friends, or Tiridates thinks they are, and that Iberian bastard can run rings round him any day of the month. If you were Mithradates, who would you support? My bet is he's in the scam up to his eyeballs already.'

Perilla was looking pensive. Both of us had stopped eating. 'I'm sorry, dear,' she said, 'but I'm afraid you're beginning to make sense.'

'Uh . . . great. Great. Thanks.' Well, where praise from Perilla's concerned you take what you can get. 'It's only a theory, mind. But it explains Zariadres's death as well.'

'Does it? How?'

'If Tiridates is our villain then killing the guy is logical. Insurance again. Zariadres was the delegation leader, and he was right behind Phraates. Now the situation's changed. With Osroes in the saddle and most of the others at least not against Tiridates for Great King in theory if Phraates does die then there won't be much opposition from that quarter, either.'

She hesitated. 'There is one thing you haven't considered.'

'Yeah?'

'Vitellius. You say he's paid for his involvement with a share of the profits from Anacus's spice monopoly.'

'Uh-huh. If what Praxa told me about the volume of trade is right then Anacus can afford to be generous. Besides, like I say, he needs to have Vitellius on board in any case to hook Tiridates.'

'Two questions, then. One, how would the payments be

made, and two, do you think he has enough influence in his own right to mould imperial policy?'

'How do you mean, how would the payments be made?'

'He wouldn't be a private citizen, Marcus, he'd be governor of Syria. Syria is an imperial province, and the emperor keeps very careful tabs on his governors, especially where unaccounted-for income is concerned. Vitellius would have an imperially appointed procurator to oversee the province's finances, and the procurator would be no fool. He'd certainly be aware of Anacus's special status vis-a-vis Syria's foreign neighbours, even although he wouldn't be able to do anything about it. So if Vitellius were receiving money on a large scale from Anacus he'd be running a real danger either of being recalled or of being tried for peculation at the expiry of his governorship.'

'Uh . . .'

'Unless – and this is where the answer to my second question comes in – he had considerable imperial backing at the highest level. Someone who was close enough to the emperor to engineer the appointment of a more amenable procurator in the first instance or give a reasonable guarantee that Vitellius would not be recalled and no charges would be made subsequently. You do see what I mean?'

Sure I did. Trouble was, I couldn't fault her logic. I should've thought of that angle myself, especially since the guy was one of the royals' drinking buddies and his name had cropped up before. 'We're back to Gaius again, right?' I said.

'Yes, dear. I'm afraid we are.' Perilla's face was expressionless.

Oh, shit.

22

I'd scarcely had the stubble scraped off my cheeks the next morning and was settling down to breakfast on the terrace when Decimus Lippillus came through the portico.

'Hi, Corvinus,' he said. 'You still interested in the crowd that hit Prince Phraates's litter?'

'Yeah!' Hey! I put down my knife. 'You've found them?'

'Probably.' He pulled out the empty chair opposite – no sign of Perilla as yet – sat down and took a roll from the basket. 'You mind?'

'Help yourself. If you're really hungry we can twist Meton's arm and spring some cheese and sausage. Maybe even an omelette if he's in a good mood.'

'No, a roll and honey's fine.' He reached for the honey-pot. 'I'd've got the guys sooner but I was looking in the wrong places. They weren't docklands lads or Transtibbies after all. Like I say I could be wrong, but my money's on a bunch of Jewish villains all the way from Ostia.'

'What?'

'Odd, right? I found out by sheer luck. The Watch commander down there's a good man, name of Publius Lanuvinius. He was round at the Pond yesterday about a big break-in at one of the harbour warehouses. The owner has a statue-copying business near the Capenan Gate, and Lanuvinius dropped in at the Watch-house to say hello in passing. We got to talking, I mentioned your problem and it rang a bell. Seemingly one of his narks told him last month he'd overheard one of the gang boasting they'd just been hired for a big job on the Esquiline. Top rate, no quibbles.'

I was staring at him. 'And this Lanuvinius didn't take it any further?'

'Come on, Corvinus.' Lippillus bit equably into his roll and honey. 'You know better than that, so don't play the outraged citizen. The nark didn't have any details, and an Ostian Watch head has more than enough problems of his own without adding to them. He sent a message to Hostilius, sure – he's the Esquiline Watch boss, if you remember – but Hostilius probably ignored it like he usually does these things; at any rate, Lanuvinius hadn't heard anything back. Like I say, we're just lucky the tip-off stuck in his mind.'

'Yeah. Yeah. You're right. I'm sorry, pal.' My brain was buzzing. Ostia was weird enough – criminally speaking, it was a different world from Rome altogether – but a Jewish gang! Shit! That opened up a whole range of possibilities. There weren't any Jews in the city itself these days, at least not officially, because the Wart had thrown them all out on their ears for persistent troublemaking. Rome's port, though, was another matter.

And there were plenty of Jews in Parthia . . .

'Corvinus?'

'Hmm?'

'Wake up, okay? I was saying I've fixed things up with Lanuvinius. He's expecting a visit from you, and he'll take it from there. Can you manage that?'

'Sure. When?'

'Today, if you can. He's pretty busy.'

'*Today?*' Well, if I started out more or less straight away I'd be in Ostia by noon, and I could always bunk down at Agron's place if things took longer than expected. Still, it was a long ride and I wasn't looking forward to it. 'Great. Thanks a lot, pal.'

'Don't mention it. How's the investigation going?'

'Not bad.'

He shot me a sharp look. 'Meaning it's turned political, right? Seriously political?'

'Could be.' I wasn't going to mention Gaius Caesar; no *way* was I going to mention Gaius Caesar! Lippillus was better off without that bit of information.

He stood up grinning. 'Very informative. You'd make a good oyster. Okay, no problem, I'm not pushing, and I'd best be getting back in any case. Say hello to the lady for me.' He paused. 'One thing, Corvinus.'

'Yeah?'

'I'm serious now, so you pay attention. These Ostian gangs, they don't play around, and they don't like strangers. Especially nosy strangers. I don't know what Lanuvinius has in mind for you, but be careful, right?'

'Uh . . . yeah. Yeah, right.'

'And give the lads at the Watch-house my regards.'

'I'll do that. Thanks again, Lippillus. I owe you one.'

'Just take care.'

He waved and left.

Rome to Ostia is fourteen miles down a good, well-surfaced road: not a bad ride so long as you take it easy, unless you're a cack-handed horseman like I am, but in broad daylight the first stage, getting across the city to the Ostian Gate, is a complete bugger. The sun was well up before I cleared the gate and got properly on my way; which meant that it was after noon by the time I reached the town itself.

The Watch-house was easy to find: an old two-storey building on the Decumanus right in the centre near the theatre. I parked the horse with one of the ubiquitous entrepreneurial kids who hang around the Market Square area, went in and asked for Lanuvinius.

'You want him personal, sir?' the squaddie on the desk asked. 'Only he's out at the moment, and I know he was planning seeing about a dodgy plaster shipment over in Picus Street this afternoon.'

Bugger. Well, Lippillus had said the guy was busy, and I couldn't expect him to be sitting in an office twiddling his thumbs waiting for me. 'The name's Marcus Corvinus,' I said. 'Decimus Lippillus at Public Pond in the city sent me.'

The squaddie's face broke into a grin. 'Oh. Right. No problem, then, the boss said you might call round. He's on his break just now, at his daughter's. She's got a cloth shop on the Hinge, about two hundred yards up from Market Square on the left-hand side. If you hurry you should catch him.'

'Great. Thanks, friend.'

I went down the steps and turned back the way I'd come, up the Decumanus. The old fort guarding the harbour and the Tiber mouth may be long gone, but the name's a reminder that the layout is still there under all the modern buildings, which means that the town's centre is a lot more visitor-friendly than Rome's. The Hinge was the other main street, crossing the Decumanus at Market Square; not far, in other words, which was no doubt why Lanuvinius took his lunch at his daughter's.

I found the place; the usual small stone-counter-and-hole-in-the-wall job between a hardware merchant's and an undertaker's business. Lanuvinia – if the woman behind the counter was the guy's daughter – filled most of it easy.

'Yes, sir. How can I help you?' she said. Nice cheerful smile, though.

'Ah . . . I'm looking for someone called Lanuvinius. The Watch commander?'

The smile broadened. She had good teeth; whatever had

caused the spread, it couldn't be too many honey cakes. 'Yes, he's here,' she said. 'Just go on through.'

The shop was full of bolts of cloth that lined all three sides a couple deep, but there was a clear space behind them big enough for a bench set against the back wall. I could see the family resemblance right away. Lanuvinius was as big as his daughter with a bit to spare: not unhealthy fat, but there was enough there for two Watch commanders, easy, certainly two Lippilluses. He was sitting on the bench with an empty plate, a jug and a wine cup beside him.

Well, at least I hadn't interrupted his meal.

'Valerius Corvinus, right?' he said.

'That's me.' I held out my hand.

He wiped his own on his tunic and took it. We shook. I thought his grip would be spongy, but it wasn't, not at all. The eyes were pretty sharp, too; they'd taken in my purple stripe and Market Square haircut at a glance, and there hadn't been any hesitation over my name. Yeah, Lippillus had said the guy was good, and Lippillus was a hard judge. That was reassuring.

'Welcome to Ostia.' He shifted up the bench. 'Have a seat. Sorry it's so cramped, but I don't usually have company on my lunch break. You want to go somewhere else?'

'No, here's fine. And I'll stand, thanks. It's a long ride from the City.'

He chuckled, his three chins wobbling. 'You're not a horseman, then? That makes two of us. How's Lippillus?'

'Fine. He sends his regards.'

He reached for the jug and held it up. 'You want some of this, by the way? There's the best part of a cup left, if you don't mind the one I was using.'

'Sure. If you can spare it.'

He poured and held the cup out for me to take. 'Now. I've

got to go over to the other side of town shortly so if you don't mind we'll get straight down to things.'

'Suits me.' I took a long swallow of the wine. Not bad. And very welcome after the ride down from Rome.

'Lippillus filled me in on the background, at least as much of it as he knew.' Lanuvinius's sharp eyes twinkled. 'Which didn't, to be frank, amount to a handful of beans. Would you care to bridge a few of the gaps at all, maybe? Just to satisfy my curiosity?'

'Ah . . .'

'Meaning no.' He grunted. 'Well, he said you probably wouldn't. All the same, he's got a lot of time for you, and with Lippillus that doesn't happen often where purple-stripers are concerned, so we'll let it pass.' Oh, whoopee. 'It's a political job, right?'

'Uh . . . yeah. Yeah. At least, I think so.'

'No need to pussyfoot there, Corvinus. That makes me feel a lot better, because political jobs I'm happier not knowing about anyway. So. Isak's got himself mixed up in politics, has he?'

'Who?'

'Isak. The gang leader. Lippillus didn't mention him?'

'Uh-uh. Just that the knifemen were Jewish. He told me you'd fill in the details yourself.'

Lanuvinius grunted again. 'Fair enough. It's a family gang – they mostly are around here, and they go back generations – maybe twenty, thirty strong. Professional, naturally. Isak's the leader, elected, has been since his father died five or six years back, although he'd already been running things in practical terms for about the same again before that. He's head brother, not the eldest but the toughest and the smartest by a long chalk, which is what counts because crime's a dog-eat-dog business in Ostia and weak, stupid leaders are culled pretty smartly, usually by their own kin. On the other hand

– or maybe the two things are connected – he's straight enough in comparison with a lot of them, which is why I didn't tell Lippillus to forget it right off when he suggested you might come down here.' He paused. 'Even so I wouldn't be doing my job if I didn't warn you to drop this now. Isak may be straight for a crook and a killer, but he's a crook and a killer none the less. Having anything to do with him and his friends when you don't need to is a bad, bad idea. You understand me?'

'Yeah,' I said. 'I understand. Lippillus said the same.'

'Fine. Just so's you don't come whining to me if you end up in an alley with a knife between your ribs. And put just one foot wrong and that's a definite possibility.'

Cheery bugger, this; all the same, if he said it was dangerous then I'd be a fool to think otherwise, and Lippillus's unsolicited warning put the cap on it. I was glad Perilla hadn't been up and around when he'd called that morning; in her present jumpy mood the lady would've had kittens. 'So,' I said. 'How do I get to talk to him?'

'You're sure you want to? Hundred-per-cent, cast-iron sure?'

'Yeah.'

'Fine.' He shifted on the bench. 'Only you play it exactly as I tell you, right? Your best bet's a wineshop near the old boatyard, name of Mamma Scylla's. I can't guarantee he'll be there, mind, or if he is that he'll talk to you, but that's your worry. Mention my name. Like I say, Isak's on the other side of the fence but we know each other and the respect goes both ways. Not that that'll help if he decides he doesn't like you or if you choose to play silly buggers, but it'll at least give you a fair chance of a hearing. Got me?'

'Got you.'

'One other thing. Suggest – just suggest – that this is even slightly official and you may as well slit your own throat and save Isak's boys the trouble of doing it for you, because they won't think even once about it let alone twice. Right?'

'Right.' Jupiter in a bucket, I must be crazy!

'Good.' He levered his huge bulk off the bench. 'Now. I have to be getting on. You know where the old boatyard is? Down near the harbour to the left at the end of a line of granaries.'

'I'll find it.'

'You'll see the slipway clear enough, two or three hundred yards along the front. Head for that. If you get lost, which you won't, ask for the boatyard rather than Mamma Scylla's. Questions in that direction tend not to be too well received, especially if the person asking them's a Roman purple-striper. Best of all, just don't ask anyone anything, find it yourself. Mamma Scylla's is the lean-to next the horse trough, fifty yards or so on the far side.' He held out his hand. 'It was nice meeting you. I hope I have the pleasure again in future.'

Shit; maybe I should just nip in to the undertaker's next door and make my arrangements now. Well, I was committed, but I didn't like the sound of this at all.

'Same here, pal,' I said.

We shook. 'Tell Lippillus I was asking for him.'

I could see, once I left the comparatively up-market area of the harbour, what Lanuvinius had meant about not asking help from the locals: if this'd been the city, the average specimen would've been definitely of the corn-dole variety, with signs of even lower social predilections like a bored-through ear or a brand across the cheek. Covering the last stretch between the harbour and the old boatyard was no joke; I could feel eyes on me all the way, and the hairs on the back of my neck were so stiff I could hear them rasp against the edge of my cloak. I had a knife, sure, tucked away at the side of my tunic belt, but I wasn't fool enough to think it gave all that much of an edge. If for reasons of their own the buggers who were eyeing me wanted me dead, then I was dead, no argument. There were at least fifty of them to every one of me, for a start.

Lanuvinius's directions had been spot-on: I saw the wineshop just where he said it would be, beyond the old slipway – abandoned now; they don't build ships of any size at Ostia any more, at least this close to the Tiber mouth – and next to a crudely made stone horse trough.

There was no point in faffing around. I took a deep breath, pushed the door open and went in.

Crowded though it was, when I crossed the threshold you could've heard a mouse fart. There were maybe a dozen punters sitting at the tables and propped against the bar. That made two dozen eyes that were zeroed in on me and the purple stripe on my tunic. Or maybe a few less, because a fair sprinkling of the punters weren't fully equipped in the optical department.

That included the barwoman. At least, I assumed she was a woman, from the length of her hair and what she was wearing. Mamma Scylla was right. Given the choice between passing within her grabbing range or Charybdis's I'd've had to think carefully myself. And even with two eyes she'd be no beauty; not if you didn't like your women built on the scale of arena chasers with a serious attitude problem.

'What do you want, son?' she said. There were a few snickers, but most of the punters just carried on staring, which was worse.

'Uh . . . a cup of wine'd be perfect,' I said. There was no board in evidence, and now wasn't the time to quibble over details. I didn't think ordering half a jug would be good policy, either. No point being extravagant when you're not absolutely certain you'll have the time to finish the stuff. Or the throat to pour it down.

Still looking at me, she reached for the jug on the counter and poured into an empty cup.

'That'll be two coppers.'

Well, I couldn't complain about her prices. I walked over to the bar like I was walking on eggshells, reaching into my pouch as I went and finding the coins by touch. The snickers died down. Now there was only silence. She took the coppers and put them into a bag at her belt. Fighting the urge not to look left or right, or behind me for preference, I took a sip. The wine wasn't bad; not bad at all. Not Alban, sure, but a long way from Gallic rotgut. 'Ah . . . I'm looking for a guy named Isak,' I said. 'He here at all?'

If I'd thought the place was quiet before, I had the impression now that my ears had seized up altogether. Forget the mouse; you could've heard a farting gnat. The hairs on my neck and scalp went into overdrive.

'He might be,' said a man to my left.

I turned slowly, cup raised. The guy was at least six-three, built like the business end of a trireme, and smiling was something he wasn't doing. I had the impression of oil, teeth, black tight-curled hair, olive skin and hard, hard muscle. Also, that the punters in the immediate vicinity had drawn back like they might when a cat at the Games had the bolt slipped on its cage.

'You're Isak?' I said.

He didn't blink. I noticed that his hands, both resting on the counter, were the size of plates. The backs weren't so much covered with hair as fur. 'That's me. What's your name and who sent you?'

'Marcus Corvinus. The Watch commander. Publius Lanuvinius.'

Pause. 'You a friend of his?'

'He told me to use his name. We're not in the same business, if that's what you mean.'

'So what is your business?'

'I need to talk to you. Just that.'

'You're talking. How long it'll last is another matter.' Someone on my other side sniggered. I didn't turn round, but he glanced over my shoulder and the guy clammed up. The silence lengthened. 'Talk about what?'

This was the tricky part. Even so, a lie wouldn't get me anywhere. 'Word is, you and your family hit a litter party some time back in the city. On the Esquiline,' I said. Somewhere behind me, a cup was set down and a throat was cleared. Isak's eyes didn't shift. 'I've got a . . . call it an interest in that. Not an official one. I told you, I'm not in that line. I just have a few questions that only you can answer. Private questions.'

'Private questions.' The eyes still hadn't left my face. 'You say Lanuvinius sent you? So he knows what these "private questions" are?'

'No. I didn't tell him. They're my business, no one else's.' I sipped the wine and tried to make it look casual. 'Just like the answers would be.'

He didn't move, but the hardness of the stare relaxed. Suddenly, he laughed, showing a set of perfect teeth like marble tombstones. 'Well, Roman,' he said, 'you've got balls anyway. And Lanuvinius is okay for a Watchman. Maybe I let you talk a little longer. As for answering questions, we'll see what they are first.' He turned to the barwoman. 'Pour us the rest of the jug and bring it over.' The eyes came back to me. 'All right, Corvinus. Let's talk. In private.'

He picked up his own wine cup and led the way to a table in the far corner. It was already occupied, and although he didn't say anything the two men sitting at it got up like someone had pulled their strings and moved quickly over to the bar. The table next to them emptied like magic too. Isak sat down and motioned to the chair opposite.

'Well?' he said when we were both facing each other.

'The guy in the litter was a Parthian prince,' I said. 'Name of Phraates.' He grunted, but his stare didn't waver. 'You knew that?'

'No. The contract was just to hit the litter party.' His tone was matter-of-fact. I glanced round; not an eye was pointed in our direction. If Isak wanted a private conversation then private it was. He hadn't even bothered to lower his voice. Evidently it was up to the other guys not to listen in. I had the distinct impression listening in uninvited would not be a wise move. 'We were told when and where, and what was the target. No names. But I've heard of Phraates.'

'Can I ask who told you?'

'A man. Just a man.'

'Roman or foreign?' That might make a difference. Sure, it was unlikely that the principal would've arranged the deal in person, but although a 'Roman' contractor – including the non-Romans Tiridates and Mithridates who were long-term residents of the city – would've had access to both types of middleman, anyone from the delegation would be forced to use one of their own people. If the rep was a complete foreigner it would point the finger at one of the embassy for sure. Not that there was any doubt in my mind that a Parthian was responsible, whether he belonged to the embassy or not: let alone the *cui bono* aspect, Parthians, even Roman-bred ones, get on better with Jews than we do. No Roman would hire a Jewish gang out of choice. There'd be too much ingrained national prejudice on both sides and too many hackles raised for either party to trust the other fully. We stick to our own villains.

Isak was studying me carefully. 'He had money to pay for the job up front and a bonus on top if we did it well. That was enough. Roman, foreign, it makes no difference to me.'

'So you don't know his name?'

'No.' The woman arrived with the jug, set it down beside him and moved off quickly. Isak poured for both of us, studiously correct. 'Names I'm not interested in. If that's what you wanted then you're wasting your time. And me, if I'm you I don't push, okay, because if I do happen to know somehow I don't tell you and that sort of question annoys me.' He sipped his wine. 'Just a friendly warning.'

Shit. Warning it certainly was; friendly I wouldn't've betted on, not given the guy's tone. Well, I couldn't've expected much else. And like I say the contractor wouldn't've worked *propria persona* in any case, so the chances of Isak fingering Tiridates or whoever by name were on the scale of flying pigs. 'He told you what the litter party would look like, and where exactly to set up the, uh, meeting?' I said.

'That's right.'

'How far in advance?'

'A day. Two days. Yes, it was two days.'

Pretty good notice. I didn't know how long the dinner party Phraates had been coming back from had been arranged, but that didn't matter all that much. Naming the particular evening would've been relatively easy; getting the time and place right exactly was something else again. Phraates could've left early, or even – if it was a good party – stayed the night: any friend of his wouldn't be stuck for a spare bed if he'd decided to sleep over. And possible routes between the Esquiline and the Agrippan Bridge might not be all that many, but there was definitely more than one. Put all that together and whoever had set the thing up must've had access to pretty reliable information; maybe even – if that was possible – someone in the prince's own household who knew his habits and who could engineer the route in advance. I'd have to have another word with Phraates himself, check if anyone fitted the bill. Besides his son, I mean: it was looking pretty good for the Damon theory here. 'So,' I said. 'You were contracted to hit Prince Phraates's litter near Maecenas Gardens and the attack went wrong—'

I stopped. Isak had sat back, and he was scowling at me. Behind my back I could hear a rustle as the incurious punters picked up on the changed vibes and decided it might be play-time after all. My stomach froze.

Shit; what had I said?

Isak's eyes were locked on mine, and they weren't friendly any more. Not friendly at all. 'We're the best in Ostia, my brothers and me,' he said quietly. 'In Rome, too. Anything we're paid to do, it doesn't go wrong. You have that? You understand, maybe?'

His Latin was slipping; his accent, too. Oh, bugger; I'd touched his professional vanity. Why the hell couldn't I just've kept my big mouth shut? 'Ah . . . I just thought . . . since the attack was beaten off and the prince survived . . . '

'If we contract to kill then we kill. Whoever the target, however many bodyguards.' The eyes were boring holes in my skull. 'If the client wants a death and pays for it then there's a death.'

'Uh . . . right. Right. No problem, pal. I was just . . .' I stopped as the implication of what he was saying sank in. 'Wait a minute. Wait one minute. You're telling me the client *didn't* want Phraates killed?'

'We were told attack the litter party. If one or two of them die then that's okay, no problem, but we don't threaten the litter itself. On that the client is very, very clear. That is the contract. You understand me? I think, Corvinus, that maybe you had better.'

Oh, fuck; I didn't believe this. It turned the whole case on its head. 'You were paid to have a quick scrap with Phraates's bodyguards then give up the fight and run?'

There was a low growl from behind me. Isak's stare didn't waver, but the scowl deepened. 'If I'm you, Roman purple-striper,' he said slowly, staring over my shoulder, 'then I watch my language better, maybe. I don't use bad words like "run". I already told you. The contract was attack the litter party, spill a little blood then leave. If anyone's hurt on our side there's blood money paid, generous blood money, but however things go we don't harm the old man. We keep our part of the bargain, always. We fulfil the contract to the letter; that's why we're the best. We fulfil it this time. To the letter. Now I think perhaps you should walk while you still can move. I don't think my friends want you here longer. Me, I'd agree with them.'

I stood up. 'Uh . . . right. Fine. Thanks for the chat.'

'Don't mention it.' The eyes were like nails. 'Give my regards to Lanuvinius. Tell him he owes me.'

I walked to the door through a silence that had razors in it. One of the punters at a nearby table got up, opened it for me and then stood aside. I went out into the fresh air and the door was slammed behind me.

Shit; that had been a close one.

I made my way back to the Watch-house, but Lanuvinius wasn't there so I left a message and my thanks, collected my horse from Market Square and began the long trip home. Not that, this time, I grudged the ride; I needed space to think.

What the fuck was going on?

23

I didn't stay over at Agron's after all, so it was late when I got back, well after sunset. Even so, I wasn't the least bit tired; in fact, what with all the thinking I'd been doing over the fourteen miles when I turned into our side street off Head of Africa my brain was on overdrive. There could be just the one explanation for the terms of Isak's contract, and for that to make any sense at all I reckoned you had to be a Parthian.

I wasn't tired; I was just angry as hell.

I took the mare round to the stables and handed her over to a yawning Lysias to rub down and put away. Then I went inside. Bathyllus was waiting for me in the lobby, as I'd known he would be, with the jug and wine cup.

'That's okay, little guy,' I said. 'Off you go to bed.' I took a long swallow to clear the taste of the Ostian road from my throat. 'The baths hot?'

'Yes, sir. But—'

'Fine. Don't bother to wake the bath slaves, I can manage to scrape myself for one evening. Oh, before you pack in see what you can scrounge for me from the kitchen. Nothing major, but if Meton's left anything cold that'd be—'

'Sir, I'm sorry, but would you listen, please?'

I blinked. You might get the occasional sniff or sarky comment from Bathyllus, but the guy's a professional to his fingertips, and real major-domos don't interrupt the master. Especially in that tone.

'Yeah?' I said. 'What is it?'

'The mistress, sir. She's waiting for you in the atrium.'

It wasn't so much the words, or the news that Perilla was still up and around, that warned me as the look on his face. I shoved the cup back at him so hard the wine spilled down his tunic and made a rush for the door.

Perilla was sitting in her usual chair by the pool, a book-roll in her lap. She looked up as I came in. One glance at her face was enough: my guts went cold.

'What's happened?' I said.

'I'm quite all right, Marcus.' She set the roll down on the table beside her. 'No damage done, none at all. In fact, they were really quite polite.'

'What the fuck has happened?'

'Don't swear, dear, it doesn't help. And sit down, please. I can't talk to you like this.'

Bathyllus had padded in with the refilled wine cup. I took it without a word and lay down on my usual couch. The cold feeling in my gut intensified.

'That's better,' Perilla said calmly. 'Now. I've been asked to ask you to drop the case. All right?'

'Jupiter, lady, will you just—'

'There. That bit's done. Now the circumstances.' She adjusted a fold of her mantle. Her voice was matter-of-fact enough, but I could see her fingers were trembling. 'I took the litter to the Pollio Library this afternoon. I'd left it at the foot of the steps and was going through the portico when two men stopped me and said – very politely – that they wanted a quick word concerning a very important matter. There didn't—'

'What kind of men?'

She sniffed. 'Marcus, dear, if you're going to interrupt with questions we'll never get finished. Now just let me speak, will you?' I subsided. 'They were decently dressed and, as I say, politely spoken, so there didn't seem any reason to refuse. I sent my maid on ahead and asked them what they wanted; to which they replied with the message I've just given you.'

Holy gods! 'They say who sent them?'

'No. I asked, of course, but they simply ignored the question and repeated the message. That, more or less, was all that happened. They left me standing and walked away.'

I knew obfuscation when I met it, and the lady was a born obfusticator. '"More or less" meaning what?'

'Just what it says, dear.' Perilla looked down at her hands. I looked at them too. The fingers were locked tightly together. 'I was . . . quite upset at the time, and I honestly can't recall any other details. They were, however, most insistent.'

'They threatened you?'

'Not as such, no, but . . .'

That 'but' was enough. I got to my feet, setting the wine cup down. 'Bathyllus!' I snapped. 'Study! Now!'

He was at my heels all the way. I opened the door, lifted the lid of the chest in the corner and took out the long cavalry sword I keep in there under wraps. Bathyllus's eyes widened.

'Sir, I don't think—' he began.

'Shut up.' I checked the edge with my thumb. 'Two things. One, I need an address for that fucking Iberian Mithradates. And don't tell me you don't know where he lives, sunshine, because a) you know where to find anyone who's anyone in Rome and b) even if you didn't originally you keep a watching brief on the master's concerns and you would've made a point of finding it out anyway just in case. Right? So give.'

Bathyllus swallowed. 'Ah . . . on the Esquiline, sir, near the southern entrance to the Lamian Gardens. The house with the blue-painted iron gates.'

'Fine. Got you. Second, tell Lysias I need a horse saddled. Not the mare, she's done her whack for today, but anything that'll move faster than a walk. Considerably faster, for preference.'

'Yes, sir.' He dithered. 'Sir, I really wouldn't advise—'

'Great. Taken on board. Now just do it, Bathyllus, okay?'

'Yes, sir. Very well.' He left.

Perilla was waiting for me outside the door. 'Marcus—' she began.

'Don't say it, lady. Don't even think about saying it.' I was still wearing my travelling cloak. The sword didn't have a scabbard, but I stuck it through my tunic belt and arranged the cloak to hide it: for a private citizen, carrying a sword is strictly illegal in Rome, and if I fell foul of the Watch purple stripe or not I was in serious trouble. They wouldn't have a hope in hell of catching me, mind, but that was by the way.

'You're going to Mithradates's, aren't you?' Perilla said.

'Yes. And if the bugger isn't behind this I'll eat my fucking sandals, so don't try to stop me.'

'I wasn't going to, dear.'

I'd been on the point of heading past her for the door. I paused. 'What?'

'If you're convinced he sent the men then you're absolutely correct.' The lady was speaking quietly, but there was steel in her voice. 'I don't like being intimidated either.'

Hey! I grinned and kissed her. When the chips are down, Perilla's no fragile pushover herself. 'Good,' I said. 'That makes things much easier.'

'Just leave the sword behind.'

'Now look, lady—'

'No. You look. If you take it you may have to use it, and under the circumstances the consequences don't bear thinking about.' She held out her hand.

'But—'

'Marcus! Please!'

Shit. In my present mood three feet of sharpened iron was not something I wanted to give up. All the same, I could see that she was right. Killing Mithradates, or even just seriously wounding him, could get me exile at the very least. And on my side I couldn't prove a thing. I pulled the sword back out and handed it over.

'Thank you,' she said; just that. Then she reached up and kissed me. 'Off you go. Good luck.'

I left her and headed for the stables.

I found the place no bother: a swanky property halfway to a full-fledged urban villa. There were plenty of lights, including torches along the outside wall itself and three or four litters with their attendants squatting in a pool of torch-light nearby killing time with a dice match. They glanced at me with the slaves' usual lack of interest as I dismounted, fastened the horse's reins to the hitching-ring and banged on the door with the flat of my hand.

Eventually, the doorman opened up.

'Take me to the master,' I said.

The guy was about to object, but then he must've seen the expression on my face and decided very wisely that that was not a good idea because he turned without a word. I followed him through the fancy lobby and the atrium, then along a corridor to the dining-room.

Dinner was over and they'd got to the drinking stage. Mithradates was reclining on the central couch in a snazzy party mantle and wreath, and there must've been six or seven other guys, but I wasn't in any mood to count and I didn't recognise any of them anyway.

The room went very quiet.

'Valerius Corvinus,' Mithradates said. 'Now this is an unexpected pleasure.'

I levelled a finger. 'I want to talk to you, you bastard!'

'Really?' He set his cup down. The click it made on the table was the only sound in the room. 'About what?'

'I warned you. My wife's off-limits. This thing's between you and me, no one else.'

Somebody to my left sniggered. I ignored him. So did Mithradates.

'I've never even met Rufia Perilla,' he said softly.

'Fuck that. You know what I mean. You had a couple of your pals hassle her today outside the Pollio Library.'

His eyes hadn't left my face. Seconds passed. Then he slid from the couch and stood up. 'We'll discuss this in private,' he said.

'Suits me, pal!'

'Excuse me, gentlemen. My apologies. This shouldn't take long.' He crossed the room, pushing past my shoulder, making for the door. I followed him out. Behind us I could hear the silence break.

The slave who'd brought me in was still standing goggle-eyed. Mithradates snapped his fingers at him and pointed to a twelve-lamp candelabrum in one of the side alcoves. The guy picked it up and the three of us walked back along the corridor. Mithradates opened a door on the left.

'In here, Corvinus,' he said. Then, to the slave: 'Leave the lights and go.'

It was a study, with the usual desk, reading couch and book cubbies. Surprisingly – I hadn't set Mithradates down as much of a reader – most of them were full. He waited for the slave to close the door behind us.

'Now,' he said. 'What is this shit?'

'I told you. You had two of your men hassle my wife outside the Pollio Library this afternoon.'

'I did nothing of the kind.' He was speaking very quietly. 'And, Corvinus, if you ever dare to call me a bastard in public again I'll make it my personal business to see that you regret it. That's a promise. Now get out of my house.' He walked back past me and opened the door again.

I didn't move. 'You're lying,' I said. 'Perilla told me the guys warned her I should drop the case. You've made that suggestion to me direct twice already, once with the help of a pack of Suburan boot-boys. As far as I'm concerned you're it, pal, nem. con. And "bastard" describes you perfectly.'

'Out!'

'First tell me about the pepper scam.'

He went very still. Then, slowly, he reached over and pushed the door to.

'What pepper scam?' he said softly.

'The one you've got going with the Armenian merchant. Anacus. Plus your mates Tiridates and Damon, with Lucius Vitellius thrown in for good measure on the Roman side.' *And Prince Gaius,* I added silently, but angry or not I wasn't going to bring that name into the conversation. No way. 'The kickbacks from a monopoly – even a partial monopoly – of the empire's supplies of pepper would be pretty substantial, wouldn't they? Worth a couple of deaths and a bit of political skulduggery, certainly worth the trouble of leaning on a no-account purple-striper in the hope he'll pull his nose out before it leads him too far for your own good. Only I'm one thing, friend, my wife's another. If you want to stop me then, believe me, leaning on her is a bad, bad idea.'

He was watching me closely like I was some sort of performing insect. Finally, he shook his head and half smiled.

'Corvinus,' he said, 'you're being incredibly silly. Not stupid, because you're far from that, just silly.'

'You deny it?'

'I don't admit or deny anything except that I'd nothing to do with hassling your wife today. Why should I bother? You don't matter, your opinions don't matter, and I'm not accountable to you or to anyone.' He took a step closer and

I could smell the wine on his breath. 'I'll tell you again, *friend*, and you just remember it. You're well out of your depth and none of this affair is any business of yours. If you choose to carry on digging then Isidorus or not, Phraates or not, fucking Tiberius or not, don't be surprised if you end up in the hole yourself and someone fills it in on top of you.' Carefully, he stepped round me and put his hand on the doorknob. 'Now. That's all I've got to say. You can leave peacefully or I can have my slaves throw you out. The choice is up to you.'

I shrugged; I'd be a fool not to admit, if only to myself, that what he'd said – and more especially how he'd said it – had planted a hook in my guts, but I couldn't let him see that. Perilla was right: intimidation was something that you just didn't accept. 'Fine,' I said, matching his quiet tone. 'So long as you don't forget that if any harm comes to Perilla, directly or indirectly, then friends in high places or not, consequences or not then one way or another, pal, I'll see you dead. Understand?'

'Oh yes. I understand.' He moved aside. 'Now leave while you still can.'

Brain buzzing, I walked back up the corridor, through the atrium and lobby and past the gaping slave who opened the door and stepped back from it like he was making way for the ghosts at the end of the Lemuria. Then I untied my horse and rode home.

I was knackered when I finally got in, a combination of physical and mental tiredness that had left me feeling like a wrung-out dishcloth. Which was a pity, because presently knackered or not I still wanted to be knocking on Prince Phraates's door first thing the next morning. That old fraud had questions to answer too, and the sooner I put them to him the better.

Perilla was still in the atrium, and the book-roll in her lap hadn't moved on any that I could see. She got up, spilling it to the floor, ran over and hugged me.

'Marcus, are you all right?'

'Yeah, sure, no problem.' I winced: the bruises to my ribs that I'd got in my first brush with Mithradates weren't up to one of Perilla's serious hugs yet. 'Uh . . . you like to slacken off a little, lady?'

She did. Then she reached up and kissed me. 'So,' she said. 'What happened?'

'He denied it.' I lay down on the couch and closed my eyes. Bliss. 'You were right about the sword, though. When I walked into that dining-room and got face to face I'd've used it on him there and then, which would've been a mistake. As things were we had quite a cosy chat.'

'You believed him?'

I opened my eyes again. Perilla had sat back down in her chair, and she was staring at me, which was fair enough considering. 'Yeah,' I said. 'Yeah, I believed him. On that count, anyway. I think if he had been responsible for your two library pals he would've said so. Enjoyed saying so, just for the fun of pushing me over the edge and seeing what happened.' I remembered that look he'd given me when I'd faced him with the details of the pepper scam, like I was some sort of tap-dancing cockroach. 'I doubt if that bastard would bother lying to anyone unless it suited him. Or maybe just amused him. Other people simply don't matter enough.'

'So who did send the men?'

'Fuck knows for certain, but your best bet's Prince Phraates.'

'*What?*' The shock in her voice was real. 'Why on earth should he do something like that?'

I told her. She was quiet for a long time. Then she said, 'You're sure?'

'Sure I'm sure.' I yawned and stretched. 'From what Isak said, it's the only explanation. And it fits the devious old bugger to a tee.'

'But—'

'Look, I'm sorry, Perilla, but can we leave this?' Giving in to that yawn had been a mistake; it was threatening to become a second, and my eyelids had suddenly come out in sympathy and decided they weren't going to stay open any longer. 'I'm whacked. If I'm going over to the Janiculan first thing I have to pack in now.'

'First thing? That's not necessary, surely? In any case, if Phraates isn't expecting you an early morning visit is terribly rude.'

I stood up; the second yawn made my jaw crack. 'That's why I'm doing it, lady. And as far as rudeness is concerned the way I feel about him currently, being hauled out of bed is the least he can expect. Plus if he was the one to hassle you then he'll be lucky if I don't do it personally with a rusty grapnel.'

Perilla grinned and ducked her head. 'Very well, Marcus. But don't be too hard on him, will you? I'm sure if he was responsible for sending those two men they exceeded their instructions.'

Right. Well, maybe, but obviously the lady still had a soft spot for the old bugger. Even so, I wasn't going to give him the benefit of the doubt. No way.

Phraates had it coming. Tired or not, tomorrow morning I intended to hand the lying bastard his head.

24

Actually, when I woke up I didn't feel too bad. Unlike Perilla, I can get by on three or four hours of sleep, in the short term, anyway, and besides the sun was streaming through the bedroom window. I slipped out of bed without waking the lady – after our late night she wouldn't be surfacing for hours yet – and went downstairs. A shave could wait, but Bathyllus was padding around so I sent him for a bread roll that I could eat on the way and set out for the Janiculan.

It was a long walk, but it stretched my stiffened riding muscles nicely. By the time I got there it was still a good hour before even the most unconventional visitor would dream of banging the knocker. Not that that worried me all that much. Like I'd said to Perilla, if I got the bastard off his mattress before his usual time then that was just tough.

'Marcus Valerius Corvinus,' I said to the door-slave when he opened up. 'I've come to see the master.'

The guy balked a bit, sure, but he let me in anyway and shot off like a greased ferret to consult higher authority. I twiddled my thumbs in the very fancy porch – murals of Leda and the Swan and the Rape of Ganymede plus a pricey-looking still-life floor mosaic – until Phraates's major-domo appeared. He gave my unshaven face a pointed stare but he didn't comment as he led me through the villa and showed me into a pleasant morning-room looking out on the grounds. Peacocks strutted on the carefully manicured lawn outside the windows, and a couple of supercilious ostriches peered over the top of the ornamental box hedge. There was a small water-clock in one corner of the room. I twiddled my thumbs again and tried to ignore the drip.

Phraates strolled in about half an hour later, wearing a dressing-gown that wouldn't've disgraced a cathouse madam.

'Corvinus,' he said, 'I'm delighted to see you at any time, of course, but don't you think—'

'You set up the attack on your own litter,' I said.

If I'd thought he'd be thrown, he wasn't. All I got was a long look and a pair of delicate raised eyebrows.

'Did I, indeed?' he said. 'Well, well.'

Jupiter on bloody skates, the bugger couldn't even manage a straight denial, even if it was a lie! Par for the course. I felt my temper slip and let it go.

'Look, pal,' I said. 'I've been breaking my fucking neck trying to make a connection between Zariadres's murder and what happened at the Esquiline Gate, and that was you all the time. You never were in any danger, or not from that direction, anyway. You took out a contract on yourself and you made sure the knifemen you hired wouldn't touch a hair of your fucking head. I ought to—'

'What you ought to do, young man,' Phraates interrupted sharply, 'is to calm down and stop swearing.' He pulled up an ivory chair that could've belonged to one of the pharaohs. 'It's too early in the morning for that sort of thing. Hermogenes' – the major-domo was hovering goggle-eyed – 'bring us some breakfast, please. In here on a tray will do. Have you eaten, Corvinus?'

'Forget breakfast. All I want is for you to—'

'Nothing elaborate, Hermogenes. But make it quick.' The major-domo bowed himself out. Phraates turned back to me. 'Now. Calmly, please. Why should you think I organised the attack on my own litter and caused the death of four my own bodyguard? I'm fascinated, really.'

'Because you knew Tiridates was trying to kill you. You wanted an excuse to tighten security, but – and Jupiter help us here – you didn't want to offend the guy by citing him as the reason.'

'Indeed?' Phraates's expression unfroze and he chuckled. 'You know, Corvinus, I think I may have said this before, but you'd make quite a good Parthian.'

'Am I right or not?'

'Of course you're right. There's no point in my denying it.'

'Then why the hell not tell me in the first place? Or if not me then Isidorus? That attack on your litter was the reason I was drafted in to begin with.'

'Oh, I'm sure Isidorus knows already by this time, if he didn't before. He does have a very efficient spy system, after all, and he's no fool.' I opened my mouth. 'And nor are you, Corvinus. I'm impressed. Really. How did you find out?'

'I talked to the boss of the gang who did it.'

'Isak? Well, well. I used a very secure intermediary, one of my Syrian freedmen. I didn't know that Isak was aware who his ultimate employer was.'

'He wasn't. Or if he was he didn't care. I just read between the lines.'

'Then I am impressed. Not least that you managed to track the man down and persuade him to talk to you, then come away with a whole skin. How did you do that, by the way?'

It might just be simple curiosity but I wasn't going to risk Lippillus and his Ostian pal getting into trouble, so I ignored the question. Instead, I said, 'Isak and his gang killed four of your bodyguard.'

'Yes.' I'd've liked to believe that the change to a more sombre expression and tone were genuine, but I wouldn't've made any bets. Phraates could give a crying crocodile a run for its money. 'Don't think I don't know what you're saying there, Corvinus, but that was necessary. To be convincing. And the threat from Tiridates was very real. Another two or three days and if I'd allowed things to take their course he might have had me.' He smiled. 'Not that I feel any ill-will towards him, mind, even now, any more than I'm sure he does for me, on a personal level. It's in the blood.'

Yeah, right; that I *would* believe. 'I don't suppose you killed Zariadres as well while you were about it, did you? Or had him killed?'

'Good gods, no! Why on earth would I do that?'

'Search me, pal. Not that a denial matters because I reckon you can lie as easy as breathe. Maybe he was Artabanus's sister in a false beard.' My anger was draining away; you couldn't stay angry with Phraates for long. He might be a devious, conniving, three-faced twister but – witness his effect on Perilla – the guy had a natural charm. 'Okay. So how did it work? Just for my personal records, you understand?'

Phraates yawned again and covered his mouth with a polite hand. 'I'm sorry. Do forgive me. I told you: I knew from my own sources – which, I may say, are quite as thorough and reliable as Isidorus's – that my nephew was planning to have me assassinated before any campaign against Artabanus could be mounted. The result, naturally, would have been that he, as Rome's other available candidate, would take my place. That I couldn't have: Tiridates would be a disaster as Great King, and besides I have a rooted antipathy to dying before my time. So I had one of my less law-abiding freedmen – his name doesn't matter – find me a suitably reliable street gang and arrange a false attack. Suitably reliable, because I had no desire either to do my nephew's work for him. Consequently, as you say, I was able to upgrade my everyday security arrangements without insulting Tiridates by publicly recognising that he was trying to kill me. In the process, of course, I obliged my Roman hosts to take protective steps of their own, the most significant of which was to enrol you on the strength. That, I'm afraid, was unavoidable. For what it's worth, you have my sincere apologies.'

'So you let me target Tiridates for the attack, knowing full well that bastard or not he had nothing to do with it?'

Phraates gave a short, barking laugh. 'Oh, Corvinus, do be reasonable! And do give yourself just a little credit! You were – *are* – completely correct. Tiridates wants me dead, he wants to become Great King of Parthia, and he is actively labouring to that end. The only difference the business with Isak makes is that I am still alive and moreover have since been in the happy position of knowing that an extremely intelligent and capable young man was working to keep me so. Personally I can't see a problem here, and nor should you.'

'So how does Zariadres's murder fit in?'

He spread his hands. 'I honestly have no idea.'

'You know Zariadres's father, or his uncle maybe, was responsible for the deaths of Peucestas's family and his own castration?'

Phraates chuckled. 'Oh, my, you have been busy! How did you find that out?' I didn't answer. 'Well, yes, I did know, as a matter of fact, and it was his uncle. A very unpleasant man, by all reports. However, if you're thinking that Peucestas killed Zariadres I'd say you were making a mistake. Peucestas – at least as I read him – isn't a vengeful person. If he'd had the opportunity to kill the elder Zariadres then I'm quite sure he would have done it. However, a nephew is something else again. Peucestas may not have liked Zariadres – I don't believe he did, very much – but I doubt he'd've killed him just because of who he was.'

'None the less, the last time we talked and I suggested one of the embassy was responsible for Zariadres's death you never mentioned the connection.'

'True.'

Gods! Not so much as a blink, let alone an apology. I'd met brass necks in my time, but Phraates beat them all hands down. 'So now I'm just wondering if there're maybe a few other potentially helpful nuggets of insider info that you're keeping quiet about.'

I'd been watching him carefully for a reaction, but just at that moment the door opened and the major-domo came in with a loaded tray. Perfect diversionary timing. Shit.

Phraates had turned towards the opening door. 'That's fine, Hermogenes,' he said. 'Put it down on the table and go, please. We'll help ourselves.' The major-domo bowed and left. 'Being interrogated does give one an appetite, doesn't it, Corvinus? And if you've come all the way from the Caelian on an empty stomach you'll be starved. My, don't these rolls smell good? I must try to get up earlier more often.'

The hell with this. 'Would you like me to repeat the question, pal?' I said. 'Or would you care to give me a direct answer first time for a change?'

Instead of replying Phraates got up from his chair. He took two plates from the tray and laid them carefully either side of the table between the dining couches. Then he selected two of the rolls and put one on each plate. Finally, he eased himself on to one of the dining couches.

'What I'd *like*, young man,' he said quietly, 'is for you to join me for breakfast.'

Yeah, well if he wouldn't be pushed he wouldn't, and there wasn't any point in annoying him to no purpose. I rose from my own chair and joined him at the table. 'Nothing elaborate' in the Phraates household obviously didn't mean what it did elsewhere, and either the guy had a vast kitchen staff poised just waiting for instructions or the tray's contents had been sitting ready for the master's summons. I suspected the former. Whatever the reason, it was quite a spread: cheese, cold meat, a honeycomb, small bowls of olives and what looked like curds. A Syrian glass jug of milk, and another of fruit juice. Some of the sliced and candied fruits I didn't even recognise. The gods knew where he'd got the fresh ones, this time of year. I broke the roll and scooped up some of the honey that was leaking from the comb.

Phraates was pouring himself a cup of fruit juice. 'Don't be too hard on me, Corvinus,' he said, his eyes on the cup. 'I appreciate your feelings, but I have to work with these people in ways they comprehend. Which, I hasten to add, is not to say I find it difficult or unpleasant. Although I've lived in Rome for most of my very long life I am not Roman. You must understand this. Parthians – and I am a Parthian, completely, where it matters – thrive on secrecy. We like to find out things about other people, especially if the knowledge affects us and they don't wish us to know, but we do not easily pass the information on to a third party. And we don't appreciate it if others do so without our permission.' He reached for the curds and added a spoonful of honey. 'After all, we can't control the third party's use of it. The answer to your question is yes, I do have information that you don't. Of course I have; I told you, my sources are very, very efficient. On the other hand, you are a very intelligent and persistent young man with prejudices of your own. There is a massive difference between telling you something which since it comes from me I suspect you might not believe and letting you find it out for yourself, in which case you will. Trust me: in the long run, although there may be certain problems involved, my way is by far the best.' He smiled. 'Now. Eat your breakfast, please. If it's any consolation, I haven't told you any lies, or no serious ones, anyway. Nor will I. That I *can* promise you.'

I left the honeyed roll where it lay, 'So you didn't send a

couple of tame stooges to hassle Perilla outside the Pollio Library yesterday?'

He'd been lifting a spoonful of curds to his mouth. He set it down sharply. 'No. Of course not. Why should I?'

'To get me off the case before I found out about your litter scam. I thought it was Mithradates, but when I talked to him I changed my mind.'

'You already knew about the litter.'

'Sure. But then you couldn't've known that, could you?'

Phraates's eyes held mine. 'Corvinus,' he said, 'I assure you – and if it helps then I'll take any oath you like – that I had absolutely nothing to do with whoever accosted your wife. Nothing. And why should I bother much if you found out about the false attack on the litter? As I said, your principal Isidorus probably knows all about it, and the small deception had already served its purpose. As far as wanting you off the case is concerned, yes, frankly, I admit to that because I don't think there's much to be gained in practical terms from your continuing. However, I am certainly not foolish enough to try stopping you by coercion, not least because I appreciate that it might have exactly the opposite effect. Better, as I told you, to let things run their natural course.'

'Then who was responsible?'

'Who knows?'

Bland as hell, and ambiguous enough for a pythoness, although I couldn't really say I'd been expecting anything else. I felt my temper slipping again. 'Pal, this isn't a game,' I said.

'Is it not? Well, Corvinus, perhaps that's another difference between your Roman view and mine. I don't say it's not a serious game; not all games are frivolous or harmless. But that's no reason not to enjoy them.'

'I doubt if Isidorus would agree with you. He's—'

'Oh, yes he would.' Phraates reached for a slice of melon. 'Isidorus plays the game very well indeed, most of the time. And he enjoys it just as much as I do.'

Bugger; I was getting tired of this. 'Look, let's get this straight. Me, I don't play games, right, nothing more complicated than dice or knucklebones, anyway, and as far as I'm concerned both of you can play this one until you go blind or hell freezes. All I want to do is find out who killed Zariadres and why, hand in my report and get shot of the whole fucking business. Full stop, draw the line and roll up the book. You get me?'

Phraates had set the slice of melon on his plate. Carefully, his eyes on what he was doing, he separated the red flesh from the rind and, with the point of his knife, began removing the black seeds. I could hear distinctly – I hadn't been conscious of it since the guy had come in – the drip of water from the water-clock in the corner.

Finally, he raised his eyes. 'Very well, Corvinus,' he said. 'I'm going to break my own rule. Just a little, you understand, and if you want a reason then I'll cite the incident involving your wife, which I most certainly do not approve of. In return you will ask no questions. Agreed?'

I nodded; the back of my neck was prickling. 'Agreed.'

'Good. You will find, then, in a small side street between the Esquiline Gate and Maecenas Gardens, a brothel called the Three Graces. The owner-manager is a woman by the name of Helen and the girl you want to talk to is Anna. I strongly suggest, for reasons you'll appreciate later, that you present yourself as an ordinary paying customer. If you need to prove credibility and credit, which you will because the Graces is a most exclusive establishment, then mention that you're a friend of Lucius Vitellius. No' – he held up a hand – 'No questions, remember, or comments. There; that's all I intend giving you. Now let's drop the subject and have breakfast properly, shall we? If you're not hungry I am.'

Yeah, well, a bargain was a bargain: I clamped my lips together and, brain in overdrive, forced myself to reach for the jug of fruit juice.

Lucius Vitellius, eh?

Shit.

25

It was barely mid-morning when I left the villa and made my way back to the Agrippan Bridge. I was thinking hard.

I didn't know what the hell connection Phraates's brothel had with things, although finding that out was my main priority. Still, the fact that Lucius Vitellius's name had cropped up again – and Phraates had dropped it deliberately – couldn't be a coincidence. We were back with the unholy alliance between Vitellius, Mithradates and Tiridates, plus Damon as facilitator and the grey eminence of Prince Gaius lurking in the wings. That all fitted. It meshed especially with what Mithradates had said about me being out of my depth. If I was right – and at this stage I'd bet a rotten sardine against Meton's missing basket of lampreys that I was – there was some pretty drastic skulduggery going on at very high levels. Phraates didn't seem too worried, mind, which on the surface was surprising because in the last analysis the purpose of the conspiracy had to be to put him in an urn before his time, but then I suspected that the cunning old bugger had more survival capability than a Suburan alley-cat. Even so—

I stopped. Shit, if Vitellius was involved then it would clear up another problem too. As far as the guys at the Pollio Library were concerned, I'd scratched – for different reasons – both Mithradates and Phraates from the suspect list. How about Lucius Vitellius? For someone in his position, organising an intercept would be easy-peasy, and his reasons for wanting me off the case would be the same as his Iberian pal's. Added to which, a slime-ball like Vitellius wouldn't have any scruples in the arm-twisting department; at least, as far as the threat went. That qualification was important. Mithradates, he was more the straightforward type: I'd seen for myself that his idea of discouragement was to take the offending punter down an alleyway and kick his lights out. Vitellius would be more subtle, and more nasty . . .

Yeah, right. If Lucius Vitellius was responsible for messing with Perilla, and I ever managed to prove it, then consular or not I'd haul the fat bastard's guts out from between his teeth.

I was level with the Agrippan Bridge now. I crossed over – it was a lot quieter than the Sublician would be, this time of day – and made my way through the Aesculetum in the direction of Marcellus Theatre and the city centre. The Palatine wasn't exactly on the way to Maecenas Gardens and the Esquiline Gate, but while I had the chance I'd drop in on Isidorus. After all, technically the job was half over: I'd found out who'd attacked the prince's litter and why, which was all that had been involved originally; the fact that I still had no idea about the whys and wherefores of Zariadres's death was a separate issue. Also, if Phraates hadn't been shooting the breeze about Isidorus knowing he was responsible for the attack already I had some pretty important questions to ask Rome's head Parthia-watcher, preferably while my thumbs were digging into the bastard's windpipe. That he'd have an explanation I didn't doubt: these diplomatic buggers always do. All the same, I wanted to be looking him in the eye when he gave me it. Knowing he was telling porkies would be just as interesting as hearing the truth.

It was a long, hard slog; the day before was finally catching up on me, and I still had a long way to go to the Esquiline. I took a break and three cups of wine in a wineshop at the Velabrum end of Tuscan Street before tackling the steps up to the Germalus, the Palatine proper and the House of Augustus. The front-man secretary – Quintus, I remembered – passed me in without a murmur.

'Ah, Corvinus.' Isidorus was behind his desk as usual, and looking genial. I wondered if he ever changed that threadbare tunic, but maybe he had several in the same condition. 'How are you? You had a pleasant festival?'

'Yeah.' I nodded to the gopher as he closed the door behind me, then walked over to the guest chair, pulled it up and sat. 'Phraates's litter was attacked by a Jewish gang from Ostia led by a guy called Isak. The prince picked up the tab for the operation himself. Now tell me you didn't know either of those things and we'll take it from there.'

Isidorus didn't blink, but his grey eyes lost their focus just for an instant and the geniality disappeared. 'Very well,' he said evenly. 'I will. I didn't know.'

Right. And I was Caesar's grandmother. 'You're lying,' I said. 'The only question in my mind is when you found out, before or after you called me in.'

Isidorus pulled at his ear; puzzled, not angry, and that was significant. If you call a man a liar to his face you expect a stronger reaction than puzzlement. 'I'm afraid you're making no sense, Valerius Corvinus,' he said. 'Why, if I already knew the details, would I invite you to help discover them?'

'Search me. But things're so twisted around in this whole business that the question stands.'

There was another long silence. Finally, he said, 'All right. I had no idea as to the identity of the gang, but yes, I did know that Phraates had organised the attack, and why. In mitigation I should say that I didn't have the information myself until two days ago, or not in any confirmed form, at least. I give you my word on that.'

His word. Right; for what that was worth in dud copper. I let it pass, though. Like with Phraates, there was no point in putting the guy's back up. 'You could still have sent me a note,' I said.

'I could. I ought to have done, but . . . well, I don't normally use this as an excuse, but I am a very busy man. I simply didn't have the opportunity.' Plausible, and there was no way I could check he was telling the truth. Par for the course, in other words, as was his whole attitude. Isidorus radiated concerned – but now slightly offended – innocence. I reckoned if he ever took to the boards he would clean up, especially in comedy. Good straight men are pure gold. 'Let me say, though,' he added, 'that I am most impressed with your efficiency.'

I grinned back at him; smarm again. That was another trait he shared with Phraates. It must go with the job. 'Nothing to do with me, pal,' I said. 'A friend of mine did all the work. I just put two and two together and came up with the obvious answer.'

'None the less, pointless exercise or not it's an impressive achievement.' Isidorus frowned down at the wax tablet in front of him. 'It really was very bad of Phraates. He could at least have dropped a hint that it was a ploy of his own and saved everyone a lot of trouble. You've seen him? He apologised, I hope?'

'Yeah. Yeah, we talked this morning.'

'And he absolved you of any further involvement?'

'No. Strangely enough he didn't. In fact, he seemed quite keen that I carry on.' I wasn't going to mention the brothel tip; no *way* was I going to mention the brothel tip! If Isidorus wanted to play secrets then it was a double-handed game. I might not be a game-player, but I knew that much.

The frown had deepened. 'My, my. Did he give you a reason?'

'No, not in so many words.'

'Hmm.' He picked up the stylus lying beside the wax tablet

and tapped it gently against his lips. 'Don't feel that you're obliged to, Corvinus. Certainly not from our side of things. And – a word to the wise – I would be just a *little* wary of falling in with Prince Phraates's wishes too readily. He's a very charming man, of course, and well-intentioned enough, but all the same . . .' He set the stylus down. 'However, doubtless you can make your own mind up on that point.'

'Yeah. Right. I can.' I shifted in my chair. 'In any case, there's still the small question of Zariadres, isn't there?'

'Indeed.' The frown was still there. 'I thought perhaps that would be your answer. Well, we called you in, as you say, and if Phraates is happy for you to continue then we'll leave it at that. However' – he picked up the stylus again – 'if – and I'm only giving you an example, of course – if you were to find that there were, shall we say, non-Roman factors involved then that might lead to certain difficulties eventually. Even embarrassments. You understand?'

'Factors like Prince Tiridates and his Iberian pal?'

That got me a very straight look. 'Yes,' he said. 'Possibly. Among others.'

'And if one of the others were a Roman?'

Isidorus's expression didn't change. 'Now there's an interesting idea,' he said mildly. 'Did you have anyone particular in mind?'

'Sure. Lucius Vitellius.'

His eyes widened and he set the stylus down. '*Lucius?* Why on earth should Lucius have anything to do with it?'

'My guess is that he has a scam going with Tiridates and an Armenian merchant by the name of Titus Anacus.' I'd expected some reaction, but the eyes didn't shift. There wasn't even a question in them. 'Shit. You know about that already, don't you?'

Suddenly, Isidorus laughed. It was so unexpected that I blinked. 'My dear fellow, did I say before that I was impressed? I'm afraid if I say so again it will be an under-statement. A very grave understatement. How on *earth* did you find out about Anacus?'

'Uh . . . '

'Never mind, it doesn't matter.' He was still chuckling. 'You're right, of course. Absolutely right. I've had my eye on that gentleman and his dealings with Tiridates ever since the unfortunate business over his daughter. He's a schemer, naturally, but his ideas are far too big for his capabilities and quite impractical. And his wife is an absolute horror.'

Bugger; he sounded convincing, too. 'Nevertheless, the scam exists?'

'To give Anacus control of the Syrian pepper trade in return for a guarantee that Vitellius would support Tiridates should his uncle die in the near future? Oh, yes. Certainly it does. In Anacus's mind at least. It's complete pie-in-the-sky, of course, but as I say Anacus is a dreamer and a gambler, and his wife's social aspirations don't help, either. The spice trade is much too complex for any single person, however rich or well connected, to hope for a monopoly.'

I didn't like the sound of this. 'So, uh, what about the other three? Tiridates, Mithradates and Vitellius?'

'Oh, my dear chap! I'm afraid they're rather taking advan-tage of the poor fellow, promising him the moon tomorrow in exchange for what they can get from him today, which I suspect is no inconsiderable amount. Anacus may be a fool in some ways, but he is extremely well off.'

I didn't believe I was hearing this. 'And you don't *care*? Jupiter, pal, an ex-consul, star of the Senate, head of the commission to treat with the Parthian envoys and future governor of Syria is plotting with a guy doing his damnedest to murder his uncle who's Rome's candidate for the Great Kingship and you can laugh about it?'

'Yes, Corvinus, I can.' The smile vanished and Isidorus

was suddenly serious. 'Listen. Vitellius is not a fool, nor is Tiridates. Anacus wouldn't be one either, if he sat down and thought things through for a change. I told you, the whole thing is a mare's nest. Also, it is nothing whatsoever to do with me or this department. A monopoly – even a partial one – in the Syrian spice market is impossible, but even if it weren't preventing it wouldn't come within my remit. My job is to look after Rome's interests vis-a-vis Parthia and the eastern client-kingdoms. Yes, these do overlap to a certain extent with economic and mercantile concerns, but spices are luxuries not essential trade goods, and anything to do with the luxury trade is guaranteed to set the emperor's blood boiling. For all Tiberius cares buyers and sellers can swindle each other to their hearts' content, and if I were foolish enough to suggest devoting even a fraction of this department's time to preventing them doing so he'd have my head by the next post from Capri. Quite rightly so.' He paused. 'So you see if Anacus allows himself to be gulled in exchange for a few nebulous promises which only a fool would trust it's no business of mine.'

'Even if Prince Gaius is involved?'

Everything went very still.

'I beg your pardon?' Isidorus said.

Yeah, well, maybe I had surprised him at that, but I doubted it. I suspected where some things were concerned it wasn't not knowing about them that fazed Isidorus; it was finding that someone else knew. I was learning a lot about diplomacy in this case.

'It's a fair bet.' I held up my hand and counted reasons off on my fingers. 'One. If there was involvement at the imperial level the scheme wouldn't be quite so crack-brained after all, and Anacus needn't be quite so gaga as you say he is. Two. Gaius is a personal friend of both Tiridates and Mithradates. Having the one as Great King and the other as king of Armenia when he gets to be emperor, which he will, would be a plus. Three, connected with two. Phraates is no spring chicken. Even if he does survive the journey and the campaign, he's not going to be around for long. Tiridates is the natural heir. Why wait, especially since you might have to do things over again in a few years' time and you can make a little on the side from not waiting in the meantime? Four, connected with three. By all accounts Prince Gaius isn't exactly the plain-living sort, and if Anacus wanted to contribute the odd copper to keep him in the style he's accustomed to then I'd bet that'd be fine by him. Five. The imperial choice isn't as clear-cut these days as it was. Sure, Tiberius is still emperor, but he's out of it in Capri. If – and I'm saying *if* – Phraates dies unexpectedly then having Gaius on the team to smooth over any wrinkles in connection with the takeover will be really useful. Now. You want to hear all that again at half speed or shall we take it as read?'

Isidorus's eyes hadn't left my face throughout. There was a long pause. Finally, he said quietly, 'We seem to have got off the subject of Zariadres.'

'His death fits in somewhere. It's the "where" part that's beating me.'

Isidorus leaned forward, placed his hands palm down on the desk and took a deep breath.

'Corvinus, listen to me,' he said. 'I advise you very strongly to forget all of this. Prince Gaius is not involved.'

'Yeah? You sure about that?'

'Very. The same goes for Lucius Vitellius. Lucius is greedy, venal and totally self-seeking, yes, I admit all that, but – as I said before, and I stress it now – he is definitely not a fool. Nor is he a gambler. He knows exactly how far he can go, and treason, which is what you're accusing him of, is well beyond his personal pale. Besides, and most important, he is an excellent diplomat and one of the few Romans I've ever met who is a match for the Parthians on their own ground. Rome needs him, *I* need him, and I have absolutely no intention of jeopardising our relationship just because he happens to take a few piddling backhanders from a pushy Armenian with more money than sense. As for Prince Gaius, as you say he is our future emperor, which is a prime reason for his *not* getting involved with Tiridates's schemes. Tiberius, although you may not think it, is still very much in charge; he's certainly well aware of what goes on, in the empire and beyond, and septuagenarian or not his mind is still razor-sharp. Gaius – and as you can appreciate we're speaking in strict confidence here – may wish things were different, but if he wants to stay in favour then he must accept the realities. In any case, he's not as self-seeking as you might think. Gaius has his limits, and they would certainly stop short of giving the Parthian throne to a drinking friend simply because he was a drinking friend.' He paused. 'So you see, all things considered Tiridates has no chance whatsoever of becoming Great King.'

'Even if he manages to murder Phraates?'

'He won't. Of that I am absolutely sure.'

'Yeah? And why's that, now?'

'Because Phraates won't let him. And nor will we.' He looked down at the wax tablet on the desk. 'Now, I'm sorry, Corvinus, but I've given you all the time I can spare. I can't absolutely forbid you to take any further interest in this business, naturally, but do think things over carefully. Whatever you decide, remember you have my total respect, and in any case keep me informed.'

Yeah, right. I stood up. Interview over. Well, if that was the best I could do I'd have to settle for it. Still, if Isidorus had pulled down the shutters on Vitellius and Gaius – or appeared to, anyway – then I hadn't: the theory made too much sense just to dismiss altogether. Besides, I wouldn't trust anything Isidorus told me the length of my arm, especially if it sounded convincing. If I was wrong then great, but I needed to find out for myself.

It was time for a visit to the Three Graces.

26

I found the place just where Phraates had said it was, in a quiet side street about halfway between the gate and the nearest entrance to the gardens. Up-market was right: it was an old, rambling property in its own grounds, with a pillared entrance at the top of a short flight of scrubbed marble steps and a front door that gleamed with fresh paint and polished brass. I knocked and a slave in a smart lemon-yellow tunic opened up. After a day traipsing around Rome I wasn't looking too well groomed, but as he gave me the usual once-over you always get in these places his eyes found the purple stripe on my tunic – I don't wear a mantle, if I can help it – and his pursed lips relaxed.

'Good afternoon, sir,' he said, stepping back. 'Welcome. If you'd care to follow me?'

Whoever had chosen the decor for the lobby had had taste. The floor mosaic was plain but good quality, and the frescos covering the side walls were a lot better than the mass-produced tat of boobs and bottoms that proprietors usually go for to put customers in the mood: a countryside scene with goats and a shepherd boy on one side, and on the other the eponymous Graces, decently clothed, with a round temple to one side. The slave led me through to the atrium: the usual pool and couches, with more tasteful frescos and a lifesize bronze just inside the door. The Graces again, this time stripped to the buff but not looking too self-conscious about it.

'Make yourself comfortable, sir. If I could take your cloak? Thank you. Some wine?'

'Yeah. Yeah, that would be great.' I stretched out on one of the couches: tasteful again, plain wood with thick, dark blue leather upholstery. 'Ah . . . is the mistress in?'

He folded the cloak carefully and laid it on the back of one of the other couches, then poured wine from a silver jug on a side table into one of a matching set of cups. 'Yes, sir. Of course. Forgive me, sir, but this is your first time at the Graces, isn't it? Then naturally the mistress will want to know your preferences before we accommodate you.' He handed me the full cup, then said delicately, 'We do by the way have excellent bathing facilities, if you'd care to make use of them.'

'No, that's okay, pal.' I sipped. Lovely stuff, but not an Italian wine, or if it was it wasn't familiar. Could be Greek – I wasn't all that well up on Greek wines – but it reminded me of Jarhades's Syrian.

'Your name, sir? In complete confidence, of course.'

'Corvinus. Valerius Corvinus.'

'Thank you.' He collected my cloak and laid it over his arm. 'The mistress will be with you shortly.'

Left to myself, I looked round a bit more. Nice place, and as I say top end of the market. There were other bronzes besides the big one, plus a couple of marble statues, all good copies of Greek originals. The fountain in the pool was in the shape of a dolphin, without the silly grin or po-faced constipated look you sometimes get on these things. And though there were plenty of boobs and bums on offer among the frescos the artist had taken care over the women's faces and the background as well.

I was no more than a quarter down the wine cup when the mistress appeared. Like the room itself, she was definitely high class: no silks or flashy jewellery, a simple, good-quality woollen mantle and plain emerald earrings.

Late forties – although she must've been a looker at one time – Greek features, an eastern colouring and slightly almond-shaped eyes. I'd guess Syrian. That would explain the wine, too.

'Valerius Corvinus,' she said. 'Welcome to the Graces. I'm Helen.' There was a bronzework chair on the other side of the table. She sat in it, adjusting the folds of her impeccable Greek mantle. 'We were recommended to you?'

Straight in, no messing, polite enough but all business. And the demand for credentials had been delicately put. 'I'm a . . . uh . . . colleague of Lucius Vitellius,' I said.

'Ah.' She nodded, obviously satisfied. 'About your requirements. We have—'

'I was interested in one girl in particular. Name of Anna. Would she be free at all?'

Had it been my imagination, or had the black-lined eyes shifted? 'Anna,' she said. 'Now that is . . . The ex-consul suggested her?'

'Yeah, more or less. If she's available . . . ?'

'Oh, Anna is free, Valerius Corvinus. And if you already know what you want then it makes my job a great deal easier.' She smiled and glanced over at the slave who'd brought me in and had followed her through. 'Ajax; tell Anna we have a guest.' The slave bowed and left. She turned back to me. 'Although please don't feel that you have to keep to your initial choice. After all, much as I respect Lucius Vitellius's judgment choosing a partner is a very subjective thing and we pride ourselves in being able to match a gentleman to a nicety. If you'd care to take a look at some of the other girls before you finally decide, then—'

'No. No, that's okay,' I said. 'Anna's fine.'

'As you wish. Then the price is five gold pieces. Payable in advance. There are, naturally, no other charges.'

Ouch; at those rates I'd hope there wouldn't be! Yeah, well, like I say the lady was nothing if not business-like. I reached into my pouch and took out the five big ones. She laid them on the table.

'The wine's to your liking?'

'It's fine. Syrian?'

'But yes! From the region near Apamea. You've met with it before?'

'Something similar. You're, uh, from Syria yourself?'

'Palmyra. Although I spent some time in Antioch.'

'The Graces been open long?'

'Three or four years. We're very well established. And, as your colleague Vitellius no doubt explained, very exclusive.'

'He recommend many new customers?'

'A few. The ex-consul is very much taken with the Graces. Understandably so.' The slave had come back in and was waiting politely. 'Ah. Anna is ready for you now, Valerius Corvinus. Ajax will take you. There will be wine in the room, Apamean, but if you have any other preferences then please say so. We have an extensive cellar. Also food and, if you do change your mind and wish to use the bath suite the furnace is hot.'

'No, I'll be okay.'

'I'm sure you will be.' She stood up and I stood too. 'Enjoy your stay with us.'

I noticed that she'd left the coins on the table. No doubt she'd pocket them as soon as I was gone, but the point was made. Classy place right enough.

'This way, sir,' Ajax said.

I followed him through into a wider hall with a staircase at the back. We went up to the first floor past alcoves with candelabra and bronzes, then along a short corridor to a panelled door. Ajax knocked gently then stood aside,

'Just go in, Valerius Corvinus,' he said. 'If there is anything further you require then please don't hesitate to ask.'

The bedroom beyond could've belonged in an eastern client-king's palace. I recognised the girl on the bed straight off. The last time I'd seen that little stunner she'd been sharing Callion's couch at the embassy dinner.

She recognised me too. Her eyes widened, then her expression settled into careful blankness. I closed the door behind me, walked over to the couch on the right-hand side of the room – it was plain cedarwood, not gilded, with red plush upholstery – and sat down. She was watching me all the way.

'Hi,' I said.

Stunner was no exaggeration. Like Helen, she was obviously an easterner, with long blue-black hair worn loose, dark eyes with just a trace of make-up and a face and figure that would've had any self-respecting artist after a model for Aphrodite reaching for his sketch-pad. Her legs beneath the short silk dressing-gown were bare. She drew them up until her chin rested on her knees.

'Hi,' she said.

It couldn't be a coincidence; no *way* could it be a coincidence, especially since she was still watching me like a cat caught with the cream and deciding which way to jump. I remembered Vitellius, in the litter going back from the dinner, saying that the first thing Callion had asked for when he arrived in Rome was the address of a decent brothel. And Vitellius had recommended the Graces, no doubt Anna in particular; which was why Phraates had very carefully linked their two names when he sent me here . . .

Everything fitted. Vitellius had fixed Callion up. Vitellius was – at least where the Parthians were concerned – Isidorus's right-hand man and a shit-hot diplomat. Or whatever these buggers called themselves. And Callion, he was the odd man out of the embassy: a Greek from Seleucia, which might well be – according to Vitellius himself – less than a spit's distance from opting out of Parthian control altogether . . .

It was the oldest game in the world. And it was beautiful.

'You work for Isidorus, don't you?' I said quietly.

If I'd sounded less certain, even to myself, I think she might've denied it. As it was, she just shrugged and said, 'He told you?'

'Uh-uh.' I shook my head. 'But it makes sense. He had Vitellius plant you on Callion when the embassy arrived. Your job was to find out all you could about Seleucia's plans for revolt. Right?'

She blew a wisp of hair from her face. 'Yes. More or less.'

'Were the other girls at the dinner in on it too? The ones with Tiridates and Damon?'

'No. There was just me.' She was still watching me closely, eyes slitted, wary.

'How about the boss of the place? Helen?'

The lips twitched. I thought she was going to laugh, but she didn't. 'Helen doesn't work for Isidorus.'

There was something there that I didn't quite catch, but I let it go for now. I stretched out on the couch. 'Care to tell me all about it?' I said.

This time she did laugh, a genuine amused laugh but with a hard edge; a woman's laugh, not a girl's. A thinking woman. Now that I'd had a bit more time to study her I could see she was older than I'd thought at first, mid-twenties, easy, and I had the distinct feeling that statue-maker's dream or not she'd be no pushover. Without a trace of self-consciousness she sat up against the headboard of the bed and brushed the hair back completely from her face, letting the silk dressing-gown part completely. No fancy gilded nipples or spangles there. Mind you, with what she had she didn't need them.

'Corvinus – that's your name, isn't it?' she said.

'Yeah. That's me.'

'All right. Let's get this clear. You've paid out five gold pieces and you want to *talk*?'

I grinned. 'It's my money, lady.'

She stared at me – she was beginning to relax now – then shrugged again and stretched her long beautiful legs out in front of her. She didn't make any attempt to close the dressing-gown. 'Fair enough,' she said. 'It doesn't matter all that much to me either way. Nor to Isidorus; he's got what he wants and my part's finished. There's wine on that table beside you. Pour some for yourself; not for me, I'm not allowed it, and that bastard Ajax sniffs your breath after a customer's gone.'

The jug and cups were heavy silver with a hunting scene on them. I reached over and poured. 'So how did you get into this business?' I said. 'The cloak-and-dagger side, I mean?'

Her eyes rested on me for a long time, considering. Then she said, 'I'm from Ecbatana originally. Artabanus had my father crucified, him personally, and my mother and two sisters died too. I won't bother you with the details. I was fifteen. I got away thanks to a not completely disinterested merchant and ended up in a cathouse in Alexandria. One of Isidorus's friends – colleagues – happened by one day and suggested I come to Rome. That was three years ago. I've been here ever since.'

'Helen doesn't know? About your link with Isidorus?'

Again that small, strange smile. 'No. She doesn't know. Isidorus – through Vitellius – sends me customers now and again. Not very often, and the result isn't always . . . productive, but he gets good value. And if I can harm Artabanus along the way then that's an extra.'

I took a sip of the wine. 'So what about Callion?'

'He was the big one. Most of the special customers are from the eastern client-kingdoms, or the Parthian satellite kingdoms at best. I'd never had a real Parthian, even the Greek variety. Isidorus knew Callion had been given secret instructions before he left Seleucia to do a private deal with . . .' She hesitated. 'With a high-up Roman. The Seleucian revolt would be timed to coincide with the invasion. Isidorus wanted details.'

'And this high-up Roman would be Prince Gaius, right?'

'Maybe,' she said cautiously.

'You don't know?'

'I'm not paid to think, Corvinus. I just do what I'm told.'

Sure, and I was born yesterday. Gaius made complete sense. A Seleucian revolt wouldn't directly harm Roman interests, unless Callion's pals were stupid enough to go down that road, which they wouldn't be. Quite the reverse. On the other hand, it wouldn't do Rome's official candidate Phraates any favours, either: the last thing a new Great King wants when he's taking over and desperate to establish his authority is an independent state across the river from his capital with widespread ethnic support throughout the kingdom and bargaining clout in spades. If you wanted to keep Parthia weak and divided, then giving Seleucia her head would be a peach of an idea. Risky, mind, and that was the point. Tiberius wouldn't go for it – he was a step-by-step, take-things-one-at-a-time man – but Gaius, Gaius was different . . .

She was watching me again. 'You know,' she said, 'this isn't very flattering. You've paid for my time and you're not even looking at me.'

I grinned. 'Yeah. Sorry, lady. Not your fault, not in the least. So. How did it go, with Callion? You got what you wanted? What Isidorus wanted?'

'Oh, yes. After the dinner.'

I almost dropped my wine cup. 'You were there the night of the murder? All night?'

She smiled. It could've been coincidence, sure, but her breasts rose clear of what little of the dressing-gown was still hiding them. 'Now that's *really* unflattering,' she said. 'You think Callion had me come along that evening just to send me away?'

Shit! 'He told me categorically there was no one else in the house that night!'

'Then he was lying. Understandable, in the circumstances. And I was gone before morning.'

My brain did a back-track to the original conversation. Hell, no; what Callion had actually *said* – under oath – was that there was no one in the house who shouldn't have been there and was unaccounted for the next morning. Which in effect was quite true. Sweet holy Jupiter, the open door! 'You were the one who drugged the door-slave, right?'

'And Callion. It was my last chance. He's a clever man and maybe I'd been pushing too hard. If I'd left things any later he'd probably have gone beyond suspecting. I told Isidorus and he authorised it.'

'What about the—' I stopped. I didn't need to ask that question any more. 'Uh-uh; the guard outside didn't matter, did he? He'd been ordered to turn a blind eye. Or if he had sloped off he'd been fucking told to.' Hell; the devious bastards – both Isidorus and Vitellius – had conned me right down the line.

'He was there. Within sight, anyway. Isidorus thought I might need a little back-up.'

I took an angry swallow of wine. The next time I met that slimy three-faced bugger if he wanted his pen and notepad back it'd need surgery. If Callion had lied or the next best thing to it, then that was fine, he had reason to keep Anna out of the business, but you don't expect it from your own side. 'The rest of the delegation. They knew you were sleeping over?'

'Of course. It was no secret.'

'Then why the hell didn't they say and be done with it? The Greek bastard was going behind their backs as well, they didn't owe him anything.' I sighed. 'No. Don't tell me. Parthian solidarity, right?'

'That and other things.' There was that look again, the one she'd given me when Helen was mentioned. 'Callion had a locked chest with him. While he was unconscious I forced the lock. The original letters he'd carried from the Seleucian senate had already been delivered, of course, but I found some other documents that were equally good. Plus the reply that he'd be taking back.'

'And then you left.'

'Then I left.'

I looked at her sharply. There was something there, something in the tone . . .

Oh, fuck. Oh, holy sodding gods . . .

'You saw him, didn't you?' I said quietly. 'On your way out. The guy who murdered Zariadres.'

She smiled and flicked a strand of hair from her right breast. 'Yes. I saw him.'

'So who was it?'

'Peucestas.'

So easy. I stared at her. It wasn't the name that surprised me – the killer had to be one of the delegation, and Peucestas had always been high on the suspect list – but the way she said it. Like it didn't matter.

'So . . .' I began.

Which was when the implication hit me.

Anna had known who the murderer was all along. Anna worked for Isidorus. Ergo, Isidorus had known all along too.

First the litter attack, now this. There was nothing left, and lying didn't cover it; the word was nowhere near strong enough. What his reasons had been – and someone like Isidorus would've had reasons, that I was sure of – I couldn't begin to guess, but the bastard had shafted me right from the start.

'Why?' I said.

'Why what?' She had her cautious, cat-at-the-cream expression on again.

'Why didn't your boss tell me? Why go through the charade of an investigation when he knew who'd slit the guy's throat five minutes after it happened? You reported what you'd seen, didn't you?'

'Oh, yes. I was waiting for the coast to clear, looking through the crack between our bedroom door and the jamb, and I saw Peucestas go past towards his room with blood on his tunic and a knife in his hand.' That came out matter-of-fact. No pushover was right: tits, a face and a body that Queen Cleopatra would've died for or not, the lady was a seriously tough cookie. 'Short of seeing the actual murder itself I couldn't've been luckier. And I went straight round to Isidorus's flat – he has one in Augustus House – as per my instructions.'

'And you think the other delegates – Osroes and Callion – knew Peucestas had done it?'

She laughed. 'But of course they did!'

Of course they did . . .

I lay back. Out of my depth wasn't the half of it: none of this made any sense, even in Parthian terms. The guy – head of the fucking delegation – had been murdered in his bed by a colleague and even knowing who the murderer was no one on either the Roman or the Parthian side gave a damn. They never had, right from the start. Plus the fact Peucestas wasn't a murderer, not that kind, anyway. That I'd swear to. Shit! What was going on? Why should Peucestas . . . ?

And then things shifted.

It was obvious. Change just one word and the whole business was clear, everything added up: why neither the other delegates nor Isidorus had been interested, why both sides wanted the case shoved down a very deep hole and buried, why Phraates had brought his taster to the dinner. Even what Phraates had been trying to tell me in his carriage the night of the *Medea*.

Change 'murdered' to 'executed'.

'Zariadres was a traitor, wasn't he?' I said. 'He was working for Artabanus. Peucestas killed him because Phraates, as Great King of Parthia, ordered him to.'

'Yes,' Anna said.

'So why the fuck could Isidorus not say so? Him or Phraates, one of the two?'

She shrugged. 'I told you, Corvinus. I'm not paid to think, I'm just a whore who collects information. If you really want that question answered you'll have to ask Isidorus yourself. Now.' She lay back. 'We've talked enough. I've my reputation to consider here, and I reckon you have about three gold pieces' worth left.'

But I was already up and heading for the door. Too right I'd ask Isidorus. By the time I was finished with that bastard they'd have to wheel him around in a cart.

27

The anger jag got me as far as the main road. Then I began to cool down and think things through.

Going to see Isidorus in this mood would be a very bad idea, even I could see that. The way I was currently feeling, I would definitely have the bastard by the throat and be shaking his teeth out inside five minutes, and to do that to a senior Roman official who has more Praetorians on call than beans in a bean-bag isn't a smart move; not unless you seriously undervalue your skin and don't mind spending a couple of years somewhere the locals trail their knuckles, anyway. Also, there was still the question of the two Pollio Library guys. I could be wrong, but with Mithradates and Phraates out of the running and Vitellius the blue-eyed boy again that didn't leave many names in the hat. Six got you ten the person responsible had been Isidorus himself. And confirmation of that little nugget was something I didn't want to get while I was within easy punching distance of the bugger's mouth.

So. Home and a consultation with Perilla. After that and a bit of judicious thought if I did still feel like saying to hell with the consequences and punching the bastard's lights out I could do it just as well first thing the next morning. I turned off the main drag that would've taken me through the Subura and headed down towards the Caelian.

★　　★　　★

Perilla was out when I got back – according to Bathyllus, a long-standing invitation to one of her literary pals' cake and honey wine klatshes – so I took the opportunity of shutting myself up in the study and spending the hours before dinner on the postponed household accounts. Like it or not, the case was effectively over; the only remaining question was how and when I handed in my final report, and I doubted that, given the circumstances, anyone would be exactly screaming for that. Besides, if I was going to be in a bad mood anyway I might as well make a proper job of things.

Proper job was right: the air in the study was pretty blue when Bathyllus shoved his nose round the door.

'It's the consular, sir,' he said. 'Lucius Vitellius. Shall I bring him in?'

Shit. That's where leading a decent life gets you. Well, it wasn't my fault. I'd avoided the punch-up with Isidorus, but if the gods wanted to hand me Lucius Vitellius on a plate as a reward then I could only be humbly thankful and take what I was given. I grinned and moved the abacus and tablets to one side.

'Yeah,' I said. 'Yeah, you do that. Oh, and Bathyllus?'

'Yes, sir?'

'If you should happen to hear any screaming or heavy thumping noises while we're in conference just ignore them, okay?'

'Ah . . . yes, sir.' He withdrew.

I checked the desk and allowed myself a little fantasising. Paper-knife: too extreme, and Bathyllus would complain about the bloodstains on the upholstery. Small hunting-dog bronze: Perilla had given me that, and if the bugger's head left a dent she would not be happy. Ink bottle: suitably shaped, cheap and easily replaceable, difficult to remove in rectal terms. Perfect . . .

Vitellius came in belly-first and beaming. 'Corvinus! Glad I was able to catch you! We're—'

'You bastard,' I said quietly. 'You and Isidorus both.'

'Oh, come now! I know you're upset, boy, but all the same—'

'Sit!'

He sat; the beam had disappeared. Now he was looking nervous, as he had every right to be: after today's events plus a couple of hours on the accounts I wasn't exactly my easy-going tolerant self. 'I understand from Isidorus that you've found out about—'

'Anna's been in touch already, has she? Fine.' I'd picked up the ink bottle and was hefting it idly. His piggy eyes locked on to it. 'Okay. Just to get things clear: I know Zariadres was a traitor and that Peucestas killed him – executed him – on Phraates's instructions. I know that Anna told Isidorus the same night it happened. What I don't know, *pal* – and let's start with this, shall we? – is why the slimy little rat let me waste my time chasing around trying to solve a mystery that didn't exist.'

Vitellius cleared his throat. 'Isidorus didn't know about Zariadres,' he said. I caught the ink bottle on its way down and leaned forward. He yelped; the chair creaked and its wooden legs scraped the floor as he pushed it back. 'Oh, he knew about the murder, but not that the bugger was working for Artabanus. Not until Phraates told him two days ago.'

'Two days. Just before your pals accosted my wife outside the Pollio Library.'

'That was a mistake.'

'Fucking right it was!'

'Come on, Corvinus! When we called you in we did it in good faith. We didn't know who'd attacked the prince's litter, Zariadres was still alive and as far as we knew he was genuine.

If you have to blame someone blame Phraates. What else could Isidorus do?'

'Tell me the simple truth when he knew it himself, for a start.'

'That's not how these things work, boy! Zariadres's death was – is – politically sensitive. You're not cleared at that level. In fact, Anna had no right to—'

'Anna didn't tell me anything I hadn't worked out for myself. You just remember that. And whore or not she's a lot more honest than you pair of charmers.' I leaned back. He breathed a small sigh of relief. 'Okay. That's Zariadres. Let's move on to Prince Gaius.' The relief disappeared. 'Isidorus was bullshitting me again, wasn't he? I was right: Gaius is playing his own game, or trying to. He wants Phraates discredited or dead or both and Tiridates crowned as Great King. Now don't even *think* of denying it, sunshine, because I'll laugh in your face.'

Vitellius was looking grey.

'Corvinus, I can't—'

'Sure you can't. I don't expect you to.' I put the ink bottle down: it had been a good fantasy while it lasted. 'Still, I'll make you a little bet. The bet is that whatever Isidorus says to the contrary – and no doubt he believes it, because devious bugger or not he's the emperor's man – Phraates won't last five minutes as Great King. Oh, sure, he'll start out crowned because that's what Tiberius wants, but not long after he'll hand in his soup bowl, probably from natural causes and well on the Parthian side of the border. And Prince Tiridates will take over. Now you want to take me up on that? After all, as Syrian governor you'll be heading the expedition. If anyone can keep the old guy breathing you can.'

If Vitellius had been grey before now he was the colour of a month-old dishrag. 'That's nonsense,' he said. 'Also, I'm insulted that you can even think that I would—'

'Fine.' I shrugged; there wasn't anything I could do about it, and maybe it was for the best in the long run, but the whole boiling just made me sick to my stomach. Gaius would be emperor soon in any case, and if a slime-ball like Vitellius thought he could get in on the ground floor by switching loyalties before the Wart was dead that was between him and his own conscience. 'So no bet, right?' He didn't answer. 'Last point. Nothing very important, but it was just an idea I had about the Graces. You go there a lot, don't you? And you recommend it to friends?'

'Yes. So?'

'It just occurred to me, from what Anna carefully didn't say. The owner-manager's from Palmyra. Or she said she was, anyway. That's not Parthia, sure, but it's east and outwith the Roman borders. I just wondered, considering that Isidorus told me categorically that there were no Parthian agents in Rome and that everything else he said was a pack of lies, if Helen could be working for Artabanus herself.'

Silence. 'Corvinus, if you're implying that I—'

I held up a hand. 'Uh-uh. No sweat. You may be conning Isidorus where Gaius is concerned but you're no traitor to Rome. You haven't the guts, pal, he told me that, and there I believe him.' Vitellius frowned, but he said nothing. 'Still, if the Graces is a sort of clearing house for information it'd be handy having one of your own people in place there, wouldn't it? Plus the fact that you could slip the Parthians a few googlies of your own on a regular basis and leave them thinking the dope was genuine. Now how about that for a theory?'

'It's . . . interesting.'

'Yeah. That's what I thought. Only if it's true then maybe you and your boss might like to know I was put on to the place by your future Great King.'

'*What?*'

He'd gone straight from dishrag grey to goggling purple. Yeah, well, it hadn't been quite in the ink bottle league, but the look on his face had been worth the effort. Telling devious sods that they've been sussed and shafted by the opposition and watching the result is one of life's more satisfying experiences. And after the way the bastards had treated me it was good to pull back a couple of consolation points.

I stood up grinning; if that was the case, then we'd had it and I'd quit while I was temporarily ahead. 'Well, I've got things to do,' I said. 'Tell Isidorus that I'll be round with a full report at some stage, written out in triplicate, and warn him to keep some piles cream and a large set of pliers handy, right? Nice talking to you, Vitellius. I'll see you out, pal.'

I walked past him and opened the door. He left meek as a lamb. If lambs clench their teeth.

Perilla was in the atrium with a short, tubby, balding guy I didn't recognise perched on the visitor's chair opposite her. Probably one of the literary klatsch dropped in to borrow an anapaest, only he didn't look too pleased about something. Perilla didn't look too happy either.

'Marcus—' she said.

'Yeah. Just a second, lady. I'll see you around, Vitellius.' I handed the outgoing consular over to a hovering Bathyllus for disposal. The bugger didn't even grunt, or so much as spare Perilla a glance. 'Now. What is it?'

'This gentleman is Gaius Minucius Thermus. I found him just about to knock when I got home a few minutes ago. He wants to talk to us about lampreys.'

Oh, shit. 'Is, uh, that so, now?' I said.

'Damn right it's so!' The little guy was glaring at me like any moment he'd go for my ankles. 'Filched from my own fishpond!'

'Ah,' I said, lowering myself on to the couch.

'Well may you say "ah", Valerius Corvinus! Luckily my bailiff managed to track down the beggar who did it and he confessed who he'd sold them to so we got them back, but all the same—'

'Hold on, pal.' I held up a restraining hand. 'Let's get this clear. My chef said he'd bought these lampreys of yours from a sale of bankrupt stock after the master of a friend of his had been killed by a falling tenement.'

Thermus bristled. 'Do I *look* bloody dead to you, young man? Or a bankrupt?'

'Er . . .'

'Perhaps, dear,' Perilla said, 'before we go any further we'd best get Meton in.'

'Yeah, right.' Bathyllus had come back from showing the consular out and he was hovering. 'Bathyllus, ask Meton if he'd be good enough to step in for a moment, would you?'

'Good gods, man, if that's the way you talk to your slaves no wonder they're running riot!'

Bathyllus ignored him and cleared his throat. 'I'm afraid Meton has already left, sir,' he said. 'I saw him go out by the side door while the ex-consul was boarding his litter.'

'And you didn't stop him?' Thermus opened his eyes so wide his hairline went back another couple of inches. 'Bloody hell, boy!'

I winced. No one – *no one* – calls Bathyllus 'boy' and gets away with it. Our major-domo froze like he'd been hit with a dozen Riphaean winters all at once.

'Ah . . . that's all, Bathyllus,' I said quickly. 'When Meton does turn up tell him I want to see him, okay?'

'Yes, sir.' He gave Thermus a long look that would've pickled an entire elephant, sniffed and stalked out. Bugger; if the guy hadn't been stiffed by a falling brick after all he'd best be careful when he did finally walk out the door.

'That fellow needs a good thrashing!' Thermus snapped. 'And as for that chef of yours—!'

'So it was your bailiff who removed the basket?' Perilla said.

'Yes. The fish were already dead, of course, but fortunately my wife and I entertain frequently and we were giving a dinner party that evening so they weren't wasted. None the less . . .'

I was getting a bit tired of Minucius Thermus. And I didn't much like being told how to deal with my own slaves, either. Even if Meton was a thrawn, anarchic, unprincipled bugger, he was our thrawn, anarchic, unprincipled bugger 'Fine,' I said. 'Look, pal, as far as I can see it was a genuine mistake, at least on Meton's part, anyway. He bought them in good faith. Whatever he paid I'll—'

'*Genuine mistake!* He told you—'

'That's between me and my chef.' I stood up. 'Now. I apologise for the inconvenience, but you've got your fish back and I'm willing to pay the handling charge over and above. Let's leave it at that, okay? You say you entertain frequently. How's your cook with Parthian dishes?'

He looked at me suspiciously. '*Parthian* dishes?'

'Yeah. They're all the rage this year at the best dinners, and Meton's a whizz. Let's say I lend you the guy the next time you have important friends round. As a sort of goodwill gesture. How would that be?'

'Hmm. Well, I suppose I might—'

'Only you've got to remember you have to crack the whip, right? Stand over the lazy bugger while he's cooking, personally, I mean, and make sure he does things just exactly as you want them done. And then have him in to the dining-room when the meal's served, so if everything's not absolutely perfect you or your guests can tell him so there and then.'

'Marcus, dear,' Perilla said quietly. I ignored her.

Thermus was beaming. 'Now that does sound an absolutely splendid suggestion, sir! If you're sure then I'll take you up on it. By coincidence we do have a rather special dinner party arranged for three days' time: the head of Aqueducts and Sewers and his lady wife. They are *most* particular about their food. Total sticklers!' He stood up. 'Well, we'll say no more about it. Our house is on Patrician Street, just before the Viminal Gate – everyone knows it – so if you send your boy round then I'd be most obliged. But do have the fellow well thrashed, won't you? After the dinner, naturally.'

'Yeah. Yeah, believe me, Meton isn't going to forget this one in a hurry.' I stood up too. 'I'll see you to the door myself. I think our major-domo may be temporarily unavailable. A pleasure to meet you, Minucius Thermus.'

I waved him off in his litter then came back to the atrium whistling.

'Marcus, that was dreadful!' Perilla snapped. 'The poor man!'

'Meton or Thermus?'

She sniffed. 'Thermus, of course! How could you *do* something like that?'

'They deserve each other.' I bent down and kissed her, then stretched out on the couch. Time for a cup or two of wine before dinner: no doubt Meton would've seen the coast was clear and slipped back in. I was really, *really* looking forward to telling him about his cooking assignment.

It was good to be shot of the diplomatic world, at least. And you never knew: Thermus might even send us an invite.

Author's Note

I sometimes wake up in a cold sweat at the thought that someone, somewhere, will take the behind-the-scenes skulduggeries of the Corvinus plots for historical fact. They're nothing of the kind, of course, and I would not – being in no way either by nature or qualification an academic – have the nerve to claim otherwise. I am, however, an inveterate *Times* crossword-solver and a sucker for conspiracy-theorising, with the result that in *Parthian Shot*, as in the other 'political' Corvinus books, I've done what I most enjoy doing: used a combination of actual events, subjective interpretation from hindsight and a quite shameless attribution of motive to historical characters to construct a work of fiction which I hope will ring true to anyone who knows anything about the period but is primarily just a story. Certainly, this applies to the main plot. Although the delegation itself was real – Tacitus mentions it in his *Annals* for AD 35, which is when the story is set – the ambassadors' names, the murder itself and all the associated details are complete inventions.

That said, those interested in such things and of a masochistic turn of mind may like to know something of the historical events subsequent to the story's ending. A small sanity warning here: although I've simplified these they do get pretty convoluted, so if you must read on then have a stiff drink first. Or, preferably, skip the whole boiling.

Phraates/Tiridates

Phraates did indeed die at the beginning of the campaign against Parthia: Tacitus attributes his death (in Syria) to an illness brought on by his determination to give up the Roman habits of a lifetime in exchange for more traditionally Parthian ones. Tiberius then shifted his support to Tiridates, combining this with a politically arranged truce between Mithradates and his brother Pharasmenes of Iberia, the aim being to drive Artabanus's son from the Armenian throne. Lucius Vitellius, now the Syrian governor, was put in general charge of eastern developments.

Beaten in Armenia, threatened with a Roman invasion of Mesopotamia and deserted by almost all his allies, Artabanus fled to the wilds of Scythia where he had family connections. Vitellius entered Parthia proper unopposed, then, having stayed long enough to see Tiridates established – although not yet formally crowned – he led his army back.

This was the point at which things began to go wrong for Tiridates. Several key nobles, unimpressed with him personally and distrusting his Roman background, boycotted the formal coronation ceremony at Ctesiphon and instead made overtures to Artabanus who, gathering what local support he could, immediately marched against the capital. If Tiridates had gone to meet him straight away all might have been well, but first he delayed by laying siege to a fortress where Artabanus kept his treasury and concubines, and then allowed himself to be persuaded into a retreat westwards beyond the Tigris. In the course of the journey, his army melted away. Finally, giving up all hope of defeating Artabanus in battle, he fled across the border into Syria with a few followers, and thereafter disappears from history.

Artabanus made his peace with Rome, possibly agreeing, as one of the terms, to send a son to the emperor as hostage.

After surviving yet another coup and restoration, he died in AD 38: whether from natural causes or not the historians do not say.

Mithradates

Mithradates was to have a chequered career. He ruled Armenia until after Tiberius's death in AD 37, but then having fallen out with the new emperor Gaius he was brought back to Rome and imprisoned. He regained his throne under Gaius's successor Claudius and despite a reputation for cruelty held it until AD 51; at which point he was challenged and deposed by his nephew, Radamistus, backed by an army provided by Radamistus's father Pharasmenes who wanted to divert the lad's designs on *his* kingdom. Radamistus persuaded Mithradates to surrender by swearing he would not harm him either by sword or poison. He then had him smothered together with his wife and children under a pile of clothing.

A charming family, the Iberian royals . . .

The Seleucian Revolt

This happened in AD 35, the year the story is set, and probably much for the reasons given. Although only just across the Tigris from the Parthian capital Ctesiphon, the city held out for seven years, for most of which time its defection was largely ignored by the Parthian 'government' while life inside its walls continued much as usual; an indication of how loose the Great King's control over his subjects really was. After a short siege and various toings and froings the city surrendered voluntarily to Artabanus's brother and successor Vardanes in AD 42.

The Magi ('Magians')

It may seem odd to find Magi outwith the gold-frankincense-and-myrrh trio, but here they are. They were more or less as I've described them: a close-knit, rule-bound, socio-religious sect at least five centuries old, currently growing in influence, who claimed Zoroaster as their founder and whose belief in the balanced opposition of Good and Evil was to become central to the official Parthian (later Persian) religion. Both the Greek and Roman establishments regarded their involvement with astrology and 'magic' – not to mention their ritual use of drugs and other dubious substances – with suspicion and disapproval, albeit, in some cases, prurient fascination: *magos* (Greek) and *magus* (Latin) have the secondary meaning in both languages of 'magician' – hence of course the English word – and as such usually occur in a pejorative context. As an interesting by-the-way – and, perhaps, as a balance for our traditional Christmas-card image – according to Pliny the Magi were accustomed to apply to their faces 'a cosmetic ointment made from *helianthes*' – sunflower in Greek, but perhaps not our version – 'lion's fat, saffron and palm wine', which they believed improved their appearance. The picture of the Three Wise Men made up to the eyeballs is not one that readily springs to mind, but it's probably accurate, for all that.

My thanks, as usual, to my wife Rona for helping me find books. I haven't needed to disturb Roy Pinkerton very much this time, but I'll add my gratitude to him in any case. Any faults the story has on the factual side – and I'm sure they exist – are completely my responsibility. I hope, if you did notice them, that they didn't spoil things for you.